Praise for The Walrus Mutterer and
LONGLISTED FOR THE HIGHLAND B

'Marries great storytelling and convincing research … always
interesting, sometimes enthralling.' ALLAN MASSIE, *SCOTSMAN*

'Haggith's woman's-eye view of the Iron Age feels fresh and
distinctive.' ALASTAIR MABBOTT, *SUNDAY HERALD*

'A gripping, haunting and, at times, visceral novel… Lyrical and
poetic prose, the author has created a convincing and entirely
believable world… One of the best books I have read so far this
year.' PENNY INGHAM, EDITOR'S CHOICE, *HISTORICAL NOVELS
REVIEW*

'Compelling … The story is visceral and visual, crafted with a
lyrical prose.' *DUNDEE COURIER*

'We see what the world was like … for the Iron Age peoples,
particularly the women … Rian is a compelling heroine …
she has insights and wisdom that we moderns may well envy.'
MARGARET ELPHINSTONE

'Utterly compelling … beautifully crafted … paints an exquisite
pen picture.' UNDISCOVERED SCOTLAND

'The language and imagery are rich, poetic, visceral, and often
moving … as strange and beautiful as anything science-fiction
or fantasy has to offer.' SCOTS WHAY HAE

'An immersive evocation of ancient folklore and ritual, this
novel's characterisation and fast pace make it a real page-turner
which will keep you hooked.' *SCOTTISH FIELD*

'*The Walrus Mutterer* transported me to an extraordinary
Iron Age world that resonated long after the final page – vivid,
memorable, and utterly compelling.' HELEN SEDGWICK

Also by Mandy Haggith

Fiction
The Amber Seeker
The Walrus Mutterer
Bear Witness
The Last Bear

Poetry
Castings
letting light in
Into the forest
Why the Sky is Far Away

Non-fiction
*Paper Trails: From Trees to Trash,
the True Cost of Paper*

THE LYRE DANCERS

BOOK THREE OF THE STONE STORIES

MANDY HAGGITH

Saraband

Published by Saraband,
Digital World Centre, 1 Lowry Plaza
The Quays, Salford, M50 3UB

and

Suite 202, 98 Woodlands Road,
Glasgow, G3 6HB
www.saraband.net

10 9 8 7 6 5 4 3 2 1

ISBN: 9781912235582
ISBNe: 9781912235599

Printed and bound in Great Britain by Clays Ltd, Elcograf SpA.

MIX
Paper from
responsible sources
FSC® C018072

For Bill

RIAN

THE WINGED ISLE

Rian couldn't sleep. She sat up in bed, tugging tangles out of her hair. It was still her best feature, the colour of amber, as Pytheas used to be so fond of pointing out. She was no longer the wraith she was when she ran away from him. Her fingers were toughened by years of scrubbing and pounding, milking and churning, grinding and peeling. Who could imagine food and herbs could make a woman's hands so rough? They were always worst at this time of year, chapped and stinging after the winter. She had yarrow butter to soften them, but never remembered to use it, always leaving it until a cut became sore. One of those nail-edge rips that refuse to heal caught on her hair with a twinge. She sucked it, worrying.

Eventually she shook Manigan awake.

'There's something wrong about that woman.' She spoke in a whisper, even though the cliff-top house walls were thick stone. Sound moved in strange ways around these buildings: you could hear voices from places you couldn't see.

She lit a lamp. They had been given a splendid room. The bed was solid, with curtains on three sides, including the one she

1

was on next to the wall. The cloth was well woven and the warm colours shone in the flicker from the wick: a deep red and mellow brown with light green patches. It made her think of rowan trees. The coverlet was a patchwork of furs that had been so warm she'd had to throw it off in the night. Despite the comfort, she had hardly slept.

Manigan grunted and groped for her hand. His thick braid of hair was shot with a touch of silver, but she still found him the most beguiling person she had ever set eyes on. Still lithe, his smile still wonky. His beard was short-cropped and it suited him. After a night's sleep he was looking comfortably tousled again, a bit scruffy, and his sea-weathered skin was more relaxed than the day before at the party. She always thought he looked like a naughty child when he was freshly scrubbed. It wasn't his natural state.

When he stirred again, she said, 'There's something not right. She gives me the creeps.'

'Who?' His voice was woolly with sleep.

'Cuilc. She's too happy. I don't believe in her.'

He opened his eyes and gave her one of his baleful stares. 'Of course she's happy. It's only the bride's mother that gets sad at handfastings. She just got herself a daughter-in-law to do her laundry for her and cut the hay.'

Rian snorted. 'Can you imagine?'

They both chuckled at the picture of Rona attempting to wield a scythe or thump a laundry tub.

'She'll have to grow up now. She'll be fine. They're good people,' Manigan said.

It was true, she knew this. The handfasting had shown the community in a good light: plenty of funny stories and more food than you'd expect for spring. The boy Eadha adored Rona and she bore a mad passion for him. The only wrong note was his mother.

She pulled her hand out of Manigan's grasp. 'What if she's my mother?'

'Ach, be quiet. What on earth would make you think that? She's not old enough.'

'How old was I when I had Soyea?'

Manigan sighed. 'Did you drink too much last night?'

She sulked for a while at that. 'Did you hear Uill Tabar is dead?'

It had been the sort of gathering where you heard news about people you hadn't seen for years. The old mystic had died, seemingly, on a boat headed for the Long Island. He'd been helping with a tack and the boom had slipped out of the hands of the boy at the bow and caught Uill on the head. He had never come round.

Manigan pushed himself into a sitting position and took her hand again. 'I see where this is going. Yes, I did. Poor old fellow. I'll miss him.'

'He never told me who my parents were.'

'No. You never did get it out of him, the old teaser.'

She tried to clench her fist but Manigan had tight hold.

'It really bothers you, doesn't it?' he said.

'I can't bear not knowing. Sometimes it feels like I'm being eaten up by it, the sense that it's just out of reach. Danuta once told me everything would change when I found out who I came from. I have to ask her. Will you take me to Assynt?'

'Is that wise?'

'I have to go. I spoke to Ishbel, you know, the priestess, and she thinks Danuta's still alive. Hasn't heard otherwise, anyway.'

'Of course, if that's what you want to do, I'll take you.' He wrapped his other hand around the one he was already holding. 'But is it safe? Bael has a bad reputation. Worse than his father. And Ussa still goes there. It's one of her haunts.'

Rian shuddered at the mention of the slaver, her nemesis. 'I have to risk facing them. If Danuta dies I'll never know. Nobody else knows who I am.'

'Ach, Rian. I've told you a thousand times and I'll tell you again, you're whoever you let yourself be and to me you're the Queen of

3

the Sea.' He thrust his head down into her belly, rocked her under him, and wrestled with his big arms until she cuddled him back.

Their leaving was sore next morning, and Rian would have willingly stayed for days or weeks rather than part with her youngest daughter. But Manigan said they should abandon Rona to her new life, and the wind was easterly and ideal for the journey north to Assynt.

Soyea and Manigan were already installed on *Bradan* by the time Rian made her way to the cleft in the cliff where the boat had been hauled up. She followed Eadha, who led his mother, his new wife and his mother-in-law down the path. His head was high and he stood, legs a little apart, hand on one hip, as Rian gave Rona a final hug. Then he wrapped his other arm around Rona's shoulder, as if to show possession. Cuilc was hovering, so Rian briefly hugged her too, and was surprised, even so early, to smell strong drink on her breath.

Trying to keep from crying, Rian turned away to clamber onto the boat. She knew she should be happy, but Rona was so young to say goodbye to. Once aboard she faced the young couple. Her daughter was alight with excitement, gazing up into the flawless beauty of her husband's face.

Cuilc stood a few steps aside, watching, and when Rian waved to her a delighted smile broke onto her wrinkled face and she raised a hand, mouthing, 'Come again soon.'

Rian nodded.

Rona was waving goodbye with both hands, then laughing turned to say something to Eadha. He stood as before, his pose struck and held, arm raised as if bearing a torch, the other clasped around Rona's shoulder.

Bradan's sail lifted and they drew away from the shore, heading south down the loch. Rian stayed at the stern, watching until the three figures turned away and strolled back towards the cliff-top tower.

ACHMELVICH

It took three days of heavy sailing to get up to the Summer Isles. The tides were all wrong up the east coast of the Winged Isle and the sea around Rubha Reidh was so dangerous they had to turn back on the second day and retreat to the nearest loch, then try again the following morning. The weather was foul, the sea lumpy and they were all soaked and exhausted when they got to the big harbour on Tanera. But it was Badger and Kino's home, so they got a warm welcome.

Rian found her stomach churning at the prospect of what lay ahead. She had to force herself to eat. She hadn't felt so sick since she'd been pregnant with Soyea and Cleat, and the sensation made her think of her missing son. It was almost unbearable.

She couldn't go directly to Clachtoll, obviously, but Badger had a sister in Achmelvich. They sent word through fishermen from Tanera and heard back that she and Soyea were welcome to visit on the quiet. As far as anyone knew, the old crone was still there at the broch, although no one had seen her for ages.

The weather deteriorated and a storm kept them all indoors for two days. Tempers were poor and stores were low. When the wind died down to a level safe to sail, it was northerly, which was no use at all. Eventually, they woke to a strong breeze gusting from the south west and it was a relief to everyone to set off.

The wind gathered up the skirts of *Bradan* and hustled her north. As they came around Rubha Coigach, the sea was jabbly and uncomfortable. Rian felt sicker than ever.

Manigan pointed out the islands of Cleat and Soyea. Rian watched as her daughter scanned the islands she and her twin were named after. She felt the familiar pang of longing for her little boy, the hole in her heart that could never be filled as long as he was gone.

'They always make me think of seals,' Manigan said. 'Cleat is a round head, bobbing in the sea, and Soyea is lounging on a rock.'

Soyea's eyes were wide taking everything in: the birds circling the islands, seals peering at them from the safety of the water.

Reaching the shelter of the islands, the sea's motion eased. They rounded the west side of Soyea and sailed past a rocky promontory into a sheltered bay. They had agreed that *Bradan* would sail on north from Achmelvich to avoid drawing attention to their arrival, so only Rian and Soyea jumped ashore onto the white sands, after a fierce kiss and 'good luck,' from Manigan.

Badger's sister lived with her husband Thormid's family in a crannog on the lochan behind the machair. Rian led the way and halted at the lochside. There were three huts on islands in the water. A causeway had been built out to the newest one, but Rian felt shy about making the crossing without invitation. She felt Soyea at her shoulder.

'There's smoke,' her daughter whispered.

'Hello!' Rian called.

'Aye, aye.' An old woman pulled the door open.

'Hello Eilidh,' Rian said. The sight of the kind face, familiar from childhood, made her voice crack.

'It'll be Rian, is it?' She waved them over. 'Come along in. Welcome.'

The old woman sat them down on stools and stared into Rian's face. 'I remember you fine. You being sold as a slave was a crying shame. I don't know how Danuta lived with herself afterwards. It nearly sent her mad, you know.'

'How is she?' Rian wanted to rush out and run to Clachtoll, but at the same time she wasn't sure that she dared to go at all.

'I've not seen her or heard anything for a while,' Eilidh said.

Soyea was looking around, wide-eyed with delight at the crannog. 'This is like a fairy's house.'

The old woman chuckled. 'No, now. Thormid's handy enough, but there's no magic in it.' Taking a step to the door, she beckoned

Rian to join her. She waved her hand towards the furthest of the other two island huts. 'The old crannog is a bit ramshackle, but you're welcome to it.'

Rian looked out at the little round water-house. Its thatch had seen better days, but it was a kind offer. 'Thank you.'

Eilidh bustled her back to the stool. 'And now you'd better fill me in on what you've been doing with yourself all these years and how you come to be with the Walrus Mutterer.'

Rian sat back down. 'Well there's not much to tell. I met Manigan that first year. He helped me escape from Ussa and took me down deep south to a place where I could be safe.'

Eilidh seemed to be waiting for more.

'And I've had children. Three.' She pointed to Soyea. 'This is my eldest and there's another girl, Rona, whose handfasting we've just been to. And a boy, who's...' Rian petered out, then mustered, '...lost.' She never knew what to say about Cleat.

Eilidh tilted her head, sympathetically, and Rian guessed that she was assuming he was dead. It was often easier to let people think this than have to explain his absence.

SMELL OF THE SEA FLOWERS

The old crannog was barely fit for pigs: dark, musty and cold, its heather thatch disintegrating. But it was surrounded by water on all sides and there was safety in that. Rian was sure Soyea must be appalled by it, but she didn't know how to make it bearable. At least it was a bright day, and the midday sun streamed in through the doorway.

Soyea set her bag down on one of the benches, then plonked herself beside it. She looked big and ungainly in the cramped space, gazing around at the wonky roof beams. 'It's like something from a story, a hut of a water sprite.'

Rian was surprised. 'It's damp,' she said.

'What did you call it?'

'A crannog.'

'I can smell the sea.'

'Yes, it's all around us.' Rian pointed out of the door 'Down there, just beyond those woods, there's a sea loch, and then it's sea all the way round to the beach.' She swept her arm around to the back of the hut. 'We're on a peninsula.'

'Can we go and see?'

They set off to explore. Rian led the way around the edge of the lochan, then through some stunted birch trees. The ground rose slightly and suddenly they were out in the open, on the edge of a rocky shoreline, overlooking the mouth of a loch. Two gulls flapped away from them. Shags stood lined up on a rocky promontory. A curious head bobbed up in the shallows. Rian pointed it out to Soyea. 'Look, a seal.' Soyea nodded and rolled her eyes, as if to say she wasn't stupid, she could recognise a seal. Then she yawned.

'Do you want to have a nap?' Rian said. 'We've been travelling a lot, we're tired, and the day's been long.'

Soyea nodded, and they made their way back to the crannog. They spread bedding on the benches and set out their few belongings to try to give the hut a homely feel. Rian found herself yawning too, and when she lay down she found sleep came easily.

She woke refreshed. It was early evening and the scent of bluebells drifted out of the woods and mingled with the seaweed tang. It was the fragrance of her childhood. Somehow Ictis had never smelt as good as this. Different trees, a different sea.

Soyea lay, mouth slightly open, on the other bed. She would sleep for hours more, if left, and then not sleep at night. But Rian wanted this chance to be alone. She had always meant this return to be the three of them: her, Soyea and Cleat. But her son had never come back from wherever Pytheas had taken him and his hole in her life still ached like an old wound. She got up, her movements cat-quiet. The door creaked when she opened it, but didn't disturb her daughter. She took herself off across the narrow causeway, through the meadows to the beach.

They spent the evening with Eilidh and her family, in a blur of news about local people. Rian struggled to put faces to the names from her memory. She worried that it all must mean nothing to Soyea, but she seemed interested. Eilidh was good at making guests feel comfortable. Still, Rian felt on edge, nervous about what lay ahead, and as soon as she found herself yawning she excused herself. Eilidh seemed to understand.

The next morning, Rian woke early and intended to take herself off to the beach again, but as she was opening the door, Soyea spoke.

'Mother?' She was sitting up.

'I was just going out for a little walk.'

'Wait. Can I come?' Soyea stretched, yawning, then swung her legs out of bed.

Rian waited while Soyea got up, drank some water and found something warm to wear. The morning was bright but chilly and Rian was itching to get out. This wasn't her home territory exactly, but it was close enough and everything was familiar yet fresh. The anticipation of what she might find when we went to the broch was tantalising, but she was frightened too, she had to admit, and this bit of distance felt safe. She needed a day to get used to being back in Assynt before she faced her past.

She led Soyea down the burn that drained the lochan into the sea. They slithered on weedy rocks and squelched through the gunge where seawrack lay rotting. Rian crinkled her nose, but Soyea took great lung-fulls of it.

'Don't get it on your clothes, you'll stink for days,' Rian said.

'I love this smell, it's alive.'

Rian shook her head, laughing. 'I've carried too many baskets of it.' It had seemed a joyful effort when she had been a child: everyone carrying the wrack up from the high tide mark to the fields together. But in Ictis it had become an annual duty and eventually a winter chore, although the smell still roused some-thing in her. It was the fragrance of tides, of seasons passing. And it reminded her of Manigan. She missed him already. She always did, particularly sharply in the first few days of his absence. She wondered how far north he would have sailed already.

They scrambled along the rocky shoreline until they had a good vantage over the loch that cut its way inland, creating a shining bowl surrounded by crags and wooded slopes. With a rasp, a heron lifted and flapped away to a safer shore and two ducks whirred off in alarm. A long, low crescent of land jutted out into the loch, on which a dozen seals lay. They lifted their heads at the new arrivals and two or three slid into the water, but the others seemed unalarmed. More lounged on weedy islands. Those in the water swamed towards the shore, a family of upturned faces – curious, welcoming.

'Hello,' Rian said. 'I've been gone a long time. This is my daughter, Soyea.' There was something in their eager glide that made them appear pleased to see her. Could they possibly recog-nise her from all those years ago?

There were six of them lying on the island close to the south shore, one flapping its flipper as if it was waving. The swimming seals dipped under, leaving ring-ripples. Then one hurled itself out of the water, its sleek, wet body curving like a dolphin in a graceful arc of flight. And again! A leap up, across the loch. Again! A series of lifts, like a needle stitching a grey thread across the water, to gather up that moment so it could not be lost.

Soyea and Rian stood side by side, sharing the freedom they had been shown. The aspen trees behind them rustled with applause.

'Breakfast?' Rian said.

'Mmm.'

They returned along a path through the woods, which were full of bluebells and primroses, their scents mingling with sea-salt. Rian stopped at one point and fell to her knees to bury her nose in the blue flowers. 'It's the fragrance of the sea flowers, that's what I've been missing most.'

Soyea nodded, bent to sniff the perfume, and seemed to understand.

As they made their way back to the crannog, Rian pointed out other flowers: thrift, vetch, scurvy grass. She gave Soyea wood sorrel leaves to chew and told her she could gather bedstraw to make their home smell a little less musty and bring sweet dreams.

'When are we going to the place you grew up?' Soyea asked, when they got back to the little loch.

'Tomorrow, or the next day.' Rian felt a twinge of terror. What would she find there? But having said it, she was committed.

SOYEA

SOYEA'S STORY

Mother wears her scars with something close to pride. On a hot day like today she'll wear nothing but her lightest underclothes and we can all see the brand on her shoulder and the marks she said she got from a flogging. She has never made a fuss about it, but nor has she been unwilling to talk about it: she was a slave and then she ran away with Manigan. She has another mark on her thigh. It is ugly and pains her when the weather is cold and wet, but she says it reminds her of her good fortune to be living in freedom. One day, she says, there is a slaver who might come looking for her, and then she'll have to hide. She has told us this so often it has become a bit of a family joke. Whenever we come home and she isn't there, or whenever we don't know where she is, we say she's hiding from Ussa. 'Check the meal-bin', Manigan will say, 'she might be in there hiding from Ussa'. Or he'll lift a pot lid and say, 'Are you in there, Rian? Come out, Ussa's not here.'

She goes off on her own quite often. I used to think it was normal, but I've learned she isn't normal at all. Sometimes she comes back with herbs. That's her excuse, collecting medicines. But often she comes back empty handed, and I can tell from her hair and her cheeks that she's been out on the edge of the ocean, and occasionally I can tell from her eyes that she's been crying.

12

Since we got here, to Assynt, she's been off walking on her own a lot, but she comes back dry-eyed mostly, so I don't mind too much. I don't know what she does on her walks. One day perhaps I'll ask her. I guess she thinks about Cleat, my brother. I hardly remember him, if I'm really honest. But he was always here. Still here but still not here. My twin. An absence.

We have been due to come to Assynt forever. Ever since I can remember it has been, 'When Cleat comes home, I'll take you to Assynt to see the islands you're named after.' Mother has promised this all my life, ever since Cleat went away with our father. We knew he might be gone a few months, but then it became a year, then two, then more. He never came back. My father was from far away. His name was Pytheas and he was taking Cleat to see his home and then they would come back. That was what was supposed to happen. Every spring we would prepare again and every year when the autumn storms began, Mother would slump. Then we would decide that they would come next year.

This year is different. I don't know if she has given up, or whether it was Rona's marriage that made her decide that this year she would take me to Assynt anyway, Cleat or no Cleat. If he ever does come, he'll be a man now.

Rona is my half-sister. Manigan is her father. She is beautiful and I am ugly. She is small and dark like a fairy girl. I am too big, with dull brown hair and a face like a horse.

Manigan adores my sister and often took her away with him to visit his family on the islands south of here. It was on one of those trips that she met the man who is now her husband, Eadha. He is like her, another beautiful creature.

I look strange because my father came from far away. Manigan says I am beautiful too. He says I am exotic. But he lies all the time. That's his role in life, telling long, elaborate stories that are made up and mostly not true, just to make some little point that could have been made with a single gesture.

Mother is more likely just to make the gesture.

They are so different it is hard to see why they get on so well, but they adore each other. I used to think that was normal, too, but I know different now. Many people are not so lucky. I am thankful that I am not married. I will not settle for less than Mother has with Manigan. I will only handfast with a man I love. Perhaps I never will, on account of being ugly and exotic. When she was my age she had already given birth to the three of us, but she says she was too young. She says there is plenty of time for me, that there is no hurry.

But sometimes I am in a hurry. I want life to offer me up a romance like in one of Manigan's stories. Maybe a handsome Selkie man will come out of the sea and claim me as his own. Or a hunter will sail in from the north and anchor himself to me. Or perhaps he is here already, living in a towering stone house beside the shore, like the one in my dream.

I only met my father once when I was very small, when he took my brother away. Mother says I got my love of writing from him. I can't remember a time before I knew how to write, and I think I recall playing with his feather and parchment, but maybe I've simply heard the story so many times it has become a picture in my head. I imagine a tall, thin, upright man, but he is shadowy, and I do not believe he is a real memory. But perhaps he is. Does it matter?

I don't want this story to be like one of Manigan's – long and tangled and with loose ends hanging off it everywhere. I want to tell you everything you need to know to keep on with it, wanting to hear a little bit more, dying to find out what happens in the end, with satisfying twists and surprises, everything linking to something else. And, of course, a happy ending. It might not be real, but it would be a good tale. That's what matters. Mother says the truth matters, but I know she loves a good story too and I sometimes think she loves Manigan because he has wrapped her in so many stories. She says there are still dozens he hasn't ever quite got around to finishing for her. She says if I want to make a good story, I should practise on some of his, and where there are bits missing or no ending, I should finish them, make them whole, then see if Manigan likes them. I'm going to try with the story of the stone. Or one of them. There are many.

Once upon a time there was a king called Ban. He was powerful, both physically and mentally. He was a brave and strategically clever warrior and had already protected his kingdom for many years when his wife bore him a son, Geevor.

I already don't like the way I am telling this tale. I want to be able to picture Ban, and to know about his wife. Perhaps I can understand why Manigan's stories are all so convoluted. He gets interested in all these things as well, and one story leads to another, and they weave in and out of each other, nesting inside one another like magic toys.

I am going to think about how to tell the tale of Ban and Geevor, and while I am considering this I shall instead relate my own history. Or Mother's story, which almost amounts to the same thing, or so it seems to me.

I was born on Whale Island in the Seal Isles, where there is a temple in the shape of the body of a whale, tended by a priestess called Shadow. Whale Island is fertile and beautiful I am told, although I have never seen it as I left it during the first summer of my life.

I am the daughter of an explorer, Pytheas, who traveled from a place far to the south called Massalia, which is part of a huge empire centred upon an even more distant place called Athens. My father spoke a language, Greek, but also other tongues. He was searching for the origins of amber, ivory and tin. Mother was a slave and he bought her with amber and that is why he is my father. He sold her again later and she ended up belonging to the chieftain of a land in the north. But there she met a walrus hunter called Manigan and ran away with him. It was he who took her to Whale Island. She was pregnant with me and my brother (she didn't know there would be two of us, of course) so she stayed with the priestess Shadow while Manigan sailed away to hunt and trade his walrus ivory.

She missed him and wondered if he would ever return, but he did. He brought her a gold bracelet and asked her to handfast with him. He did not seem to mind the fact that she had a son and a daughter by another man. Nor did he mind that she was a runaway slave with brands on her shoulder and thigh. He loved her and she loved him.

My brother Cleat and I were born just after Imbolc. Manigan went away north to hunt walruses, but he came back in time for Beltane and they handfasted, leaping the sacred fire together in the whale temple. At the end of the summer hunting season, he took Mother and the two of us south to Belerion, to a tidal island called Ictis where the Spirit Keepers live. They made an offering of a walrus tusk to the Keepers and Manigan's Great Aunt Fraoch took us all in and gave Mother a role in the temple so she would feel she belonged. She and Manigan were given a hut to live in and they spent the next winter there, by the end of which Mother was pregnant again with my sister Rona, which is an island near to where Manigan grew up.

All three of us are named after islands, which seems appropriate, as we are all separated from each other, no matter how close we seem or try to be. Mother and Manigan are different; they are joined together. Even when Manigan travels away to hunt or trade, which he does a lot, Mother seems somehow still to be linked to him. She talks about him as if he is just on the other side of the fire even when he is far away over the ocean, as if a causeway still connects them, the way Ictis is joined to the mainland.

There is a story – I don't know how real it is – that we stayed on Ictis while Manigan went away to hunt every year, because Mother was safe there from Ussa. She is the trader who first bought my mother. They say she still wants to take Mother back into slavery, but back then she could not, as long as we were protected by the Keepers. That's the story of my life, in essence: hiding, caged with Mother, trying to believe in her fear.

THE BEACH

Mother and I get up early to walk to the place where she grew up. I don't know quite what to expect and I am pleasantly surprised. It is a long walk, but splendid, full of wonderful corners. It seems to waken my mother out of her despondency as each feature we encounter brings her back to some incident of her childhood. This place is full of happy memories for her.

We walk the main track from here down to the beach and then head north up to another, smaller, lovelier beach at the far end of which is a shrine to the Goddess. It is still early when we reach there and the moon is beaming across the sea from the west, into the shrine. It is so beautiful, it is impossible not to worship. I begin to speculate that Mother has been planning this for days, just so we could watch the moon set over the ocean.

The moon seems to be guiding us on this journey. On our voyage north to the Winged Isle, one beautiful evening we sailed into a bay and anchored just off a small island. It was protected to the west by an even smaller island, silhouetted by the setting sun. The full moon rose out of the eastern landmass and its silver beam rippled across to our boat as if it was a blessing. We poured a few drops of mead onto the shining water and Mother sang a strange song I had never heard her sing before. Then Manigan spoiled it all by groping and kissing her and telling her how much he loved her. In front of me! I wish they would keep it to when they're alone, in private, but Mother says he has been away so much of their lives, they must squeeze every drop out of the time they have together.

For me, though, it was a moment to be respectful, to allow the moon herself to be the centre of our attention. I focused on her white orb, slightly dented, a day away from full, like a bone button, not quite a true circle but all the more beautiful for its flaw, easier to be with than perfection.

Right now, Mother's having one of her holy moments. 'The cave is sacred,' she says, as if that was not obvious, 'it is one of the yonis.'

I nod. I don't know why, but I'm not interested in doing a ceremony with her, here, with the moon sinking into the sea.

'Are we going to your broch?' I must sound petulant. She doesn't notice.

'After we have made a blessing.'

'We already made one this morning.'

She ignores me, gathering shells and bits of weed, a washed-up stick. I can't help but do the same. It is not worth a fight.

'Good,' she says, when she sees the feather and the intact cockle shell, like a butterfly, that I find. I pick up a scraggy bit of dry seaweed as well, the first thing I set my eyes on. It's slimy and I regret it. And then I see a skull, a small bird's brain case, with beak, and I drop the wrack and lift the bone delicacy. It weighs nothing at all.

Mother gives a little gasp when she sees it.

'Beautiful. Perfect.' Her rapture is pleasing, and a bit infectious. With this skull, I do feel as if I now need to do something formal. I am holding flight in my hands: a bird's brain and feather and a shell in the form of wings.

I follow mother into the cave, and I lay down my offering and wish I could fly away, to be free like my sister, to be unleashed from my mother and her constant penance.

'You'll fly soon enough.' She is reading my mind as usual and she has spoiled my ceremony. I leave. I can see myself in her eyes and no doubt she is thinking I have 'flounced off.'

She stays. I hope she will ask forgiveness for me from the Yoni spirit. I ask myself, under my breath.

On my own I could have made myself a nice ceremony, a gift

to the spirit in there, and I would have listened for the Goddess to speak to me. But I can't hear anything when my mother is eavesdropping on my thoughts.

I wander back down to the edge of the sea and watch a soaring gannet. It dives, allowing itself to fall like a dead weight, and as it hits the water, spray splashes up as if a rock has fallen. What must that feel like? Terrifying. Exhilarating also. Another plummets, and then another. Then they lift themselves up out of the waves and with their big, strong wings they power up again, skywards. One flies towards me and looks down with its beautiful yellow head, its long, graceful black-tipped wings outstretched. I reach my arms out, showing the bird my full wingspan in greeting, and wish myself up into the sky. As it beats out to join its fellows, I am there with it. They rise to meet us, flanking us, wings in synchrony, up, up into the blue, blue sky. It is glorious. We soar onwards, now in a line, now like an arrowhead shooting away into whatever is beyond.

'If you want some time alone in there, with your gifts…' Mother is beside me. 'I'm sorry if I presumed to know your thoughts.'

I shake my head.

'Then we can carry on, whenever you're ready.'

'I'm ready.'

'I'm glad you're here, Soyea.'

'Which way is it?'

'Up there.' She indicates the sheer rock face to the north. 'There's a lovely path, or there used to be.'

We make our way up around a strange pooling of water in the sand. 'It's never the same twice,' Mother says. 'Nothing lovely ever is.'

Why is she talking? I want her to quieten down and allow the world to talk instead, in smells and colours and the sounds of other animals.

'There's a dragon along here,' she says, 'and we might see an otter, or at least the signs of it. You know my old medicine pouch?

That was an otter I caught along here, well, not really me, it was Drost that set the snare, but I found the otter in it.'

She points out bright green mounds where the otters come to mark their territory with spraint. Although I don't ask her for details, I get the full story of the capture and killing of the animal and how she learned to cure a skin.

There is a pool of dark water, like the pupil of an eye, and around it a mat of short, tight grass of the greenest green. I stare into the water. Eventually she stops talking and we both stand there gazing silently down into the blackness.

'Is it magic?' I say.

'Ask the otter.'

I glance at her and see she is not looking at the pool, but away to our left. And then I see it too: the sleek, black catlike creature bounding across rocks towards us. Either it hasn't seen us or it doesn't care that we are there. Perhaps it knows we mean it no harm. It is on a journey, stopping to peer into dark gaps under rocks, sniffing occasionally, but intent on its way, beautifully purposeful. It gleams. Its pelt is far more vibrant than Mother's bag, which is soft and smooth. This creature is glossy and has burnished-brown glints among its fur. Its bright eyes dart, pretty little head cocking to one side or the other. It is more alive than anything I have ever seen. No wonder its spraint post is such bright green. Everything about this animal is more intense than the world normally is. Mother and I are stock still as the otter seems suddenly to decide to attend to us. It looks up, and scrutinises us as if trying to decide what to say to such an intrusion.

'Hello,' Mother says. The otter stares at her, and then at me, and I swear it has murder in its eyes. It would eat us if it could.

'Are you wondering what we would taste like?' I say to it inside my head. This seems to decide the matter of our inedibility and it turns and scampers off, flowing across the steep crag as if the gaps and holes among the boulders did not exist. I marvel at how footsure and in possession of this place it is.

We walk on to a place where Mother says the dragon lives in a sea cave under the cliff, but I only see the waves melting over the rocks. 'It is sleeping,' she says. 'We'll have to come again another day.'

I stand looking out to sea. It is grey and flat. The moon has set into a bank of cloud that is drawing across the sky like a blanket slowly pulled up over a bed. The sun lights everything from the east, but I can see it will soon be engulfed.

'What's the matter?' Mother asks.

I cannot tell her how it feels to be in her world, where everything is new to me but familiar to her, and delightful or disappointing depending on how it has changed since her childhood; where everything is meaningful to her but meaningless to me; how alone I seem here, how empty my life is, how everything I have and do is shaped by her and how I drag along behind. I am just a net hauled in her wake, heavy with fish that she wants to catch, encircled by seabirds she has attracted. I want to empty myself and be free. I want to be alone. I want to be myself. I want to be someone else than who I am here. I am stifled by breathing the air she has already breathed. I think of Rona, who has escaped, and though I'm glad to be free of her irritating presence, I'm discovering in her absence that she used to shield me from Mother.

'Nothing,' I say.

'I suppose it's all new and strange.'

But that is not it. It is not new or strange at all. It is imprinted all over with her footprints and handprints. It is all old and all known. It is second hand. It is hers.

I am quiet and kneel down to peer at the flowers. At least they are fresh. She looks searchingly at me then shakes her head a little, turns, and walks on.

RIAN

CLACHTOLL

When Rian and Soyea reached the mouth of the salmon stream, Rian paused and thought about Manigan. For years now, he went off out to sea like a migratory fish and, as reliable as a trout, he always returned. Over and over he had done this now, sailing north to hunt, then back south to rejoin her. They had spent so many winters together, there could be no doubt he would come back safely, and yet there was always a sliver of worry that she couldn't shake off.

She showed her daughter where to slither down the slippery crag to the river, as if it had been only yesterday when she had been here last. They splashed across the easy shallows down by the shore, then cut inland up the far side of the busy torrent and along a track through woodland. There were birds singing in the treetops at first, but as the cloud covered the sun they fell quiet and the brightness of the morning dulled.

Beyond the woods was grassy land, cultivation and a few smoking huts. Rian was tense, holding herself upright as she walked. They were getting close. Did she really have the courage to go back to that place? Soyea was looking around, wide-eyed, with her customary curiosity. Rian took a deep breath. She was no longer the foster child who was sold by Drost. She was a mother now. Her daughter was becoming a woman she was proud of.

As they emerged from the woods, Rian waited for Soyea to look left, and enjoyed the look of wonder on her face as she saw, for the first time, the extraordinary cleft promontory jutting out into the sea.

'Clachtoll,' she said. 'Rock hole. It gives its name to the whole place.' She pointed ahead to the tall stone tower. 'Look.'

Soyea blinked. 'Is that the house?'

Rian nodded.

'You never told me it was a broch.'

She shrugged. 'It was just the new house when I was growing up. I didn't know it was special then. I presumed they were everywhere.'

'I'm hungry,' Soyea said.

Rian was too, and tired. It was further than she remembered and it had been hard going on the slippery coastal path, but she said nothing. She felt sick with dread at the sight of the big stone building, yet maybe Danuta was still there. She let that longing tug her onward. They passed a group of huts and mounded strips of field surrounded by wattle fences. Cattle ranged about, black and hairy, with huge horns and a wild look in their eyes.

Soyea made to coax one to let her stroke it but Rian knew that would be a long, long game, and urged her to press on. She pointed out the sandy beach on their left. Soyea said she didn't think it was as pretty as Achmelvich. Rian didn't care. She tried to focus on the flowers. The air rang with the sound of gulls and swallows zipped about among the cattle, just as they had always done, so why did she have such a feeling of dread?

They passed a girl, a bit younger than Soyea, with a prod in her hand. She was trying to persuade a cow to stop grazing, without much success, and she smiled a warm, shy smile, with no trace of recognition. Of course not. Yet Rian knew exactly who she must be. She was the image of Duileag as she had been back when they were both girls. She stopped, and wondered whether to say something, but then walked on. The girl and Soyea shared a glance and smiled again. Rian was pleased. Perhaps there could be new friendships. Perhaps old acquaintances could be rekindled.

They made their way onto the peninsula, the broch becoming more and more imposing as they approached. Rian gestured towards the sheltered pool beyond it, where several boats were moored, but she couldn't find any words. Her mouth was dry. It was eerie that there were no people milling about or even animals, although there were signs that pigs had been churning the ground. Sure enough, as they got even closer a large boar came grunting towards them. A sow with piglets joined the boar and they crowded around them wanting food, or as if questioning why they were there. It was a strange welcome party. Rian wished she had a stick. The sow was leaning in on them and squealing, smearing mud on their skirts. The boar was aggressive. Rian aimed a kick at the boar's throat that kept the big pig marginally at bay while they made their way to the gate. It was a stout wattle affair, lashed firmly in place to ensure no one could intrude easily. The pigs were maddening, butting against them, hungry. Rian worked away at the knots in the rope until the gate opened, and with a few more kicks and a rapid dash and slam, they were inside and the pigs were not.

Rian called out. 'Anybody home?'

Soyea struggled with the ropes until Rian returned to help her. Soyea had never got the hang of knots, and Rian didn't understand why not. She had tried to teach her many times, but Soyea's hands didn't seem to be able to remember what to do.

They were at the broch. The stonework was still stunning, the tower daunting close up. And it was surrounded by a maze of new walls: cells, bunkers, sheds. Smoke trailed out of a low stone building but there was remarkably little activity. Rian was trying not to give away her fear to Soyea. She needed to be brave in front of her daughter, but the brooding silence was alarming. Why was there no dog? Soyea kept close to her, frowning.

Rian stopped by a new curving wall and glanced back towards the gate. She tried to moisten her mouth and speak as if this was normal. 'This used to be my house,' she said. 'It's changed a lot.'

They continued circling through the labyrinthine stonework. 'What is with all these walls?' Rian said to herself.

And then they reached the tower entrance. At least the fine wooden door, ajar, was still the same.

Rian banged on it and called again. 'Anybody home?'

There was still no answer.

DANUTA

Rian pushed open the door into the narrow passage between the walls. The wicker inner door was hanging open off snapped hinges. It was dingy inside and smelt of cow dung and urine. A thin little cat rubbed around her ankles, miaowing. She leant down to stroke it, absently, and it tried to bite her hand as if it was unused to friendliness.

Rian could feel Soyea at her shoulder as she made her way through the stour. The mud floor underfoot and low, ramshackle wattle overhead made the room seem more like a byre than a house.

'Come in,' said an unfamiliar voice.

Soyea clutched Rian's wrist. Rian could feel her heart pounding. Her eyes were taking a while to adjust to the gloom, but she made out a skinny woman sitting in a chamber opposite the door, up a few steps, across the muddy floor. She shifted and the yellow pool of light from a tallow lamp lit her wan face. She had a leather garment across her knees and was mending a tear in it with a big, clumsy needle and thick thread.

'It's a lovely day out,' Rian said. Who was this, and why would

25

anyone be sitting indoors stitching by lamplight when they could be outside in the brightness?

'I'm sure it is, and I'm stuck in here with the crone.'

It was impossible to tell how old this woman was. Her face was lined. She wore a baggy tunic and tatty skirt and her hair was covered by a woollen scarf as dark and grimy as the rest of her clothes.

'Is Danuta here?' Rian asked.

In answer, the woman gestured to a dark hole in the wall to their left. Rian's shoulders lifted and her neck tightened. She glanced round to Soyea and raised her eyebrows.

'What's your name?' she asked the woman.

'They call me Donnag here.' She didn't lift her gaze from her stitching, as if it was not really her name, just a temporary inconvenience.

'Are you Bael's wife?'

The woman looked at Rian, clearly wondering who she might be, and gave the tiniest of nods. Her face was etched with sadness and her eyes were dark, yellowed and sick-looking. Inside that bundle of clothes there was little of her. Whatever curiosity she may have, she didn't express it as a question.

Rian said, 'I grew up here.'

Donnag gave another, almost imperceptible nod.

'Is Danuta well?' Rian was trying to sound like she was just making conversation, not as if she was asking a question of life or death.

Donnag gave a tiny shake of her head and blinked. This minimal gesture conveyed clearly enough that there was serious illness in the building, and until now there was no help and nothing that could be done about it. Rian didn't know how she could possibly deduce this from one look at her, but she did. Donnag's gaze lowered to the leatherwork on her lap; it was clearly a difficult task, one of many difficult tasks that weighed her down. Rian ushered Soyea towards the room in the wall.

She pulled aside the curtain across the doorway. It was dark inside. The smell of stale urine intensified. The air was dense with sickness.

'Danuta?' Rian's voice was soft, like a child's.

There was only a whimper in response.

A little light filtered into the chamber. Rian crouched beside the low bed, where Danuta's face peered out from a bundle of fleece and blankets, shrunken and wizened, her eyes deep in their sockets, but still speedwell blue.

Rian swallowed, then managed to speak. 'You're still alive. I'm so happy to see you.' She wasn't too late. Yet in her mind Danuta had always been as she had last seen her, eighteen years ago. She had seemed old even then, although hearty and strong, but now she was a vision of death.

'Rian.' The crone's voice was little more than a whisper, but it had a note of joy in it that made tears come into Rian's eyes. A bony hand scrabbled out from inside the covers to reach for her face. The old woman struggled to shift but Rian stilled her.

'You don't need to sit up.' Rian took her hand with both of hers and lifted it to her cheek, then kissed it. She couldn't stop the tears, didn't want to.

'Don't cry,' Danuta whispered, and then chuckled, and the smile on her face was such a beautiful crumpling that Rian felt she would burst with love for her. Then a cough caught the laugh and a terrible wheezing hack engulfed the old woman. Rian feared she would surely die.

Eventually her coughing eased. 'Rian.' Her voice was a whisper.

'I was afraid I would be too late.' Rian reached for a handkerchief and blew her nose.

'They've not quite managed to finish me off yet. And who's this with you?'

Rian turned. Soyea was standing just inside the doorway, shock on her face.

Rian supposed she had never seen anyone look so ill. She

27

gestured to her to come close. 'This is my daughter, Soyea. Come and meet Danuta, my foster mother, the only mother I ever knew.'

Blinking, the girl stepped towards the bed.

'Soyea.' The crone's eyes were eating her up. 'You know what it is?'

She nodded. 'The island.'

Danuta beamed first at Soyea, then at Rian: an ancient smile, yet somehow as fresh as one of the seashore flowers.

'I had a twin brother, Cleat.'

Rian watched Danuta digest this, her eyes shifting between the two of them. Rian knew Danuta could see that this was painful for her.

'You must have many stories.' Danuta clutched Rian's hand and in that touch was all the optimism, the ability always to be positive even when everything was wrong, that had kept her alive all this time. And then the terrible coughing started again.

Rian pushed Soyea ahead of her out of the chambered cell into the centre of the broch and swept her hand up over her forehead. She breathed deeply, then pulled her hair back into a bunch behind her neck, tugged a ribbon out of her pocket and tied it. The effect was stern, she knew, but she was ready to work.

She turned to Soyea and looked her steadily in the eye, speaking in a murmur. 'I didn't expect her to be alive. I may need to stay here for a while. She needs care. Are you willing to stay and help?'

Soyea gave one of her noncommittal shrugs, which Rian decided to treat as assent. It made no difference anyway. It was obvious that she had to be here. The place was a mess, as if no one had treated this hearth as their home for some time. Danuta needed to be looked after.

'I may have to be rude to our hosts.' She took a few strides to where the quiet figure sat mending, and raised her voice. 'Donnag. Danuta needs a hot drink. May I light your fire?'

'The embers died ages ago, Buia might have some.'

'I can make it.'

Donnag looked down blankly, as if she was asleep.

'Would you mind if I build fire in the hearth? Is there someone else's permission to ask?'

Rian was trying to avoid a desecration but it was not clear Donnag appreciated the situation. Who had let the hearth fire die? Who cooked here normally? Rian didn't wait for Donnag to answer. She was already on her knees, pulling her spark stone from her pouch, teasing fibres of cotton grass into a light fluff.

Donnag put down the leatherwork. 'I'll go and get Buia.' She stood like an old woman, shuffled to the entrance arch. Before she bent to pass through it, she turned.

'Who are you?'

'Rian.' She struck a spark. The cotton grass flared.

'Rian.' Donnag gave no sign that the name meant anything to her. She ducked through the passage out of the broch, leaving the door ajar.

'Can you find any firewood?' Rian asked Soyea. 'Try there.' She gestured to the doorway.

As Rian fed the flame, coaxing birch bark and twigs into burning, Soyea rummaged and soon found a stack of birch logs in one of the antechambers of the passageway. There was not much kindling but that was never much of a problem to Rian. The fire wanted to burn for Danuta, it was easy. She had water heating within a few minutes and sent Soyea to get more fresh water from a well outside. By the time she returned with the bladder filled, Rian was rummaging in the wicker bedding trunk.

Muttering about the things she needed, she handed Soyea cloths and blankets to take into Danuta's room. When the water boiled, she set some mint and meadowsweet from her pouch to infuse in a pot and refilled the kettle.

Soyea seemed happy enough to help. She was a good girl and liked to be useful. They went in to see Danuta, who was dozing.

29

When she woke, Rian told her she had a brew for her cough. She let Soyea hold the cup to her lips and watched as her foster mother and her daughter encountered each other.

Danuta sipped, then smiled that crumply smile. 'Mother bless you, Soyea.' She looked into the girl's face. 'You are a handsome young woman.'

'No, I'm not. I'm ugly.'

'Psht. How old are you?'

'Seventeen.'

'You'll be a beauty in your twenties. You're striking. And you're modest and don't think too much of yourself. That's never a bad thing. Is your mother good to you?'

Soyea nodded, frowning. Danuta winked at Rian.

'You're still as beautiful as ever, Rian.'

This time it was Rian's turn to say 'Psht'.

'Is this it for children?'

'There's Rona, a bit younger, and already handfasted. But nothing more after her, sadly.'

'The father?'

'Rona's father is Manigan, the Walrus Mutterer.' Saying his name, the words were sweet in her mouth.

'So the rumour was true.' Danuta smiled. 'Is he good to you?'

Rian warmed at the thought of him. 'When he's with me, he is all a woman could ask for. But he is married to the ocean first.'

'And Soyea?'

'Do you remember the Southern man who was with Ussa?'

Danuta opened her eyes wide and looked at Soyea again as if understanding her 'striking' appearance, her strange coloured skin and wiry hair.

'What was his name again?'

'Pytheas.'

'You've so much to tell me, little bird. Can you forgive me for not protecting you?' There were tears in her eyes. Rian saw the memories were painful for both of them. The coughing started again.

'We must do something better for that cough.' Rian looked about her. 'Where are your herbs?'

Danuta gestured vaguely upwards into the loft space to the right of the doorway, where baskets and bundles were stacked. Rian rummaged about for a while, then said, 'How long have you been like this? There's nothing fresh here.'

Danuta's eyes were closed and she didn't respond.

'I'll see what we can do for you.' Rian took a breath. 'I know you're tiring, but I must ask. Donnag, is she nursing you?'

'That girl is a bone picked clean of all flesh. She cannot look after herself let alone another.' There was anger in Danuta's voice, quiet as it was.

'And Buia? Where is she?'

'Out there somewhere in her own place. I don't know what's the matter with her. Sometimes for a few days she will be here and she looks after me but mostly I don't think she is in this world. I can't walk, Rian. I am a burden on them.'

'And Drost?'

'He has gone west.'

For a moment Rian thought she meant he was in the Hebrides, then she understood he was dead. The relief made her feel she could breathe fully for the first time in years.

'But Bael is still here?'

'When he is here, he is here. When he is not, he is not.'

So there was still cause for caution. She didn't want to think about it.

'Well we're here now. I found some clean bedding for you.'

She arranged some sacks for Danuta to sit on and they lifted her out. She weighed nothing. They stripped the bed. The bedding was foul, the heather beneath it needed replacing but for now they just put down a cleanish hide Rian took from the main room and let Danuta lie back again.

Then it was time to think about something to eat.

BAEL

The dim light faded as someone entered the passage. The bowed figure straightened up and Rian tensed. She would have recognised him anywhere, even in this gloom. He blocked the doorway like a dog down a badger hole.

She measured out a cupful of barley and tipped it into the cooking pot, then put down the cup. 'Hello Bael. How are you?'

His laugh was a bark.

'How am I, Rian? Aye. That's a question, that is.' He scoffed at her. 'I'm very well, thank you.' He spoke in a boy's voice, as a child is taught to say it, mocking her. Then in his normal voice. 'I'm getting low on barley, that's how I am.'

'Well I wish you a good harvest this year.'

Rian's voice was calm. She would not be intimidated by the boy who was horrible to her as a child. He might be the son of the man who sold her into slavery, but she was a woman now and Drost was dead.

'This is my broch and you might as well hear it from me. You're not welcome, coming here, getting in the way of my wife.'

Rian interrupted him.

'Danuta is sick. I will stay as long as I can be helpful to her. She needs a healer.'

He might have been surprised by her forcefulness, but he backed quickly into deep sarcasm, clearly a place he frequented.

'A healer, are you?' He used the formal form of you and made a mock bow.

'I am not a healer, no, but I have not forgotten what she taught me and I'll repay her in the usual way.'

'Not in my house.'

'Yes, in your house.'

It was still unclear what this man looked like. He was silhouetted. But this provocation brought him into the space, so the light improved as he stopped blocking the door and it was a surprise to Rian that he was not more ugly. He had one eye that didn't open properly, yet despite that he had his father's good looks, with strong cheeks and high, wide brows, and he was dressed in a fine, decorated leather jerkin and high boots. There was something of the dandy about him, but when he spoke, his mouth narrowed into a sneer.

'You're not welcome, I tell you.'

'Danuta has welcomed me. I will not go unless she asks me to, except to gather herbs.'

'The old bitch can get her own herbs.'

'While I am here you will not talk about Danuta that way.'

'I'll talk how I like in my own house.'

'Danuta's your grandmother. You should have more respect.'

'You talk just like her.'

'Thank you.'

'Boring and bossy. I'll tell you one more time you're not welcome and you can go of your own will or I'll throw you out.' He laughed his barking laugh again.

'You're not intimidating me,' she said. Soyea was backing towards the wall between Danuta's room and the doorway, looking as if she would like to be able to vanish or at least make a quick getaway. Rian didn't blame her. Bael's snarl was enough to make anyone want to run away. But for her sake, if nothing else, she had to be strong and resist him.

'I'm making porridge for Danuta and my daughter. Shall I make enough for you too? And Donnag?'

'I don't want your stinking food. You'll probably try to poison me.'

Rian let a pause come and pass, while she thought how to respond.

'I'll make a bit extra so there's some left over in case Donnag would like some.' She tried to make it sound as if she was simply talking to the porridge pan, as if Bael was no longer there.

He stood with legs apart and his chin jutting forwards, ready to bite back at the next question or remark thrown at him. Rian's avoidance of his aggression left him nothing to chew on, so he turned to Soyea.

'Another generation of ugly bitches.' He looked her up and down and although she must have been shrinking inwardly, she didn't show it. 'You must have been fucking a bull to sire that one.'

'My father was Greek. That's why I look different.' This was what Rian had taught Soyea to say to the children who mocked her. She hadn't heard her say it for a few years.

'My father was Greek.' He repeated it back in a high voice. 'That's why I look different.' Then in his usual voice. 'The freak can talk.'

She nodded 'I like talking. It's how we show other people what we're like.'

Rian was proud of her for saying that. She was so brave. And as Bael didn't reply it became clear what a powerful thing it was to have said. He couldn't merely sling it back. It had pierced him, and Rian saw that most of what came out of him was a kind of shield, an external casing of harsh words. He was like a crab, all shell and claws but soft and spineless inside. The pincers may be dangerous but as long as one could stay out of their range, he had no agility, and no inner strength to sustain an attack.

'I'm not staying here to be insulted. Mind you're not still here when I get back.' He ducked out through the low doorway.

Soyea turned to Rian, who lifted her eyebrows and smiled.

'That was Bael.' She stirred the porridge.

'I'm sorry about that boy,' a little voice said. Soyea peeked into Danuta's chamber. Rian listened in from the hearth.

'What?' said Soyea.

'I'm sorry about Bael. He's rotten. Don't let him upset you.'

'You don't need to be sorry.'

'I heard what you said to him. You're a wise one for your age, aren't you, little bird?'

Rian could hear that she was smiling in that cherubic, crumpled way again, and she realised why she called her own children 'little bird'.

'Rian's making porridge,' Soyea said. 'It's a lovely day. Do you want to go outside later?'

'I've not been outside for a long time.' Her voice sounded wistful.

Soyea stuck her head out of the doorway. 'Can we take Danuta outside later?'

Rian began dishing porridge into bowls. 'Maybe another day. When she has a bit more strength.'

Danuta managed a few mouthfuls. After Soyea's bowl was empty, Rian stayed with Danuta while Soyea went to wash the porridge pot and bowls. The food seemed to have tired the old woman. She closed her eyes and dozed. Rian was content just to sit there, in her presence, treasuring her.

Soyea returned with the bowls. They were new, decorated with a strange, rather beautiful dimpled pattern Rian had not seen before.

'Who made these?' Soyea said. 'They're lovely.'

Danuta opened her eyes. 'Donnag does them like that. It's the island style.' She gestured in the direction of the sea. 'She's from the long island.'

Rian would think of the scrawny woman differently now she knew she made these pleasing round bowls with delicate, rhythmic patterns.

'I'm sorry about Bael,' Danuta said to Rian.

Rian said nothing.

'He was never a good brother to you.'

'He's not my brother.'

Danuta's face lit up. 'Did you meet Uill Tabar?'

Rian's mouth twisted, and she chewed her bottom lip. She said nothing, but nodded.

Danuta reached for Rian's hand. 'I'm glad you met him before he died, Rian. So you know.'

'I don't…' Rian said. 'I still don't really know.'

'Didn't Uill tell you?'

'Soyea, would you like to put the bowls back?' This wasn't really a question, more of an order. Soyea couldn't hide her disappointment. She must have known there were important things to be said and that she would miss them, but she picked up the bowls and spoons and took them out into the main room of the broch and dumped them by the fireplace where the embers were cooling.

'Oh Rian, I'm so sorry about that day,' Danuta said.

She was crying, and Rian didn't know how to make it all right. She sat still, staring at the floor as if no one else was there.

After Danuta repeated her apology, Rian took her hand and stroked it. 'No point in being sorry now,' she said, wanting to ask about her parents, but tongue-tied in the face of Danuta's sorrow.

Neither of them spoke for what seemed ages. Eventually Rian said, 'We should go back to where we were staying. I wasn't sure I'd be safe or welcome here, so I asked them for a hut in Achmelvich. Eilidh is letting us use a crannog. We left some things there. If we're really going to be welcome here…' She petered out. The look in Danuta's eyes was all she needed. 'It's my turn to look after you. We'll come back tomorrow.'

They had tired Danuta enough. The old woman looked exhausted. They made sure she was comfy, and then left and made their way back along the coast. Rian tried to suppress the agony of being so close, and still not knowing what Danuta had to tell her. Why hadn't she simply asked? What was there to fear from knowing?

RIAN'S FATHER

The walk back to the crannog seemed far longer than it had been on the way there that morning. Rian sometimes stopped to point out where the sea had eaten the rocks at the shore into amazing shapes, but mostly she stomped along, not wanting to talk. She put Soyea ahead of her and let her pick out the path, so she would get to know it. From behind her, Rian could see her taking in the landscape, the dazzling sea.

At the beach, although she was tired and the sun had set, Rian headed towards the shrine but the tide was too far in to reach it. She stood as close as she could and called a thank you, then she made a gratitude blessing on the sand, arranging shells and weeds into the pattern of a flower. She got Soyea to help, looking for shells in the dusk; although she rolled her eyes as if she felt Rian was treating her like a child, she obeyed, and even improved the design.

When they got back to the crannog, it was almost dark. Soyea began questioning Rian about Danuta. Rian smiled at her but said, 'I am tired, little bird. I need to think about everything I heard today. We'll talk about it another time, I promise.' She lay back on her bed and closed her eyes. She heard Soyea shuffling about as sleep began to overtake her, and roused herself.

'Soyea.'

The girl glanced at her.

'You know how to look after yourself, don't you?'

Soyea frowned. 'What do you mean?'

'Nothing, really. It's just that even people who want the absolute best for you can't always protect you. You need to be able to look after yourself.'

'What are you saying?'

Rian wished she hadn't started this, but she also felt compelled to make her daughter understand. 'Danuta wanted to protect me, but she couldn't. I want to protect you, but I may not always be able to. You may need to be your own protector.'

'Don't worry, Mother. I can keep myself safe.'

'Good.'

A frog croaked outside the crannog, a rhythmic sound that soothed Rian as she let sleep wash over her.

In the morning, Rian tiptoed out early to spend some time alone on the beach, thinking about Cleat. When she returned, it was time for food. The fire was smoky. Trying to wake it, she breathed on it until her eyes watered and a flame eventually licked a birch stick. She shook oatmeal into a pot and added water. The flame puttered out. She reached for her blowpipe and puffed the reluctant flame back into existence, but laying a stick across it snuffed out the fledgling burn. The fire shouldn't be this unfriendly. Soyea would be awake soon. It was necessary to have some food ready for her. They had a big day ahead of them. Was that so difficult? She blew again down the pipe, willing the embers to wake up. A trickle of fire mustered itself and this time the birch stick caught and held the flame, allowing itself to be eaten. She put the pot on the stone nearest and nudged it towards the heat. The flame sputtered but held on.

She heard Soyea scuffling in her bed and looked to see if she was wakening. When she turned back, the flame was out again. Dead. It shouldn't be so difficult to make a pot of porridge on a spring morning. It just shouldn't be so difficult.

Her third attempt to light the fire succeeded but it left her feeling rattled.

Even though it was another lovely morning, as she and Soyea set out on their way back to the broch, she was nervous. They paused briefly at the shrine at the beach, then pressed on. She needed to return to Danuta and wondered if she would be strong enough to ask about her mother and father. She must be. She had waited so many years, but now suddenly she couldn't bear the prospect of waiting another day.

It was all quiet at the broch. Rian opened the door and called, 'Is anyone there?'

Donnag appeared from the guardroom. 'I am.'

'Is Bael here?' Rian asked.

Donnag shook her head.

'Where is he?'

'I have absolutely no idea.' She sounded as if this was often the case. She stepped aside to let them enter, stood watching for a moment, then left without a word.

They made a drink, then Rian and Soyea took Danuta out into the sunshine. Her legs were spindly and weak, but she managed to shuffle along, bent nearly double, held up by the two of them. Outside, she blinked and her eyes streamed. Rian sent Soyea for deer skins and a sheep fleece to make somewhere comfortable to sit where they could see the sea.

When they were all comfortable, Danuta sat stroking Rian's hand, a blithe expression on her face. 'Tell me, what happened when you met Uill Tabar?' Her voice was thin and breathless.

'Manigan knew him. But he's dead now,' Rian said.

There was a pause, as if both Danuta and Rian were waiting for the other to speak. Rian shuffled, staring out to sea.

Eventually, Danuta said, 'Did he tell you about your father?'

'Not really. All I know is that he was a slave as well, apparently.' Rian turned to Soyea. 'I'm afraid you are from a lineage of slaves.'

'Noble ones, if nobility matters to you,' Danuta said.

'What do you mean?' Soyea was sitting on the ground, looking up at the two of them perched on the low wall at the base of the broch.

'Uill said my mother got pregnant with me when she was young, same as I did with you,' Rian replied.

'And she was a slave too?' Soyea asked.

'I'm not sure. I don't think so. My father was the slave. I don't know what happened, but it was some sort of disgrace.'

Danuta crossed her hands in her lap. 'I do know, and it's about time I told you. That girl, your mother…' She licked her lips and lifted her chin.

'What was her name?' Rian asked.

'I wish I could tell you, but it was kept a secret even from me, to preserve her reputation.' She clenched her fists in frustration. 'But I can tell you who she was, and she was no slave. She was a headman's daughter on the Winged Isle.'

Rian's eyes widened.

'So you're a princess,' Soyea said.

Danuta chuckled. 'Well, almost.' She turned to Rian. 'It was Farspag, your father, who I knew. I didn't know her really. She was just a wee girl who fell in love with him, and who wouldn't? He was the strongest, most handsome youth you could imagine. He was the son of a slave-woman, Magris, but everyone knew he was Fergus the Chieftain's son, and Magris herself was no ordinary slave. Did Uill tell you this?'

Rian shook her head. She daren't speak for fear of interrupting Danuta's story.

'Well Magris was the daughter of the leader of a land over the Sea of Eriu. He was beaten in a battle that Fergus fought when he was young. Magris was captured and Fergus took her as a slave. He treated her like a trophy, but she never forgot she was someone powerful and she did everything to remind him.'

'What was she like?'

'Oh a splendid figure of a woman. She was red haired, like you, and tall. I think Fergus was frightened of her. She oozed magic. I've never known a shaman like her. She could sing so strangely, the stars would fall from the sky at her feet. Animals adored her; dogs would walk for days to pay obeisance, horses would throw their riders and gallop up to her. Whenever she went on a boat they said dolphins would come and dance around it. She had pet birds that brought her fish and flowers. She had few friends but she didn't seem to care. She would take men to her bed and they would emerge like boys. Fergus tried beating her to make her do his bidding, but it was like trying to tame a badger. She was invincible. And her son, your father, was the same.'

There was a pause while a coughing spasm shook the old woman. Rian stroked her back until she was able to continue.

Her voice was a croak. 'I used to see it in you too, Rian, when Drost would try to order you around as a child. You'd listen to him and then you'd do just what you were planning anyway, as if that was what he had demanded. Magris used to say, "My soul is stone. You can never break me." And Farspag was another stone-souled child. He was a beautiful boy, white-haired and always big for his age. Fergus himself was a handsome man, and Farspag had his big bones and his green eyes. You have his eyes.' She stopped and peered into Rian's face.

'Tell me more about him,' Rian urged.

She chuckled. 'He was a trouble maker, and he caused mayhem in Fergus' household by organising all the boys into a gang. They were like an army, with Farspag in the lead. They would borrow Fergus' horses and ride out hunting together and bring them back all in a lather. Eventually Fergus gave up trying to punish him and sold him to a trader, one of Ussa's ilk. He ended up down the coast there, with the chieftain of Glenelg.'

'What was his name?' Rian asked.

'Oh goodness, I forget. Ruaridh, I think. It doesn't really matter. He was a big jovial character with red hair. Farspag was made part of a building squad, because he really knew how to handle stone. I don't know where he learned it, maybe it was the stone in his soul.'

Now Rian understood why she had always felt she had rock inside of her. Her eyes egged Danuta on.

The old woman's story was flowing now. 'The old chief tamed Farspag by giving him building work and he became the head of the team of stone masons who built the broch there. Your mother was the daughter of the big house. She was fifteen and as pretty as a rosebud.'

'And she fell for the stone mason?' Rian said.

'That's right. I don't think there was anything the old man could have done to stop them, and her mother was dead by then. Nothing could have kept the pair of them apart. Even if she had been locked in a dungeon Farspag would have found a way in. Unfortunately, she was promised to the son of another big family. There had been endless conflicts over who had control of which bit of shoreline and who could fish where. The idea was to bring everyone in the area together in one clan to keep the peace, so she had been promised to him since she was young. But he was a good bit older than her, you know, and he made a big thing of the purity of his bride to be. He was powerful, but he was ugly, and a slip of a thing compared to Farspag. I don't imagine she was very impressed by him.

'Anyway, the inevitable happened, she got pregnant, and she was terrified about what would happen to the baby if anyone found out. So after you were born she tried to do away with you. That's when I got involved.'

Danuta paused. It was incredible that someone so old and frail could have so much of a story inside her.

'What happened?' Soyea said.

Danuta looked down at her, as if surprised that she was there.

Rian was chewing her lip and gazing out to sea. 'Uill Tabar said she left me on the beach and the sea must have brought me here.'

'Uill Tabar makes up what he doesn't know. I found you on the beach. I was there at the birth. At Imbolc there was a gathering at Brigid's Cave, and I traveled down to it. I was one of the sisters who helped to deliver you in secret.'

'Is that why you were there? For the gathering?'

'Aye. I was there with Buia. It was her maiden day. I had hopes for Buia back then, that she would follow me and become one of the sisters. I took her to all the great rituals. You know. How much of this does Soyea understand?' She turned to the girl. 'Are you initiated?'

Soyea shook her head, uncertainly.

'Anyway, Seonag the Priestess was helping her to have her baby without anyone finding out, for Magris' sake more than anything.'

'What was her name?' Rian asked.

Danuta tutted. 'I wish I knew. We were introduced to her as Cara but we guessed that wasn't her real name. She was a silly slip of a lass: a pretty thing, but vain and meek. Seonag would have let her bring the child up within the sisterhood if she'd wanted to join us, but she just wanted to pretend the child didn't exist, as if she was still a maiden, as if Farspag was a fairy man, not a real one, as if all that the men wanted to believe about her was true. Seonag hid her at her place near the cave for the last few months, making out she was doing a special purification before the marriage, as Brigid's spring maiden. Well, shortly after the birth, she walked to the beach to get stones for the healing fire and came back and said she had slipped and you had been caught by the sea and washed away and drowned. But I'd been following her. I was watching what went on, and that's not what happened at all. She put you down at the water's edge and turned her back and walked away. And I went down there after she'd gathered her basket of stones and stomped away back up the hill, and I rescued you.'

Danuta smiled at the memory and Rian reflected on what she had heard. Eventually she said, 'Are you tired? Do you need to rest?'

'Rest for what? You're here. I've been waiting to tell you this for years. Can you imagine, Rian, ever since Ussa took you away I've been regretting that I never told you before you left. It's been gnawing away at me.'

'Why didn't you?' Rian didn't look at her.

'I swore on my life to Seonag that I'd not tell while her husband was alive, to protect the girl's reputation.'

'How did I come to be here, with you?' Rian's voice was higher than normal.

'I carried you back up to Brigid's Cave and by the time we got there you were howling. The girl refused to have anything to do with you. There was a scene. It was dreadful, but there was a young mother there from the north end of the island whose baby was nearly weaned and she let you feed. Seonag had you stay with her for the next few months, and you fed from one breast after another, and then before long we had you drinking goat's milk and you probably moved onto solids earlier than any child ever has. I guess you knew it was your only chance of survival. I don't know why I stayed with you. Strictly speaking you were the priestess's problem as it had happened on her patch, but she was a busy woman and not obviously one for caring for a baby, and I loved you. You know Mara, Drost's wife, had always wanted a little girl, but all her daughters died before they came to term. You reminded me of what our family didn't have, and you had such trusting eyes. And you were strong. A fierce, tough little thing. And then Farspag came to Brigid's Cave to see you and that settled everything. Ruaridh wasn't stupid. I think he had drawn the obvious conclusion and sent Farspag packing.

'He was raging when he found out what the girl had tried to do. And he had a temper on him that boy, it was frightening to watch. Between Seonag and me and Farspag, we decided to take you both away from there, father and daughter. I knew his building skills would be welcome with us, and I wanted to look after you, so when I returned home I had the two of you in tow. And this fine tower is the result.' She patted the stone under her.

'My father built it?'

'Aye.'

Rian turned to look at Danuta, frowning. 'Why did I never know before now? I don't understand why it was kept a secret from me.'

'I promised. Everyone was frightened of the girl's father and if he had found out you were here, well, who knows what would have happened.'

44

Rian said nothing to that.

Then Soyea asked, 'What happened to Farspag?'

'Of course, this is your story too, isn't it, little bird.' Danuta smiled. 'I'm sorry to say he barely lived to see your mother toddling. When people from over the water saw the job he and the team made of the broch here, they wanted him to go over and build for them. He never really got on with Drost. He drank too much and he'd goad him, or Drost would think that he was having a go at him when he was cracking jokes. Anyway, he went off to the long island to help build a tower there and never came back. He fell off. It's dangerous work. There were suggestions he was maybe not sober at the time. He had a tendency to lark around, show off. I don't know. There were different stories about it. All I can tell you is he never returned. It was the death of his mother as well, and that was a sorry loss. You'd have been three years old and by then you were well settled here, so you stayed, even after Bael was born and Mara died. Until that day. Oh, little bird, I'm so sorry about that day.'

SOYEA

CLACHTOLL

We take Danuta back inside, and Mother sends me off to wash bed clothes where a stream flows out of a lochan nearby. They are flimsy and reeking, but there is soapwort near the stream and I soon have them rinsed out and no longer filthy, if not exactly spotless. I hang the blankets on a line that I presume is for such a purpose. I am anxious to get back. I am no doubt missing important conversation.

But when I bow into the broch again, Mother and Danuta are quiet. Danuta has had a wash and is wearing a clean slip. Mother is carefully combing her hair and the old woman's eyes are glazed over. I am frightened by her but also fascinated. It is a horror I could never have imagined, that a body so ancient could still contain a spark of life.

'Perhaps you could make a little porridge Soyea,' Mother says.

I am about to protest but there is such an atmosphere, it is almost like being in a sacred space, that I back out. There is a chest by the hearth and I find a filthy cooking pot and a spirtle. Everything needs to be washed. I put three sticks on the fire to keep it alive and take the pot outside to scrub it with bog heather.

As I return, a weird-looking woman appears. I think she has come from the hut where I saw smoke earlier. She looks half-witted and pale. Her legs are swollen and she waddles, rather than walks. Her hair is thin and straight and plastered to her forehead as if she has just got out of bed.

'Who the hell are you?' She looks at the pot in my hand and back to my face.

I tell her my name. I am closer to the entrance of the broch than her and now I feel awkward. I cannot pass through the entrance ahead of her so I stand aside, but she doesn't seem intent on going in. I need to get in to tend the fire. Perhaps she will know where I can find some oats.

She is looking me up and down as if I have stolen something and have it secreted about my body.

'What are you doing with that pot?'

'I washed it.'

'Why?'

'To make porridge.'

'Who asked you to make porridge?' She takes a step towards me.

'My mother, for Danuta.'

'Rian, you mean.' She takes another step and I can smell her breath. It is rotten. I want to move back, away, but the broch wall is behind me. I nod, and wonder if she is dangerous. She doesn't meet my gaze, her eyes are fixed to my left, which makes me want to look over my shoulder, as if there's something behind me I have not seen.

'Do you know where I can find oats?'

'What do you want oats for?'

I am definitely scared of her now.

'To make porridge.'

'Why are you making porridge?'

Her eyes focus on me at last, and they are wild and lost. I duck into the passage entrance to the broch. She tries to grab me but I slip out of her grasp. I'm too quick for her and she is uncoordinated. I burst in on Mother and Danuta.

'There's a woman out there.'

'Is Buia here now?' Mother says mildly.

Danuta is back on her bed, eyes closed.

'I don't know where the oats are but I found this and cleaned it.' I show her the pot.

She comes out into the main room, takes the pot from me and sets it down beside the fire. Then she goes to the chamber in the wall opposite Danuta's room and pulls a sack down from the stone shelf. From another she picks a stone jar without even checking to see what is in it. When she hands it to me I see it is salt.

'Nothing has moved in eighteen years,' she says. 'Amazing, isn't it?'

I am fascinated to have met Danuta, who I've heard so much about. She is the source of Mother's herbal knowledge. This is as close as I have come to having a grandmother. I remember when I was little being so jealous of the children who had real families, proper families, with fathers who loved them and grandparents, aunts, uncles, cousins. There were none of them for me. For us. Just Mother and Rona. And the endless waits for Manigan and then the disappointment, not knowing what all that waiting was about.

Manigan, he's like hay fever. He turns up just as things seem to be going well and he gets up my nose. His mouth says things to me that sound innocuous enough, but I'm not blind. I can see what he thinks of me. I am not his, not really. Whoever my father was, Manigan hated him and so I am like a little doorway into the part of him that hates. Mother says I bring out the worst in him. She says I should avoid annoying him if I can, but I get sick of creeping about when he is there, as if I am not allowed to exist. Especially as Rona can do or say no wrong as far as her Daddy is concerned. Mother says, 'We love you both equally,' but she may as well say the rain falls inside as well as out. It doesn't make it true. Rona is adorable and you can't help but love her, but Mother has to try to remember to love me and Manigan has never known how.

It doesn't matter.

I don't need love. Only weak people need to be loved. I may

not be beautiful, or elegant, or talented at dancing and singing, but I am strong. Mother says I take after a tree. What Danuta said about Mother's grandmother, that rang a bell with me. We have stone souls. Stone is even stronger than wood. Stone is stronger than everything.

Perhaps this is why I am getting used to the broch. I have made myself a comfortable bed in one of the alcoves between the walls. Mother showed me how to make a fresh heather bed for Danuta. I was amazed by how comfortable it was, so I made myself one yesterday. I gathered heather, bundles and bundles of it. It smells sweet, and it's springy, much more pleasant than straw.

We have organised the pigs too, set up some hurdles to pen them around the back so they don't make so much mess. They have a clean bed of straw and they seem happy about it, grunting and squealing, turning round and round in circles to make it into a big nest.

There is so much gathering to be done. Each day we go out cutting, bundling, stripping leaves. I wish I had a proper basket to carry herbs in. Everything here is old and damaged, mended, mended again, coming apart. But the broch is starting to smell like home, with drying bunches hung from the rafters and rustling trays of leaves and petals. Later, there will be berries and mushrooms to gather, but for now it's all about drying herbs. There are seaweeds too. I don't know most of them. I wish Danuta could get down to the rocks to show me what's worth gathering and what's not. She knows everything. I thought Mother was pretty good at the herbs, although I wouldn't admit it to her. But the old woman can tell from the scent on my hand what I've touched, and she has a rhyme or a story to help you remember what everything is good for.

Today Mother and I are going to the woods. Donnag has her arms in a bucket of clay and looks almost happy.

Danuta asks me to go and get Buia because she has a nose for herbs and mushrooms. She talks about her as if she is an animal, a favourite pig, perhaps. I am scared of Buia, of her madness.

She has her own hut. It is no bigger than a sty. I do not want to enter but when I rattle the hurdle door and call her name she says, 'Come in, come in, welcome.' Suddenly she is there pulling it open, tugging me inside. It smells rancid. There are bones everywhere. The roof is lined with them, as if she has been deliberately thatching herself in with them from the inside. A lattice of bones of all kinds, from the huge leg bones of cows to the light wings of birds. Skulls hang on strings from the rafters. There is a pile of ribs and vertebrae taking up the right-hand side of the hut. On the left is her bed, a nest of grungy fleece. The side opposite the door has her hearth. It isn't central. Everything is wonky. There is a gap in the wall above it and I can see the sea. Smoke drifts out through the hole.

She propels me to a stool beside the hearth and pushes me down onto it. She is stronger than she looks. She curls herself into her nest and smiles wide-mouthed satisfaction. She has captured me! She doesn't seem to need to talk to me. She takes a dead bird up from the floor into her lap and resumes plucking its black feathers. When she turns it, I see it is a cormorant. I sit, mute, watching her wiry hands tug at the feathers, one by one. She lets them drop around her, occasionally looking at me and nodding, as if I am saying things she agrees with, wise words. I swear she is listening to my thoughts, tilting her head as if in question and then nodding at my answer, all the time plucking, plucking.

I say, 'Danuta says we've to ask you to come to the woods to look for herbs.'

'No, no, no, no, no,' she murmurs, turning her grey head in slow refusal. 'Today I'm flying in the sea.'

I think that's what she says.

'Danuta says you're good at finding things in the woods.'

'No, no,' she says. 'I'm flying.'

She doesn't meet my eye, looking past me out of the gap in the wall. I watch her hands, tugging at the plumage of the cormorant.

She is a pale mermaid with a black tail of feathers.

'The sea!' She gestures out of the hole. 'You see?'

Her eyes glimpse momentarily at me, then away, as if I am dangerous to look at. But she is looking for an answer to her question and when I nod, she nods as well and smiles the wide smile. We return to the silent conversation where she agrees with all my non-statements and I answer her non-questions satisfactorily.

My stomach churns with fear of her, but she is so clearly capable of great magic I dare not move until she tells me I can go.

'Today, it's, you're…it's the sea. But some other day, would you show me the woods?'

She stops plucking, her shoulders slump and she stares me full in the face, grimacing. Then her eyes close and she grunts, like a pig, twice, loudly, then says, 'Rootle, rootle.' Opening her eyes, she frowns at me. 'What are you? Otter? Weasel? Otter?'

I nod. I'd rather be an otter than a weasel.

'Otter goes away now.' She turns her head.

I get up from my stool. 'I'm going.'

She nods. 'Flying, flying,' she says, in a squeaky voice. She brushes me away.

I get out as fast as I can and close the door behind me. The thin cat sneaks around the side of the hut.

Mother is waiting for me, sitting on the stone platform outside the broch. I am pleased to realise she was within earshot. I wish I'd known when I was in there, but perhaps I would have been even more frightened if I had been aware she was on sentry duty.

'She's flying,' I say.

'Oh well, we can go on our own.' She pauses. 'I wonder if it's worth me asking her?'

I shrug.

She strides over to the door, raps once, calls, 'Buia?' and opens the door. I don't hear what she says but Buia's response is clear.

She shrieks, 'Get out! Get out! Get out!'

Mother is spat out of the hut, reeling. Then she turns to me as if nothing has happened and says, 'Basket?'

It is on the platform. I was forgetting it. I grab the decrepit object, vowing to make a new one if I can find some good willow. Mother has her own with her and I'm jealous. I try to think where the one I made last winter went but I can't remember. I must have left it somewhere. Then I recall: I gave it to Rona, of course. Rona always ends up with the best of everything.

I shall make a new one.

RAMSONS

'It's a good day to see what we might gather in the woods,' Mother says. 'It'll be too early for any of the mushrooms, even for birch slippers, but we'll see.'

It rained earlier but now the clouds seem to be dissolving away. There are thrushes singing and nettles everywhere. I want to stop to gather them but mother walks on, beyond the fields and the grazing land, back towards the woods. She doesn't talk. I'm glad about that. I don't need to know what she is thinking about and I don't want to tell her my thoughts either.

I can't stop seeing all those bones in Buia's hut. There were so many. Thousands. How many animals died to give her all those bones? Does she kill them? Why did she let me in but scream at Mother? How dangerous is she? What are the bones for? Do I dare ask her? Are any of them from humans?

I don't like the woods here as much as the shore. They aren't like any woods I know: stunted and scrubby, most of the trees tumbling around, branching from the ground with no trunks to speak of. There is no space in here. Of course there are no fungi, but I can't help looking. When I was a child, mother used to tell me about the little pixie people who camped underneath them, putting up their tents in the woods to shelter from storms. I used to check under every mushroom to see if I could spot one of the little ones and I still vaguely worry that I am making them homeless when I pick them, ripping the roof from over their heads. Is this just a story told to children?

Mother points out ramsons. Once I know what I'm looking for I see the white flowers everywhere and my basket fills quickly. I find myself among a mass of them, so I can pick and choose just the young, succulent leaves. As I finish gathering from one clump, I look up and another cluster catches my eye. The fragrance is deep and powerful. I am not thinking of anything but selecting the best.

And then I realise I am alone. I call, 'Where are you?'

No answer.

I holler it more loudly.

There's no response. Just a green tangle of birch and hazel trees and sallow bushes in all directions.

'Where are you?' I shout again. I sing it out, so my voice carries, but the rustle of the leaves in the treetops muffles it and if there is an answering call it is smothered by them too. The trees crowd around me, peering down at me, clutching at me. They are no longer guardians of treasure. I understand that they were laying out the white flowers as temptation, as bait, to lure me onwards and trap me.

'Where are you? Mother?'

Only shuddering leaves answer, and a thrush, mocking me.

'Maaaa!' I howl, like a child. 'Maaaa!'

Which way did I come? I have been turning around so much I don't really know. The trees are all different but all the same, all completely unfamiliar, or perhaps all ones I've seen before. I know I should be methodical, but I find myself bashing through the woods hollering, spooked, like a woodcock battering through branches trying to escape their clutches. Where has she gone? Why has she left me here?

I find myself at a stream and my feet sink into mud. I grab at a tree but I'm up to my knees in sticky black wetness. My basket up-ends and all my leaves scatter. Part of me wants to cry, but a bigger part of me is furious and I lunge out of the mud roaring and swearing with a glorious spewing of foul words. It's like being a boar. I'm a crazed animal. It's monstrous and exhilarating at the same time, to be so full of rage and to allow it to explode out of me.

I stomp about, a squall of fury, growling and berating the unfairness of my life.

But then I am just wet-legged, and she is there on the bank above me, watching down, with that know-it-all smile on her face.

'Don't laugh at me,' I shout. 'Where were you?'

She shakes her head and still that smile lingers. 'Whatever is the matter?' she says, or something like that.

I hate her.

'You left me.'

'No, I didn't.'

'Why didn't you come when I shouted? Or answer? I thought I'd lost you.'

'Calm down. We just got separated while we gathered. It's not a big panic. These are friendly woods.'

'They're not friendly. They're dangerous. Look what they did.' I spread my arms, pointing to my spilled harvest, much of which is floating away downstream. I am biting back tears. I won't let her make me cry. I am too angry with her for leaving me and if I weep, her victory will be complete.

'That rotten stream.' Her sarcasm is thick. 'Come on. You got lots, let's not lose them all.'

It's as if it's all normal again, the way she talks, but I'm not sure I'll ever be able to forgive her.

'I'm sorry,' she says. 'I know you hate me when I get out of earshot in the woods.' I hate her for knowing what I'm thinking. I want her to get out of my head.

'Don't be grumpy with me.'

She has a cheek! 'Stop telling me how to feel.' That shuts her up.

We don't speak much on the way home. Home? That big stone tower.

RIAN

HIDE

As Rian and Soyea made their way out of the woods towards the broch, they met a hurrying figure. It was the girl they had seen tending her cow on previous days.

'You have to go back,' she said. 'Hurry. My mother sent me to tell you Ussa's at the broch. She says to ask Eilidh to hide you.'

The girl's speech came out in a blurt, like she had been rehearsing it. Rian stared at her, frozen, then looked wide-eyed out to sea as if expecting to see *Ròn*, Ussa's boat, sailing towards her. Her heart raced and she had to breathe deeply to keep control.

'Oh by the Goddess will I never be free of her?' It was barely a whisper, not intended to be heard by either girl. In a normal voice she asked, 'Who's your mother?' She tried to sound as calm as if the girl had merely commented on the weather.

'Duileag. I'm Duileag too. I've got to go.' She turned away, then back, and smiled at Soyea as if seeing something in her she recognised. 'Good luck.' Then she scampered away.

Rian swivelled and placed her palm flat on Soyea's shoulder. 'Back to Achmelvich.' She dogged her daughter's footsteps, trying to hurry her without creating alarm.

Eilidh was waiting for them. 'Thormid was out fishing and saw the trader's boat. He came to tell you but you'd gone. But I see there are folk looking out for you in Clachtoll as well. Unfortunately you can never tell who'll take Bael's side. Come.'

She led away into the woods that ran down to the shore of the rocky fjord stretching inland. Rian gestured for Soyea to go ahead of her. If necessary, she would act like a lapwing, limping, hanging back and flapping about as if injured, to enable her daughter to escape.

They hurried after Eilidh along the leaf and twig strewn path, not speaking until they reached a little stone shelter among some bouldery scree. Beyond it was the shore, with a space cleared of rocks where a boat could be hauled up.

'I'll come back later and tell you what's happening,' Eilidh said. 'We'll find a way to make out you've gone south again, never fear.'

Sure enough, before the afternoon had begun to dwindle into dusk, the stout woman reappeared, chuckling, with a basket of food. Rian and Soyea ate and drank gratefully as Eilidh reassured them that *Ròn* had been seen sailing for Coigach.

'Thormid went and complained to Bael that his good-for-nothing brother-in-law Badger has stolen a boat and sailed away south with the two of you. Seemingly Ussa was more than ready to believe that any associate of your man is nothing better than a pirate and off they went in hot pursuit.' She thrust the basket of rolls at them. 'Dig in.'

Soyea swallowed and took another.

Rian shook her head. 'I don't know how we can thank you.'

Eilidh waved her hand. 'You'd do the same. I know you would.'

Soyea was frowning. 'So how did Ussa know Mother is here?'

Eilidh smiled. 'News travels fast here. She was over on the Long Island, apparently.'

'Bael may have sent word,' Rian said. 'I wouldn't put it past him.'

'So does that mean we can't go back to the broch?' Soyea was pale.

'Don't be frightened, little bird.' Rian patted her arm. 'My days of being cowed by Bael are over. If Ussa turns up again, we'll make ourselves scarce. I know this area far better than she does and there are plenty of places to hide.'

'And you have a good number of us who will do what we can for you, never fear.' Eilidh offered Soyea the rest of the rolls from the basket. 'Take these with you and get away back to the broch. Danuta needs your mother and you.'

SOYEA

BROCH

It's amazing how quickly I feel I belong here. Is it amazing? I don't know. I just do. I have my space, my cubby hole between the walls.

There's a big room inside where the fire is, where everything goes on, and where the herbs and fish and mushrooms that we have gathered hang from the rafters. And then there is the outside world. Between these, I have my heather bed, my fleece, my nest. I haven't got used to the idea that Mother grew up here and my Grandfather built this tower. I can reach up from my bed to the stones, laid cleverly over each other to make a pleasing curve over my head and down to my feet.

Danuta is sleeping and Mother has gone to pick herbs again, I do not know where. She wanted to go alone. So today I am making pottery with Donnag. I like her.

We roll out the clay, which she brings in a bucket. It is heavy. She says she dug it up from the stream bed between here and the beach and it is good clay. The slimy brown mud is surprisingly firm under my fingers, but whereas she seems able to smooth it into forms, I am clumsy with it and find it hard to shape. It squashes. It resists what I want. It gives the impression of being malleable but then, as I am bringing it up into a curving bowl-shape it disintegrates, or crumbles, or tears, and I am left with clay lumps, bad thoughts and nothing to offer to the flames.

Meanwhile she makes cups. We could do with some plates, but I do not know her well enough to suggest what she might make, and as I flounder with the clay she creates drinking vessels, one after another, a clutch of palm-sized, identically curved cups, arranged in a neat line. They are without handles or ornament, except for the ridiculous pinches she puts in. They are repetitively misshapen. I watch her make one after another as if she were an insect, mindlessly repeating its action, making a perfect shape and then ruining each pot with the same distorted pattern.

'Why do you do that?' I say. 'They are so perfect until you dent them.'

'You must not try for perfection,' she murmurs. 'Only a goddess can make a flawless thing.' Her voice is so quiet. It is a wispy, dried out voice, and it fits her frame. She is frail in every way. There is no more flesh on her than on Danuta and she seems brittle, feather light, as if she could easily break up and blow away in a storm. Yet she handles the clay with confidence and there is surprising strength in her hands.

I have the urge to cover her in clay, to flesh out her bony body with it. Perhaps that is what she is doing, creating a substitute in clay for the muscle she does not have in her own limbs. Her big eyes peer out from the caves of her eye sockets, strange lights above the thin cheekbones, the narrow chin, the scrawny neck.

'And anyway,' she says, 'it makes them easier to hold. Our hands are not symmetrical.'

It seems sad to me, a shame. She looks at the struggle I am having with the bowl I am trying to make. She comes and stands behind me and reaches around from the back. Her hands cover mine, guiding me to shape the clay. The pressure of her palms across my fingers transfers to the pot. It helps. The bowl curves, the clay smooths.

'There,' she says. 'Cut the top.' She puts a thin blade into my hand, and somehow without touching me, her hovering fingers guide it around and across, slicing an even cut, and the bowl stands, as near to perfect as I dare to imagine.

'Do I have to dent it?'

'Not if you don't want to,' she says.

I don't want to.

'Put it with these ones to dry.'

'How long will that take?'

'A few days.'

'And then?'

'We'll fire them.'

'In here?'

'No. You'll see.'

'What now?'

She points to the bucket of clay. 'Make another.'

She is already shaping something big.

'Can I make a plate?'

She shrugs. 'Better to try the same again if you want to learn, but...' Her shoulders nudge up and down again and her voice shrinks away. 'Do what you want.'

Something in the way she says it makes me willing to take her advice, and I make another bowl, more carefully and successfully this time, my hands remembering the pressure she applied. It goes wrong in places but I manage to correct it. The clay begins to seem a bit less as if it has a mind of its own. My second bowl is not as even as the first one, but it's all my own work.

She gives a grave nod at it. 'And again,' she says.

'I'm hungry.'

'Oh well.' She really seems not to care less what I do.

I make a third, but the base is too thin and it breaks, and I've had enough when Mother appears, ducking in through the broch entrance. She seems surprised to see what we're doing.

'How's Danuta?' She looks at each of us in turn.

I remember I promised I'd look in on her but I've been so engrossed by the potting I forgot. I leap to my feet to dash into her chamber to check she's all right but Mother beats me to it, turning away from us as if we have been doing something filthy. I can see her thoughts in her turned back, her pointed footsteps. We are untrustworthy. We are negligent.

I stand, halfway between Donnag and Mother. I look back at Donnag. She is immersed in her clay-shaping. Mother may as well not exist. Her arrival has left Donnag completely unmoved whereas waves of shame and anxiety are breaking across me. I follow Mother into Danuta's chamber.

'I'm sorry,' I am saying, as I walk in. 'I got engrossed. Donnag was showing me how to make bowls, how to work the clay.'

I peter out once I see Mother is holding Danuta's hand. Her eyes are closed. She is pale, small, still. Is she dead? I have a bird in my chest.

All mother says is, 'Shhh.' I sit down on the stool.

She is pressing Danuta's wrist. Then she touches her throat. 'Danu?' she asks. 'Are you sleeping?'

There is no sound from the woman on the bed, but I hear her breath rasp. At least my neglect hasn't killed her. I breathe out. But Mother remains tense.

'Have you looked in on her at all?'

'Once,' I lie.

'And was she awake?'

I shake my head. I can't speak.

'Perhaps she's tired. We'll leave her.' Mother has her sanctimonious voice on. I loathe it. There'll be something else later. She looks at me, but as I am sitting and she is blocking the light I know she can barely see me.

'We'll leave her in peace,' she says.

Isn't that what I've been doing all day?

She pulls the curtain aside and steps out. I get up to follow her. I risk an anxious look at Danuta, the old woman nearly killed by my neglect, and where I expected a near corpse, I see a face looking brightly out at me. She winks!

'Your first pot?' Her voice is a crackle, but it's alive.

I nod.

She gives an approving blink. Then her eyes drop to the cup beside the bed, and the wrinkle of her nose says everything.

'Do you want something?' I ask. 'A fresh drink? Some soup?'

Her eyes lit at the first suggestion, a frown came with the second. She says something I can't catch but her eyes pull me in.

'Mead,' she says. 'Get me a honey cup, my honey.' Then her face crumples in that way she has of collapsing into herself with humour.

'Mead?'

She blinks twice. I pick up the half-empty cup of herb tea, whatever it was, seeing the fly in it now, and carry it out into the space where Mother is examining the pots and Donnag is studiously ignoring her.

'She wants a cup of mead,' I hand her the cup.

Mother spins around. 'What?'

'Danuta asked for mead. Do you know where I'll find some, Donnag?'

Donnag gives a characteristic shrug that ends with a gesture towards a chest behind her left shoulder. I go and open it, but there's nothing in it but empty flasks.

Mother has gone into Danuta's room.

'There might be some up there.' Donnag points up the stairs.

'Where?'

She shrugs. 'Look about.'

I go up the stone staircase between the walls and emerge out onto the first floor. There's a wooden chest right at the top of the stairs. I rummage in it, but it's all fleeces and rugs. It's dark up there, so I go back down for a tallow lamp, light it from the fire and return.

On one side there is curtained-off space. It's Bael and Donnag's. Opposite it a clutter of baskets and boxes is stacked up on the wattle floor. The prospect of finding anything among it is daunting, but I'm also curious as to what could be lurking in all those wicker and wooden containers. There is a lot of pottery lying around: some of it broken, but much of it intact and probably unused, by the look of it.

I start rummaging. Under a bundle of untreated fleeces, there are creels of fishing gear: nets and floats, bundles of sailcloth and hides, twine and sinew. It's a lot of useful material for anyone with boats. There are two boxes of iron tools, perhaps for stone and wood-working, the signs of industrious activity. Nothing much like this seems to be happening here at present, but this pile of mallets, adzes and awls makes me realise that there have been people here at some previous time who made things. I shift a bundle of hide and two more baskets of rope. The next wooden box is more promising: it is filled with ceramic flasks stopped with leather. I pick one out. It is weighty enough to be worth investigating further. The box is too heavy to carry downstairs so I pull other bottles out of it. They are all full and made of two distinct types of pottery: one chunky and crude, the other more like the fine patterned work I see Donnag producing. I wonder if she made them and if so, who made the other. I remove one of each and push the box back where it came from. There are four or five such boxes and an oak cask, and between them a chest. Again, I have to shove hides aside to get to it. It has a metal clasp that is stiff, but after a bit of a struggle I manage to open it. As I lift the lid the clasp breaks off. The lid clatters closed. I am left with the bronze hasp in my hand and I feel awkward but now it's done, I want to know what's in the box.

'What are you doing up there?' Mother calls.

'Snooping,' a male voice says, just behind me.

I almost jump out of my skin.

It's Bael. 'Breaking into boxes that are none of her business. Thieving, I'll warrant.'

His stench is there with him, his pale skin and hooded grey eyes, too close to look away from. His face is distorted by the damage to one eye and his mouth lifts on one side into a sneer. He is leaning against the wall between me and his chamber, dressed in his finery, as if he thinks he is handsome. Presumably he was in there all along. He's not as near me, really, as I felt he was when he spoke, but he has a way of making me feel he is in my space.

'I'm looking for mead. Danuta asked for mead.'

He nods and points to the bottles. 'And there it is. You've found it.'

He doesn't need to say what follows from that, to ask what else I'm looking for, to make me feel guilty.

'There's a lot of sailing gear here,' I say.

'Yes. Maybe you haven't noticed there's a big sea on the doorstep.' His voice is lardy with sarcasm.

I pick up the bottles and lamp and step towards the staircase. He steps that way too. As I reach the top stair, he has closed on me. He grabs my wrist and pokes a finger under my chin so I look up at him.

'Ugly creature, aren't you?'

He snuffs out the lamp and clamps his hand on my left breast. Under his breath, he says, 'Even ugly people fuck.'

I pull away from him, clutching the pottery flasks, my face blazing, breast burning. I'm down those stairs as fast as I possibly can be, and I know from the quizzical look on Mother's face and Donnag's scowl that they're suspicious about what I was doing. There's nowhere safe in this house at all, I realise, except perhaps Danuta's bedside.

'I found these.' I put the bottles down beside Donnag. 'Shall I open them?' She gives a barely perceptible twitch and I look to my Mother, who nods. I need a knife to undo the sinew fastening of the nicer one. Once it's off, I sniff the contents. It's sharp and I don't recognise it, but I don't think it's mead. My uncertainty must show on my face.

'What is it?' Mother says.

I hand her the bottle. She smells, then wrinkles her nose.

'Horrible.'

Donnag speaks up. 'My father calls it his elixir of life. It came from his house.'

Mother looks at Donnag in surprise. 'Do you like it?'

Donnag shakes her head. Mother re-stoppers the bottle and places it back, closer to Donnag, as if to signal that it is her responsibility. Donnag appears completely uninterested.

'Shall I put it back?' I offer, although I don't want to go back up there.

'Open the other one first,' Mother says.

I pick up the other bottle. It's the more crudely made and I manage to untie its thong without cutting it. There's a leather cover and inside it a wooden stopper that comes out with a pop.

It smells of honey. This is what we're looking for. I nod and smile.

'Where's Danuta's cup?'

I spot it beside the fire, put the mead down and take the cup outside to empty it.

FIN

The light is silver on the sea; a band of ripples shimmers, illuminated through a gap in the cloud. It is raining to the north, a mesh of grey, and the hills at the back are swathed in mist. I wonder what it means, this enclave of brightness beamed in from the sea. Waves murmur on the rocks below. A gannet soars, then dives like a knife plunged from the sky, throwing up a plume of white spray. I watch it surface and lift itself laboriously from the water and flap away and up in a curve, and I imagine it searching and searching for prey in the vast glittering ocean below. I want to fly away with it, to get some glimmer of a fish worth following.

I notice a sail on the horizon. It grows. Whoever they are, they're not just passing.

I take Danuta's cup inside and say, as nonchalantly as I can, 'There's a boat coming in.'

Mother takes the cup. 'What sort of boat?'

I shrug. I have no answer to that question.

Donnag looks alarmed and rushes out. She is soon back, calling for Bael and asking him who it might be.

He storms down the stairs strapping a weapon on, shouting, 'How would I know, woman?' To Mother he says, 'If this is more of your sort they'll get the welcome they deserve.'

She simply gives him a cool stare.

I keep my eyes to myself, but once Danuta has her mead, I slip back outside to watch the approach. It's *Bradan*. She is unmistakable once she's close enough to see the height of the mast and the flag up above the main sail. Manigan calls it the gannet's tail feather. I don't know much about boats but I've always thought that was stupid. The sail is brown, there's nothing of the gannet about the vessel at all. It's just fancy words, like all of Manigan's talk.

My feet stick to the ground. I know I must tell Mother but I don't want to. I try to will the boat away, but of course it doesn't work. It keeps on, growing bigger as it gets closer. I can see that there are four men on it now. The sail is coming down. It is down.

I know how a caged animal feels.

Mother appears. I don't have to tell her. 'It's *Bradan*.' She is alight, or as lit as she ever gets. There's something like a girl in her that comes to life whenever Manigan is nearby. It makes me sick. Mothers are not supposed to be childish. Should I be happy for her, that she is still in love with him when plenty of women her age are sick of their men? I can't be. That is what I want for myself but it seems mawkish and stupid at her age. She rushes indoors. She'll be trying to make herself look how she thinks he wants her to.

In fact, she is out again in no time. She was just getting a shawl. 'Stay with Danuta,' she says.

So I am to be ordered about now that Manigan is here, is that it? She runs off down to the shore where they'll land. At the big rock she stands for a moment and looks out at the boat, and waves, and one of the men raises his arm in return. That'll be him, watching for her.

Bael is down at the shore already. I don't suppose he'll give Manigan a particularly warm welcome. I rather wish I could overhear it.

I slip back into the broch and go in to see Danuta.

'Is this her man coming?'

I nod.

'You don't look as pleased about it as she does.'

There's no need to answer.

'How's your mead?'

'Just the thing.' She smiles that ancient smile. 'Come here.' She pats the covers. 'What do you know of the ways of the Mother?'

I sit down beside her. I can see she is deadly serious.

'Do you mean the ceremonies?' I feel completely ignorant. She is looking at me with her tired, wise eyes.

'Aye, the rituals are part of it. The stories are another. You lived with the Keepers. Did they teach you anything about the Sisterhood? The herbal lore?'

I shake my head. 'All I know is what Mother showed me. We took part in the ceremonies for the seasons. I was the Spring Maiden one time and I watched at other times, when they let me, when they were calling in the ancestors. But I don't really know anything.'

'You know more than you know,' she says. 'Now her man is here, Rian will be busy. I am old. I need to pass on my knowledge before I die. Buia is too vague, I have given up trying to teach her. Your Mother could have been a leader, but she has her own path now. Donnag does not want to learn. She fears it. But you, I sense you could, if you want to, be one of the Sisterhood. You have an open mind. You have a good soul. You're smart. You know the ogham. Think about it.'

The broch is quiet.

'What do I have to think about?'

'Whether you want to learn the mysteries of the Mother.'

'Of course.'

'It may be hard.'

'So? Life is hard.'

She chuckles, patting my hand. 'You're old and wise for one so young.'

There are voices outside. It's strange the way you can hear whatever is said just outside the door so clearly inside those thick walls. There's that one spot where it happens. I can hear Manigan's laugh and, 'You've no idea how much I've longed for your cooking, my love.' Not exactly secrets worth overhearing.

I mime a repetition of his words, and Danuta shakes her head.

'It's a great love that lasts like theirs, you know. She says he's a good man.'

I feel a bit ashamed then, for being so bitter. 'He doesn't like me.'

'You're not his.'

'Exactly. Rona is always better than me in every way.' I pause. 'He just appears and expects everything to stop for him, everyone to dance to his tune, everything to revolve around him and then he's gone again. He's hardly ever here and then when he is it's as if he's King.'

'That's not just him,' Danuta nudges me. 'That's men in general.' She has a wicked smile. 'Don't let him get to you. When he's gone, I'll teach you some of the women's ways and you'll never need to worry about men again.'

When he ducks in through the doorway I feel armoured somehow, and I manage to smile at him, and he is charming as he always is. Behind him there is a boy, no, a man, a pale-haired, slender young man. Manigan and Mother are almost dancing and she is introducing him to Danuta. The pale man lowers his head slightly.

'Hello.' His voice is deep, and soft as fleece. 'I'm Fin.'

'Soyea.' I bob a welcome. 'Come in. You are welcome.'

'Thank you. I'd better bring things up from the shore. I'll be back soon.'

He is turning to go.

'Do you want some help?' I say.

'Come and see, if you like,' he replies.

I follow him out, shoo the pigs around the back of the broch and shut them in their pen, then walk with him back to the shore, showing him the best route, as it isn't obvious. There is such a network of little paths and awkward stones everywhere.

'I love it here,' he says. 'The mountains, everything.'

'You can't really see them from here.' I had almost forgotten about them. 'But when I first came here, I thought this was the most beautiful landscape I'd ever seen.'

'It is. When was that, when you first came?'

'Just this spring.'

'Is that right? I was going to ask how the winter was.'

'No point.'

'You seem at home here, as if you belong.'

I look round at him, surprised. How can I look like that when I have only been here a few weeks? His pale blue eyes are on me, and I daren't meet them. I hurry on.

At the shore there is a mound of gear up above the high tide mark. A gull is trying to rip the top off a basket, which presumably contains fish or something that smells equally enticing. A strange little furry animal with a long tail is shrieking at it. It is on a long string, standing on a bundle of wet clothes and bedding beside a roll of brown hide and two huge tusks.

'What's that?' I point at the animal.

'My monkey.' It has run to him and is climbing his leg. He unties its leash and scratches its head. 'Down.' It jumps to the ground. 'Good monkey.'

It hides behind his leg and peeks out at me. It's adorable.

'A successful hunt,' I say.

'Did Manigan ever not have?'

Badger shouts something lewd from the boat. I wave back.

'Don't encourage him,' Fin mutters. He chases the gull off and I pick up the basket. Then he crouches in front of the big bundle of wet gear, heaves it up onto his shoulders, grunts, and sets off back to the broch.

Badger is off the boat again, up to his knees in water, shortening the rope attached to a boulder on the shore. The tide has a long way to come in. He'll be there a while.

'Shall I bring you something to eat?' I shout to him.

He gives me thumbs up and calls me an angel. I've always liked Badger. He's funny and kind, and although he's lewd and smelly, he means no harm.

Kino is lying on a flat patch of grass a little distance from the shore, apparently sleeping.

'Is he all right?' I call, pointing at him.

Badger indicates with his upturned hands that he has no idea. I go over, put the basket down, and nudge him with my foot.

He grunts.

'Are you all right?' I say.

He opens his eyes and fixes them on me.

'Booze. Grog. Hooch. Ale. Mead...'

'What about it?'

'Drink. Booze. Grog. Hooch...' He repeats his litany. He is haggard and filthy. I leave him to his own devices. He will no doubt make it to the broch eventually in search of his heart's desire.

I hurry after Fin. As I catch him up, I see how tall he is. He has big, tough boots of leather that make his feet look huge at the end of his long, spindly legs, with their scraggy woollen leggings sticking out of an outsize leather coat. His feathery hair wisps up above the load on his back. He has no hat.

At the broch entrance he dumps his bundle and straightens up, then takes off his coat. The monkey immediately sits on it and he ties its leash to a post.

'It's warm.' He smiles. Now his outer garment is a big woollen gansy. It must have been made for someone else, for although the sleeves are the right length, the chest is baggy and short. I can picture the man who should have been wearing it. He is shorter and chunkier than Fin.

He sees me looking at it. 'Badger's.' He pulls the hem down, ineffectually. 'I'd have frozen without it, but it doesn't fit.'

I have an urge to make him something warm that does fit him, and I find myself trying out thoughts of what colours it could be, what pattern I could make it, whether I have some fabric already woven that I could use, or whether knitted wool would be the warmest thing. I want to make this stranger something snug and cosy. Why is that? I want him to touch the texture of a garment I have made for him. I want him to pull it over his head, let that soft hair flop down over it, those slim hips be kept warm. I stop myself. What am I thinking of? But as soon as I let go my attention, my mind is back there, wondering about how to clothe him properly. He looks like a big child, I say to myself, but when have I ever had any desire to make clothes for children? Never. This is something new.

PIGNUTS

I go inside to find some food to take to Badger. I butter a half-dozen bannocks and find a chunk of cheese. Mother and Manigan are with Danuta. Manigan is talking, as always. I interrupt him to offer him a bannock and to show Mother I am feeding the guests she is ignoring.

Danuta says, 'Are the pignuts worth gathering yet, do you think? There are usually lots up the path to the Shaman's cave. It would be a good treat for the sailors.'

Manigan agrees.

'You might see some herbs worth drying.' The old woman gives me a smile that must be meant to remind me of our earlier conversation. 'Take my basket.' She points to the corner.

From the look on Mother's face I see it's a great honour.

I thank her, blushing. It might not seem like much to anyone else, but it feels to me like the beginning of my initiation. It is a kind of test. What herbs can I find? I know so little of what grows here.

'Mind you keep your focus on the dinner!' Danuta's eyes are twinkling and I'm not sure why.

'Your boy might fancy going too? What do you think?' Mother is addressing Manigan, of course, not wondering what I might think of the idea, although, for a moment, I thought she was referring to the boy as mine and I knew exactly why.

'Aye, take him, and stay out as long as you can. You never know, you might lose him.'

'You're so cruel.' Mother is laughing at him.

I don't know if he's joking or not. I can never tell with Manigan, and half the time it turns out he is, but I don't find him at all funny. Like now.

But then he turns to me. 'Poor Soyea. You don't want to be burdened with a lout like that. He'll ruin your nice quiet walk.'

'I don't mind taking him.' If only to spite you, I don't say. But it's true. 'If he wants to come, he's welcome.' I grab the basket.

'There's a load of smelly fish out there,' I say. 'The seagulls are desperate for it.'

'We can smoke it later,' Mother says.

When I leave the broch, Fin is already nearly back, bowed down by the roll of hide. Behind him comes Kino, with the tusks, and I know exactly what he'll be asking for when he arrives. He can ask someone else.

I say to Fin, 'Is there more to bring?'

He shakes his head, putting down his load.

'I'm going nutting. Do you want to come?'

He seems to think about it, looking around for other options. His monkey is asleep on his coat. He says, 'Why not?'

It takes me a moment to realise this is assent. I take a bannock down to Badger, who makes the inevitable rude remarks when I tell him we're going for nuts, then we set off away from the shore.

I lead the way across the pastures and corn fields and along a path into some birchwoods. It is cool and green in the shade. As we come around a bend, three roe deer bound away from us, brushing vegetation aside like cloth.

Fin lopes along behind me, not saying anything, which suits me fine. I have nothing to say to him either, and now he is here I am a bit embarrassed. For a while I regret inviting him. On my own, I could be singing, or telling myself a story.

I point out some flowers along the way but he isn't interested. They are so many lovely colours now: milkwort, so deeply blue; lousewort, pink; and tormentil, yellow and everywhere.

Near where the path divides, one going to Achmelvich, one up to the Shaman's cave, there are ramsons and sorrel leaves for salad.

'It's going to be a good dinner,' he says.

'Are you hungry?'

'Always.'

'I've more bannocks. I was planning to eat them when the basket is full, but we can have them now, if you like.'

We sit on rocks by the side of a stream and munch the rolls. Then we carry on. The path follows the stream up the glen, and we're soon among thinner trees where the understorey is thick with flowers and herbs.

The feathery leaves of pignuts are thick here. Our pace drops as we keep stopping to dig them up. We have to stay close because there's only one basket. I like the way he holds his cupped hand out to empty it as I proffer the wicker container. As we repeat the action, it becomes more and more like a dance; an offering, acceptance – his gift, my thanks. He acts it up a little bit, and it makes me laugh. I curtsy with exaggerated gratitude. I like the way he smiles mostly on the left side of his face.

We're concentrating on digging up the nuts, eating a few of course, but largely they go in the basket. There is a trance-like state you get into while gathering; the plants you're after seem to multiply as your eye gets used to spotting them. Everything else in the world fades out of focus. There are just pignuts, the digging stick and the basket.

Then something makes me look up, and I see the bear, in its own foraging trance, munching and snuffling its way towards us.

Fin is near enough for me to reach out and touch him on the sleeve. He turns, and I put my finger to my lips then point out the bear.

He freezes. His face has alarm written all over it, eyes wide, brows raised, mouth agape with the last intake of breath.

'Greetings to you, Furry Sister.' I hope I sound strong, but friendly.

There is no response, and I guess I'm too quiet, so I raise my voice. 'Big Sister, Hairy Paws,' I call out.

Her ears twitch and she lifts her snout.

'We're nutting too, I hope you don't mind us taking a share.'

She's listening to me, so I carry on, calling the first things to come into my head.

'I'm Soyea. I'm not from these parts originally, but I'm staying with Danuta in the broch. This is Fin, he came here on a boat with Manigan today. He's not had fresh vegetables for ages. We're very pleased to meet you.'

I go on in this vein and the bear seems to be paying attention. When I pause, she keeps her head up for a moment, then lowers her muzzle to the herbage again.

I look round at Fin. He has closed his mouth but his eyes are still wide with fear. I am thrilled with all that this encounter signifies, but he has drawn his knife.

'No need for that,' I whisper. 'She's just doing the same as us.'

'We need to back off,' he hisses.

'If we keep upwind of her, she'll know who we are.'

He is shaking his head.

'She'll not hurt us.'

'How can you be sure?'

'Sister Hairy Paws,' I call. 'We're coming down this way.'

She lifts her head again, her furry ears swivel, and I move out into the clearing, circling around so that the wind will take our smell to her. Fin follows, tiptoeing.

'Off we go now. It was lovely to see you.' We are almost directly upwind now and she raises herself onto her hind paws, her mouth wide, breathing in our smell. I know she doesn't see too well, but she will know everything about us from our scent. She slumps back down, turns her back on us and saunters away.

'Goodbye Sister,' I say.

Within moments she has gone. Her big hairy rump has swung away, grass and bracken have closed behind her, and we look into a wooded space that hides her and who knows what other mysteries.

'She's gone.'

'How do you know it's "she"?'

'I don't know. She's small.'

He nods. 'You're not scared.'

'No.' I'm digging again. My fingers will be muddy for days. I crunch on one and smile at him, then swallow. 'She's our spirit sibling. There's nothing to fear.'

'Who told you that?'

'Mother, I guess. All I know is, "Never fear a bear unless you're between him and his food, or between a cub and its mother, or otherwise being rude."'

He's not looking at me. 'I don't trust any bears,' he grumbles. 'Have you seen their jaws?'

'They're more scared of us than we are of them.'

'I've seen bears that show no fear at all.'

'Where?'

'In the ice.'

'Manigan talks about them. They're white?'

'Yes. Huge. They just want to eat you. I'm terrified of bears, sorry.'

I'm surprised that he is so candid about this fear. He's so different from Manigan.

'I'll keep you safe, don't worry.'

We both laugh. I feel big and brave.

He doesn't seem at all ashamed of his fear. 'Manigan calls me a coward.'

'Manigan never has anything good to say.'

'Except about your mother. Rian does no wrong.'

We exchange looks that leave me in no doubt we understand each other perfectly, then walk on for a while. I have an urge to go down to the shore of the lochan. There are flag iris just coming into flower and I dig up some roots. I love the blue dye they make. I look at Fin, who's watching the surface of the water. His eyes are flitting as he tracks the flight of a green dragonfly. The insect alights on a spearwort, green and gold shimmering together.

'That's surely a spirit messenger,' he murmurs.

We stroll around the loch edge to the outflow where the brown peaty water pours out in a series of steps, pooling, swirling, then tumbling down more rocks. Each little pool is a garden of mosses and ferns. We follow the stream down and pause where trees overhang a waterfall; a tangle of willow, a glossy holly and a rowan stretch out over the white cascade.

Fin speaks and I have to turn towards him to hear him over the splashing torrent.

'Where does it go?'

'I don't know. The sea?'

'It's like time. One day,' he gestures from one pool down to the next, 'then another day.'

'And eventually we die,' I say.

He nods.

There's a crag on the far side of the stream where rocks have fallen recently. As we clamber over them, I say, 'These dropped off that cliff after heavy rains last winter. This used to be an easy path, Donnag told me.'

'Everything flows,' he says. 'Everything.'

'You don't think anything stays the same?'

He shakes his head.

'The ocean?'

'All flow.'

I think I see what he means.

I stop at the next patch of level ground and he comes and stands beside me, close enough that I can reach up to his cheek and bring his face down to mine. I have never kissed a man before. I feel the force as the two of us flow briefly into one.

By the time we get back to the broch, Bael is at odds with Manigan. It starts with bickering about how much food we are collectively going to eat and whether it is reasonable to expect such hospitality at this lean end of the year. I sit with Danuta, listening in. She is asleep, or pretending to be. I have some sympathy for Bael, after all it is a long time since harvest and we are a substantial crowd of people, with big appetites, who have descended on his household without being invited. Manigan is acting as if it's his right to be here. When the men reach a blazing argument about slavery, I head outside. The last thing I hear is Mother's shrill voice. 'Put that weapon down.'

I find Fin sitting on the seaward side of the broch feeding pignuts to his monkey, tossing them across rocks and making the animal scamper about for them. It's a beautiful evening, the sunset painting clouds the colours of orchids and clovers.

'I have been talking to Buia,' he says. 'Or at least, she was talking to me.'

I don't want to pass any kind of judgement. Her hut is close by. I gesture to it. 'Is she there?'

He shakes his head. 'She went off. She told me about you, your father, your grandfather.'

I sit down on a rock, where I'm able to see him without facing directly. I look at the sea, but also at him. His hair is like the clouds at the end of a spell of fine weather. There's a band of sunlight across the sea, too bright to gaze on. 'He was a slave, my grandfather.'

'She says he built this broch. Is that right?' He pats the stone under him and tosses another nut at his monkey.

'His mother was a witch. My great grandmother. I only just found out myself.'

'Buia said she was a healer. The best there ever was.'

There is something so kind about him. Talking isn't easy, not like this, about myself, but I don't want it to stop.

'She was a slave as well.'

'But you're not.'

'I don't know. Mother's still running away.'

'From my aunt.'

'Ussa's your aunt?' My ribs tighten.

He gives a big puff of breath and throws three nuts in quick succession for the monkey, so it has to scamper back and forth. 'She's so embarrassing,' he says softly. 'Crazy with greed.'

He hands me a nut. I hold it in my palm and the little animal creeps towards me, glancing between my face and my hand. 'I've never seen her. Just heard about her all my life.'

'Did you never meet her on Ictis?'

'Nope. Always hiding. Then she stopped coming.'

'Fell out with the Keepers, I suppose. She falls out with everyone in the end.' He sounds as if he is sorry for her.

'Is she mad or bad?'

'How do you tell?' He is looking at me.

I think of Buia and of Bael. One has feathers in her eyes, the other iron.

The monkey grabs the nut from my hand and scampers to Fin's side.

DESTINY

Next morning it is a blue, breezy day but the boat is being packed again. I lug the butter churn outside.

Mother comes out wearing winter clothes: stout boots, thick coat and the hide leggings she wears for traveling. It's all completely incongruous for this time of year. She's carrying a bundle wrapped in fleece.

'You're going with them.' I don't sound as amazed as I feel. I try to keep an even rhythm with the handle of the churn.

'Yes. I'm...' She stops. 'Will you stay and look after Danuta?'

'So I don't get to go?'

'Do you want to?' She puts her bundle down.

'Where are you going?'

'North.'

'Where?' I give the butter paddle a bit more force.

'Walrus hunting.'

Of course I don't want to go.

'I thought you'd rather stay here,' she says.

'On my own.'

'You'll not be on your own. There's Danuta and Donnag. You're old enough... I thought you'd like to be independent. Free of me.'

'You thought.' I don't know what else to say. But I put what I am feeling into the handle of the butter churn. I thump it round and round, hard.

Mother looks ridiculous in her leather coat. She must be sweating. It's a day for bare arms.

'It's been such a swift decision by the men. I had to make my mind up quickly. I've always wanted to go north with Manigan, but when you were children... You're not a child any more, Soyea.'

'And by the time you were my age you were already a mother. I know.'

'I thought you'd be pleased.'

'You didn't ask me though, did you? You're just dumping me with this bunch of no-hopers to go off with him.'

'This is my home,' she says.

I stop beating for a moment, then restart, harder than ever, sloshing the milk into a new rhythm.

'I'll miss you, but we won't be gone long. It's never more than a month or so at this time of year. Danuta will teach you so much.'

I don't say anything. I want to stay angry with her but I know she is right, which is just as annoying as her being wrong. I have wanted her to leave, to be alone, to be free of her, to make my own decisions, and I know Danuta intends to let me into her secrets. It will all be so much easier if Mother and Manigan aren't here. But I am exasperated that she is right, and I am not going to let her have the satisfaction of seeing it.

'Go on then.' I thump the butter round and round.

'Give me a hug, Soyea. Stop that, just for a minute, please.' She is crying and trying not to.

I stop. 'Have you told Danuta?'

'Yes, I've said goodbye.' She comes towards me, stretching out her arms and reaching them around me in her stupid, thick coat.

'It's like hugging a cow,' I say, and she laughs, and I can't help but smile a bit.

Fin and Manigan are loitering just outside the door. Mother notices them and pulls away as Manigan steps towards us. He puts an arm around Mother's waist and with the other he squeezes my shoulder.

'I'm stealing your mother away. You're a free woman. I guess we've both got what we wanted.' He pats my upper arm as if I'm a pet animal. I want to hate him.

He spins Mother away and she turns back to give me a watery smile and a pathetic wave.

'Come and wave us off.'

'No rush,' says Manigan. 'It'll take us a while to get ready to sail.'

They head away down to the shore. Now there's only Fin, watching me.

'It's been good to meet you.'

'Good hunting.'

He nods and I nod back. He makes no attempt to touch me, which is fine, and although I want him to say something else, he doesn't, which is fine too, in its own way. Better that than Manigan's endless drizzle of words. He turns and strides away, the long, thin shape of him diminishing towards the boat. I fit the rhythm of the churn to his steps, like a drum, and add a chant of safety under my breath, a secret charm.

And then I try to put him out of my mind. It doesn't take long to discover I can't, of course.

When I cannot see the people on board any more, but before the boat has passed around the headland, I return to the churn. When the butter firms I heave it back indoors. Danuta is coughing so I go in to see her and give her a cup of the herb-flavoured mead Mother prepared for her.

'You'll have to tell me how to make this.'

'It's mostly self-heal, yarrow and Brigid's balm boiled in milk. I've lots of recipes if you're keen. I'll show you how to make the mead too, and how to take the honey from the bees, that's more important.'

'I want to learn how to heal people.' I've never really known this, but as soon as the words are out of my mouth I feel certain that it's my destiny.

Danuta pats the cover. 'You know, what might just heal me is some sunshine. It'll make me feel better, at least. I can smell it on you. You're like a buttercup.'

I help her out of bed, support her as she totters out of the broch into the sunshine and hap her up in a blanket to keep the breeze off her frail old bones. I sit down beside her.

'I've never known anyone of her age love a man like your mother loves the Walrus Mutterer. She's daft as a maiden for him, isn't she?' She cackles.

'They're apart so much.' I can't believe I'm justifying her.

'He told me he is jealous of you getting to spend all your time with her.'

'And I envy him for being free.'

'Like he said, you both had what the other wanted.'

'It's been like that for years.'

'It's a wonder you got on as you did.'

I turn to stare at her. 'What makes you think we got on?'

'Oh, did you not?' She is all innocence.

I laugh, and wonder if I should tell her everything, but just say, 'No.'

'Well, he's gone.'

'He's gone.'

'And by the time he gets back you'll be well on the way to becoming a healer.'

HERBS

My study of herbal medicines begins by making a series of concoctions for Danuta: a coltsfoot expectorant for her cough, poultices of elder leaves and figwort gathered when the tide was coming in for her aching joints, and a sleeping draught of broom flowers, primroses and valerian root, which smells divine. Some of these she seems to have no confidence in, but they turn out to be useful for all kinds of other things. I realise I am getting an intensive study in making up ointments in different ways. She's a good teacher, and one day when I am peeling off a waxy poultice she smiles and says, 'People always want the potion or the ointment, but the treatment's just as much about feeling someone's hands on your skin, the massage.'

'You mean I might as well be smearing dripping on you?'

'Aye, although it wouldn't smell so nice.'

We laugh together, then she takes my hand. 'But don't forget to make a little request to Brigid in your head, for she's the one who'll guide you best in healing. Go and pick some of her balm and think about what that means to you.'

The weeks pass quickly. She gets me to shift her bed to the fireside so she can supervise my work. Each day I get up early to go out for a walk looking for new plants, either those I don't know or things Danuta has told me to look out for, and each day there's a new flower in bloom. Today I found clanicle and bog bean. What is prettier than bog bean? Such fluffy delicacy, growing out of black mud. It makes me feel there must be good hiding in even the most wicked and foul-tempered soul. I am sure there are guiding spirits opening up buds when they see me coming, offering up their secrets. I try to listen to them as Danuta tells me to. I make pure decoctions of many plants and drink them, meditating on the flavour, trying to distil meaning from their taste and smell, committing to memory everything I can of what the old woman tells me of the magic of each herb. I have begun a collection of sticks with the names of plants carved into them in ogham script, to guide my thinking about them.

Often there are rhymes to help me remember, like 'raspberry leaf gives pain relief'. I love the wordplay most of all and make up many of my own verses. They are just for my own fun, for they contain secrets I cannot share with anyone, but they help me remember the lore. My best one is 'reed roots and elder fruits, let them bubble for breathing trouble'.

One day a man comes in, knocking on the door as he opens it. 'Hello. Anybody home?' He stops as he sees me. 'Oh, excuse me.' He tilts his head in a bashful way. 'Is Bael here?' He looks around.

I shake my head and expect him to leave again, but Bael's absence seems to be what he wants, and he comes in and steps towards me. 'I don't know you.' He is looking at me curiously.

I start to my feet.

'No, don't get up, I didn't mean to disturb you. It smells good.'

He gestures to the pot on the fire.

I'm making a shellfish soup with ramsons and butter. As I stand I realise how tall he is. He's a giant of a man, with a weather-beaten face. I look down. His feet are huge.

I make for Danuta's room, where at least I'll feel safe, but he follows me. I find myself pressing back into the wall to avoid him.

He stoops to enter, his frame almost bent double to get in. When he unwinds, his head almost touches the vaulted ceiling. He smiles down at Danuta. 'You're still with us!'

She reaches an arm up to him. 'Alasdair!' She says his name as if it's a favourite food. 'You get more handsome each time I see you. Soyea, do you know who this is?'

I can't see past him to make eye contact with her, but before I can speak he has swung round to me.

'Soyea! So you're the daughter of Rian? I heard a rumour she was back and has daughters named after islands. What do you make of Assynt?'

I swallow, wishing the wall would push back and let me escape. 'All right.'

'I'm sorry, I'm intimidating you. Barging in like this. I'm just putting my head in to see how Danuta is. I'll not stay.'

'You'll stay as long as you like,' Danuta says. 'Alasdair's chief. He lives in a fine place over there at Rubh an Dunain. Your grandfather built that as well as this.'

'Is that right? Your grandfather? Well, well.'

'Would you like some ale, Alasdair? And something to eat? Do we have an oatcake to offer him, Soyea? She makes lovely cakes this girl.'

He grins. 'You know me, Danuta.'

'Fetch the man a cup of something, little bird, if you don't mind.'

'But not if it's a trouble,' he says.

'It's no trouble.' I slip past him out to the hearth and pour ale, sweetening it with a little mead, a big beaker for him and Danuta's favourite cup for her. I set out a plate of oatcakes and cheese.

The effusive thanks when I take them in make me blush. He has sat down beside Danuta.

'When they said Rian had a daughter, they didn't tell me she was so lovely.' He takes a bite of an oatcake and his eyes widen as he chews. 'Delicious!' His mouth is still working. He takes a second bite.

'She's clever, eh?' Danuta fixes her dimpled smile on me and I'm finding one squeezing its way onto my face too.

The big man lifts his mug and with a 'Slàinte', takes a slug. He swallows. 'Well, it's good to see someone taking care of you, Danuta. I can reassure a few folk. You know,' he turns to me, 'I'm glad Rian's back. You're welcome. And the Mutterer. He's all heart, from what you hear, and what a seafarer.'

I look back at him blankly.

'The poor man was almost thrown out of here by Bael.' Danuta rolls her eyes. 'That boy still has no idea of hospitality.'

'He's not a boy, Danuta.'

'Oh, I know, I know. I despair of him, though.'

Alasdair chomps his way through another oatcake and finishes his ale, while Danuta tells him about Mother and I and all we've tried to do for her. It's embarrassing, but pleasing all the same, to be so appreciated. I find myself liking the big man, and I relax a bit. He has a verve that reminds me of Manigan and somehow this casts my stepfather in a better light than usual. I almost feel proud of him as Danuta and Alasdair discuss his exploits out hunting on the northern ocean, and how thrilled he was to be taking Mother away with him.

As if he is reading my mind, Alasdair turns to me. 'There are good people in this community too, you know. Though I'm here with a warning. There's a thief about. We don't know who, but there are things going missing. We had a ceilidh a few days back, a big throng of folk, and afterwards some things had gone for a walk, valuables, you know, a couple of bronze cups and my wife's favourite necklace. It makes you sore, to think someone here would do such a thing. It gives you a bad taste.'

Danuta shook her head. 'That's awful. Who'd do such a thing?'

'Well I don't want to go casting aspersions, you know, but that trader's in the area, the one-eyed woman.'

'Ussa.' Danuta grimaced. 'She's not welcome here.'

'Aye. That's no surprise. But your lad Bael is thick with her sometimes, you should know that. And she has slaves with her. I wouldn't trust them as far as I could throw them.'

'His father was in thrall to her as well.' Danuta rubbed her forehead as if it was hurting.

'Sorry to have brought bad news.' Alasdair looks abashed.

'No, no. It's best to know these things. We'll keep our eyes open, won't we Soyea?'

I nod.

Alasdair nods back at me, gravely. 'Good. I'm going to be going over to the Long Island tomorrow. Any messages?'

'Oh yes. I'd like you to ask the Wren to visit us. And Donnag may have some too. Soyea, could you go and ask her?'

I head out to find Donnag who puts on a rare smile at the suggestion of being able to make contact with her people and rushes in to see Alasdair.

Otherwise our life is quiet. Only Bael disturbs it with his huffs and tantrums, but he goes off for days at a time. I don't know where and I don't care. It is always better when he's gone. I hate him more than I have ever hated anyone.

Danuta closes her eyes when he comes in, and after a particularly bad night of his brooding presence and the ranting that gets more and more angry as his flask of drink empties, she asks me to take her back into her chamber between the walls. It is cooler in there and dark, and I am worried that all the improvements to her health that she has shown since she took up her place by the fireside will fall away. But she says she is weary.

She wants some peace and quiet. I position her in there so she can still see the fire and its light, and so that sunshine can reach her through the doorway.

He comes in one rainy day in a foul mood. I hear his voice raised in his room upstairs. I can't hear Donnag's responses, but when he returns he is in a rage and he strides over to where all her newly made pots are laid up drying by the fire. He upends the tray and stamps on them. Pottery smashes in all directions.

I run to my room.

THE SISTERS

A few days before midsummer Danuta tells me we'll have some visitors and we must prepare for them. Donnag gets excited, or as close to it as I've ever seen her, when she hears one of the names of the women who may be coming – The Wren. She is Donnag's great aunt, apparently, but from the way she breathes the name it is obvious that she is special.

I am sent to Achmelvich to tell Eilidh that The Wren is coming for midsummer, and her reaction is to hug me and kiss me with delight. Such effusion makes me even more intrigued.

Donnag and I work together to air bedding and make enough oatcakes to feed a fleet. It's good that we do, because when the women come they arrive en masse, fifteen of them, ranging in age from five to seventy-five. I have never had so much fun in my whole life. Bael flees, I don't know where, but Buia emerges from her den and becomes almost like a real person, instead of the ghost we are used to. Donnag seems terrified, making excuses to rummage about upstairs for things, hiding from the constant babble of conversation.

Danuta gets us to carry her bed out again and holds court at the hearthside like a queen. Everyone treats her with absolute respect, even awe. I am proud to be beside her, apprentice, assistant, nurse, whatever I am. I feel like her granddaughter. In other words, I feel like a princess. But more than anything, I feel like a woman. I tend the fire, boil water, heat soup. I am in the centre of it all.

Most of the women are a blur of busily obedient workers, but one stands out because she is by far the oldest and does absolutely nothing from the moment she arrives. She barely needs to stoop to enter the broch and crosses directly to Danuta's bed, where she clutches her hand and beams a toothless smile. She perches like sunshine on Danuta's bed, legs crossed, nodding approvingly as all the preparations for the women's visitation are made, receiving a bowl of soup second only after Danuta and refusing everything else offered to her. I find it hard to take my eyes off her. She is pale as a moth but chirpy as a wren. This is The Wren, of course.

When Donnag emerges from upstairs, she goes straight to the bed and kneels before her. The old woman cups her face with her hands, then leans forward to kiss her on the forehead. Donnag speaks intently to her, and she says a few words. After a while, Donnag bows her head, then goes off to sit in her favourite spot on the stairs, barely visible, but able to watch what is going on.

There's a woman my mother's age, maybe a bit younger, who takes total charge of practical things like food, beds, even toilet arrangements for the whole crowd of them. They have brought the sail up from their boat to make a tent. This woman, Arna, gives everyone else tasks. I have never met anyone so commanding but no one seems to mind her being like that. She is strong, grey-haired and big-boned, and she makes me think of one of those dogs that runs around barking at all the other animals, making them do its bidding. And they are all surprisingly biddable. She leaves me out of her orders and even apologises to me once, 'for the intrusion into your space,' as she puts it, in her big voice. 'We'll do everything, don't worry, we've no intention of being a burden on you. We've brought everything we need and we'll leave you everything we don't use.'

After we have all eaten and the dishes are cleared, I can allow the fire to ease for a while. The old woman asks me to sit by her. She quizzes me intently about all sorts of things: my mother, my life so far, what I know about herbs and why I feed the fire the way I do. If my answers are too long, she interrupts me and asks a different question, and some of these are very strange. She asks me where I think my monthly bleeding comes from, what would I think if I found a frog in the house, how to comfort a cow if its milk stopped coming, what age the sea is – that's one of the strangest. I get a lot of the answers right I think, but some of them wrong. What to say to a wild boar if you meet it in the woods, for example.

I don't know, so I say, 'I wish you many nuts.'

'Nearly.' She pats my knee. 'You thank him kindly for leaving some of the acorns to grow into oak trees.'

'We'd just say, Oak Thanks,' Danuta interjects. She's been following the interrogation intently without interrupting, and now she has managed to break in she adds, 'We found an oak cask up there that you'll be happy about.' She points above our head and winks at me. I go and fill a flask with mead and make Danuta her usual yarrow and self-heal concoction.

The Wren takes hers neat. It's too sweet for my liking, so I water mine down, then I take the rest of the flask to Arna and tell her there's more where it came from. To my surprise, she turns it down, saying they won't abuse our hospitality by drinking something so precious. I insist there is plenty, but she is firm. I relent only after she promises that they'll all drink heartily the following night. All the women have gone except her. I ask where they've gone, and she smiles and shrugs and says, 'Where women go.' I want to ask her what she means but she shoos me away. 'Go and talk to The Wren. Mind and treat her like your honoured guest. You'll not regret it. There's time enough to meet the rest of us tomorrow.'

The Wren and Danuta are chuckling about something when I come in. They allow their laughter to die away like a tumble of stones coming to rest on a slope of scree. I have never seen Danuta enjoy herself so much. I see the fire needs attention, so I feed it three sticks in the way Mother taught me.

'You're a good fire keeper,' The Wren says. 'Your mother showed you well.'

I bow to her. 'Thank you.'

'You'll do. You've more to learn, but we all have, even Danu. Isn't that right?'

Danuta smiles. 'More than ever. I'm forgetting more than I remember these days.'

I know this isn't true but I don't know how to argue with her without sounding rude. I say to The Wren, 'I don't think I've ever asked her something she doesn't know.'

'And I gather you've asked plenty.' She and Danuta chuckle.

I'm embarrassed. 'I like learning.'

I must sound put out because Danuta says, 'Don't take it the wrong way, little bird. I'm happy with all your questions. They make me feel old and wise and young all at the same time. Your curiosity has been a tonic to an old woman at the end of her life. You remind me so much of your mother, bless her, and listen little bird, you know I did wrong by her?' She is sitting up in bed and speaking with an intensity I have never heard her use. 'I let her be taken away. I watched while that monster sold her as a slave. But I'm going to do the right thing this time. You must have the chance she never got. I call you child, but you're not. You're a woman now. You've the heart and the head to be one of the Sisterhood. Your body's ready. You'll do, as my friend here has said.'

The Wren nods. 'You're not polished, shall we say, but there's the beauty of the raw stone in you and I'll happily set you in the ring.'

It dawns on me then what they're telling me.

'You mean I'm to be initiated?'

I look between the two smiling crones.

'But I don't know any magic,' I blurt.

'Shame on you. The whole of our Mother's way is magic,' says

Danuta. 'Show her your sticks.'

I fetch the sticks I've been making with herb names carved into them, and The Wren handles them lovingly, reading every one, naming them. 'Nettle, woundwort, sneezewort, clanicle, sorrel…' I am on tenterhooks to hear what she might make of them.

'You know enough,' says The Wren eventually. 'And in your own words, you love to learn. We are all just beginners, and like the spider and the salmon, we play our part in the great world-weaving. Tomorrow, if you're willing, you can join our merry throng and share some solstice secrets.'

'Will I have to leave here?'

'I don't see why. If you want to visit any of us you will always be welcome. We each have our own path in life. The Sisterhood is not a burden.'

I am smiling so much my cheeks will ache later. I have been chosen! Rona has always been the favoured one – the little one, the pretty one – but this time it is me! I remember, at last, to be polite.

'I am honoured.' I kneel and bow before The Wren. 'May I fill your cup?' I reach for the mead flask and she chortles.

'Yes, you'll do.' She proffers her beaker and when I've filled it, she holds it up. 'All the sweetness of our Mother to you, Sister.'

There is a bang on the door, and a full-throated female voice I don't recognise. 'Greetings sisters!'

Pushing her way into the broch is a woman in a huge white fur coat, with a black leather patch over one eye. She stands in the entrance with both hands on her hips. 'I thought I'd find something happening here if I came for the solstice.' Her voice is deep and smooth but the face it is coming out of is hideous, and the combination makes me shudder. I know immediately who this must be, and I watch, fascinated, as she looks around her.

'You're not welcome, Ussa.' Danuta says.

The Wren pushes herself to her feet with surprising force and steps towards Ussa, her hands out in front of her, fingers making a little gesture of riddance with each step.

As if she's surprised but unable to help herself, the big woman takes a shuffle back, and then another until she bumps against the door.

The Wren keeps on towards her, saying nothing.

Ussa's gaze settles on me. 'I know who you are.' She points at me. 'I'm watching, you see. I know things.'

'Goodbye.' Danuta is completely calm.

The Wren is almost touching her, fingers flicking.

Ussa backs around the door, turns and ducks out. She is gone.

The Wren makes a final waft with her fingers, then returns to her seat, sits down and sighs deeply, before turning to Danuta and carrying on talking as if she has done nothing more serious than put a wasp out of the house. I find I am trembling, so make myself busy at the hearth.

In the morning I am initiated. Eilidh puts a wreath of summer flowers on my head and I dance the Moon Dance with the Sisterhood in the solstice ceremony for the first time that white night. I can't reveal anything about it of course, but it is wonderful, pure, wild magic. I emerge the next day feeling like a butterfly after a long pupation.

Before she leaves, The Wren draws me aside and speaks gravely to me. 'Danuta will not be long for this world. Take care of her for us all.' She gives me some special herbs to put in her mead if she seems to be suffering.

Too soon, Danuta, Buia, Donnag and I are waving the women goodbye. There's a light easterly breeze that is perfect for their crossing, and although it's cloudy, I feel as though the radiance they have left me with could outshine the sun. When their boat is no more than a fleck on the horizon, I turn to the broch. It too has changed over the past two days. It is my home. I find myself thinking of Rona, wondering how she is getting on in her new place and whether the broch she is living in feels like home to her. I hope one day she will visit me here, and I wonder how I will make her feel welcome.

RONA

RONA AND EADHA

My name is Rona and in time I will show that I am capable of great things. My man, Eadha, too. Ever since we first met at that distant cousin's handfasting, I knew he was the one for me and that we would be marvelous together. And we will be.

Today, we have come to Brigid's Cave to spend time with the priestess, Ishbel, learning the Lyre Dance. No one has danced it for generations. It has become merely legendary. We shall revive it, so it can be wonderful again.

It is so exciting! The right place, the right time, the right everything: blood, age, partner, teacher. It is as if everything has been waiting for this moment. We shall dance the world to happiness.

It is my destiny to come to live here on the Winged Isle and bring the dance back to life. It has been a month now since our handfasting and I don't miss Mother and Soyea one bit. Not even Father. Sometimes I feel a bit lost, not really knowing anyone here very well, but I have Eadha now and he's better than all of them put together. I chose him because, like me, he is not happy with humdrum existence. He is willing to strive. He seeks a better future and sees that we must work for it.

How the lyre shines in the lamp light! Its wood gleams, the strings shimmer and the sound it makes is like starlight and moonbeams reflected on flowing water. It makes your blood ripple inside your veins and waves crash in your heart. It really is the music of love. It is impossible not to be moved by it. It is impossible not to move to it.

Ishbel plays like a goddess. We follow all of her instructions to the letter. I am not allowed to tell anyone else what we do. So much of what we are learning is secret.

First we bathe in the dome tent getting fresh, our skin softened by steam. Ishbel gives us a blade and I carefully scrape Eadha's beard away. I only cut him once, a little bit under his ear, and he says it doesn't hurt. The sensation of the blade on his face is so intense: the smoothness of his skin under my fingers; the curve of his chin, his cheekbones, his lips; the weight of his head in my hands. Our longing to hold each other is almost unbearable, but we know that we are cleansing ourselves for the ceremony and that we must hold apart from each other. I cut his hair to a curve around his neck and it curls so much more now than it did when it was longer. He looks magnificent now. You can see his cheeks and his beautiful mouth. I can't stop kissing that mouth. Each time I catch sight of it, I want to reach for it, touch it with my own.

After I shave him, he plaits my hair. All these tender things we have to do to prepare – it is heavenly and excruciating, holding back from what we really want to be doing with each other. But Ishbel is watching, or if not actually here all the time, we know she could come in at any moment, and she is very clear in her instructions that we must abstain from what she calls 'any intimate caresses'. And we are obedient. We both want to do this so much.

That's what I love about him most, the way he shares the passion for this ritual. I think he is perhaps even stronger in his belief of what it all means than I am. He has thought about it more deeply, over years and years. He and Ishbel have talked about it forever. I hear them sometimes and wonder if it matters that I do not have this knowledge. She says it doesn't. She says I have other wisdom, and what I bring is an instinct for the music. That feels right. I do not dance with my mind. I sometimes sense Eadha thinking too hard and allowing his analysis to get in the way of his body. Whereas with me, the rhythm is everything and I cease to care what any of it means. But of course I do care. I care with all my heart and I can give it all my heart because I am dancing with him, who has all of my heart anyway. I am not making sense, perhaps, but I hope you know what I mean.

We giggle about it as we dress, the way we are so desperate to touch each other, yet must cover up our skin in our costumes, denying ourselves and each other, for the sake of the dance. He looks so gorgeous in the leather jerkin, his bare arms and upper chest muscles somehow accentuated by its lines, the shape of his legs, buttocks, groin, smoothed and held by the tight hide. He says the same of me. The leather dress is like a second skin. I can feel how it makes my movements lithe and smooth. I love the way the straps on my legs stretch and flex as the muscles work. There is more of the costume to come, Ishbel says. Horns for our heads, once we have learned to make the movements properly and built up the strength in our necks to carry them. It is all getting so exciting. Each day we learn a little more, practise harder, make progress towards the day we will be ready for the ceremony.

And of course, after we have practised and eaten and changed back into normal clothes and set off home, alone, together, we can't keep our hands off each other. We can't wait for a right time, can't bear the prospect of arriving back home, having to be civil to Eadha's mother, listen to her sickly moaning and groaning, talk to whoever may have called in. There is always someone staying and it isn't seemly to rush straight off to bed and even then we have to trap the wild noises of love inside because there is embarrassment about being heard.

So we stop in the woods, lay coats down under a birch tree and allow our bodies to do what they need. We are like a single animal, our instincts and rhythms seem to be so perfectly attuned, and when we join our bodies together we seem to move into some spirit realm. Surely no two people have ever been so perfectly in love, so blessed. We are able to touch something entirely divine when we fuse. He makes me feel so alive, so vibrant, so beautiful. It's a level of ecstasy I am certain no one can ever have felt before. That's why we are so right for the ritual. We will channel love into the earth so powerfully that nothing will ever be able to fail again. Ishbel says I shouldn't make claims like this, that we are just two leaves on the tree of life, but I know that we are not just any two leaves. We're the golden ones. We're the seed from which something perfect and beautiful will grow.

When I try to express this to Ishbel, she says, 'Watch such pride, lest it fell you.' So I am careful where I put my feet, and make sure not to lose my balance.

When we get home there are no visitors after all, and Cuilc is happy to see us home safely, smiling at what we tell her about the dance. Obviously we just reveal a fraction, none of the secret parts. She seems proud of what we are doing. Of course, she finds something to complain about: mice in the rafters keeping her awake at night, eating holes in the roof. We promise to go and find a cat tomorrow. Someone is bound to have some kittens. It will be a lovely thing to do.

After Cuilc goes to bed, I drink my foul tea, which Ishbel says will stop me getting pregnant before the ritual. It seems to have worked so far: I bled last week. I'm pleased. I don't want a squalling baby sucking at my breasts, keeping me awake at night, hanging on my back all day or crawling around my feet, like Mother had at my age. I don't want anything to get between Eadha and me. We are complete together already. There is no room for a child.

Cuilc's right. I can hear the mice scratching up there, and squeaking. But I think I am tired enough to sleep anyway, and if not, Eadha will take my mind off everything. Even if he's snoring, I know the touches that will have him awake again in no time.

Eadha says we must treasure this time, for it may not last, but I love to dream of the future. He says if we hanker after harvest when the seed is being sown in spring soil, then we may go hungry later. We must watch for weeds, he says. He talks of the dangers of pride. I don't altogether understand him.

But when I say, 'let's dance,' he agrees, and when I say 'let's swim,' he agrees, and when I say 'let's learn the mysteries and always live by the wisdom of the priestesses and druids,' he agrees and kisses me and I know I am blessed to have found him.

This morning we walk early, just because it is a perfect day: quiet, almost windless, just a ruffle of breeze to stroke your skin and shimmer the surface of the loch. We stroll hand in hand along the shore path, down over the stream where they built the little stone bridge last winter, and up through the woods. We step from one sun-dappled spot to another, stopping often just to kiss.

Our walk takes us up onto the ridge where we can look out to sea. It is a sheen of fabric for a fairy queen, with a gemstone necklace of islands. If I could wear clothes made of the colours and textures of this place on a day like today, I would be happier than a lamb. As it is, I have Eadha, who makes me feel like I am dressed in the most glamorous outfit even when I have thrown on my raggiest dress.

This island is the most beautiful place I have ever known. I'm sure I'll never tire of exploring it. Every day the light is different and there are so many colours and textures on the hills. And what hills! On today's summit we practise the dance. Our necks are getting strong. Soon we will be able to try it wearing the horned headdresses, Ishbel says.

In the evening, she comes to the broch with her lyre. Aonghas, one of Cuilc's cousins, has sailed over from Rum. A few others come round and Cuilc cooks up a delicious sauce of fresh herbs to eat with trout that someone caught from one of the mountain lochs. I'm a bit nervous about what to say to all these strangers, so

I concentrate on making bannocks. I hate cooking, but I can do bannocks reliably enough and hungry people are always grateful for them. I bake a huge quantity to make up for not cooking otherwise. Cuilc grumbles at me for using up the flour and goes on about how short we are running on grain, but it's getting mealy and it needs using up, and a big batch means I won't have to make more again for a while. Cuilc says the more I make the more people eat. So what? If we're generous, others are generous back. Just look at the fish. If we weren't known as a house where food is shared with open hands, those fish would have been taken elsewhere. Cuilc likes to claim it's her tasty sauces and pickles that draw folk in with meat. Eadha tells us we're both right – ever the diplomat.

After we've eaten, Ishbel plays her lyre and Eadha gets out his drum – how different it is from the Cave Music! I had forgotten how good it is to dance a jig and sing the simple songs. I could sing all night.

Tomorrow morning they will all leave. Cuilc is going with Aonghas to see his wife, who is sick. Cuilc isn't well herself, but she is enjoying herself so much, dancing and singing, so when Aonghas suggests she return with him she allows herself to be persuaded. Ishbel has given her some herbs to take and we encourage her to go, telling her it will do her good to see some other people. She is old, and she needs to see her oldest friends. But mostly we're pressing her to join them because it means we will be alone!

RIAN

SAILING NORTH

Rian's place on *Bradan* was beside the helm. If they ever needed to tack, she took the mainsheet through to the other side of the boat and fastened it there, while Kino, Badger and Fin did the heavy work at the mast and the bow, and Manigan had the tiller. She had her manoeuvre down to a slick, relaxed set of movements. Most of the time they didn't need to change course so she could simply look around at the huge, empty expanse of the northern ocean.

Manigan was attentive to her, and she had never been so happy, afloat in this dreamscape with time to listen to his stories. She was well wrapped up against the cold, though it was really not as cold as she had expected. In any case, no amount of chill would have perturbed her. The open sea was so beautiful. There was no land to be seen anywhere, no other vessels, nothing but their little boat and the infinite ocean.

Was it infinite? She didn't know but she wanted to believe so. And if the ocean itself was not, it blended and mixed with the sky, which surely was.

Beside her, Manigan was 'muttering on as usual', as he put it. He always had a tale to tell and she finally had the chance to be there, prompting him. She didn't need to know what would happen in the end, she just liked the sound of his voice. And here she could really attend to the telling of the story, accompanying him on his journey inside the tale, with grunts and nods and little questions about what he thought something meant or an observation of how it linked to real life.

The tale of the sea horse finished, and she laughed and he fell silent. For a while there was only the hush and fizz of waves and wake.

She looked round at him. His hair was greying but his face was still that of the only man she had ever wanted to touch. He was gazing out to the west, where the satin surface of shimmering ripples met the grey lightness of sky.

'Will we ever reach the edge?' she said.

He bent forward and kissed her. 'Rian, you speak so little, but when you do it is a kind of poetry. Look out there.' He gestured out to the horizon. 'Is that the edge? Is that what you mean? What a beautiful question. I don't really believe in it as an edge, no more than I believe that you and I are separate. There is ocean and there is sky, but there is no line where one stops and the other begins. There is a space where they merge. We can be aware of it sometimes, like when a tempest or a storm makes them blend in chaos or when stillness settles, mist rises and sky falls. But I've come to realise that the horizon is always an illusion. I have spent half my life sailing towards it and sailing away from it and the forwards direction never took me any closer and the retreat never found me any further away.

'So yes, it looks like a line but it's not really an edge. The sea is a body and the sky is a body and between them is a plane of touching. All over that surface of the sea, all over, the sky is reaching in and the ocean is reaching out. See its ripples, even in such calm as this; it is reaching, pushing itself up, while the sky is stroking it, kissing it, rubbing itself over the skin. The sea reveals the sky to itself, reflecting it back, playing with its light. What lovers they are, what passion they have for each other, what a love it is to witness. And just as when our skin touches, we are no longer separate, we have no edges, our breath, our pulse, our soul is shared, it's the same thing with them. We only see the horizon as a line of separation because we cannot really imagine a joining of such vastness, such perfection.'

She thought about this for a while, then said, 'Pytheas believed we live on a ball. He tried to explain it to me once.'

'Did that man think he was one of the gods, to be able to see the whole world and know its shape?'

She breathed out slowly. They never spoke about Pytheas because of Cleat, it was too upsetting. 'Perhaps.'

'He thought he was a superior body. He gave that impression anyway.'

'He was in awe of you. He said there are three kinds of people in this world: the living, the dead and the mariners. He thought you were a spirit man.'

' Rian, there was only one reason he was interested in me and that was because ivory was worth something to him. He had the same greedy glint in his eye as the rest of the traders. No object really means anything to those people, they just see it for what they can get for it.'

'Is that why you hated him so much?'

He sniffed and tossed his head. 'You know exactly what my problem with him was. He took Cleat and never brought him back. He stole your son – the only son I had. What is the Mutterer to do without a son? I love you Rian, I have never loved another the way I have loved you. But you have only given me Rona. I say "only", and that is cruel. Rona is my most precious, my songbird child. I adore her pretty little soul. But I need a son. I cannot train her to kill, I cannot teach her the wisdom of the oceans, I cannot pass on the Muttering to her, not that she'd want it.'

'You could teach Soyea.' Rian said. 'She'd honour the tradition.'

'It is forbidden for a woman to know the Muttering. It is not merely the physical strength required in the killing, it is the need to face the Old Gentleman of the Sea, man to man. How could a woman cut the penis bone off a walrus and live to tell the tale? And for that matter, how could a woman tell the stories of the stone? I must pass them on too, to someone who can tell them in his turn.'

'You told me some.'

'Aye, I've told you bits, but there's more that I haven't told anyone.'

'It's gone now, though. Isn't it? It's not your burden anymore.'

'No, it's not mine anymore. But I had it for years and years and the stories are part of me.'

'You never did tell me exactly how you lost it.'

'Did I not? I was probably too furious. I never want to spoil the time we have by getting het up.'

He paused and took some breaths, as if readying himself for an exertion. 'You know how the Queen Bitch, cousin Ussa, followed me around like a horsefly in summer trying to get it?'

She nodded.

'Well one day, just like a horsefly, she bit in before I noticed her and took it from me.' He settled himself on his bench. It would be a proper story.

Fin had woken up. He perched himself within earshot, listening. Rian frowned, reluctant to widen the close circle with her man to include the lanky youth, but Manigan nodded approval.

'You might not have heard this one, Fin, but you need to. I was on *Bradan*, this very boat, at an anchorage off the Long Island, in a sheltered loch called Marabhig, hiding from a north-westerly gale. It was midsummer and so it never got dark. The crew had landed to go in search of food and drink. I always seem to have crew with insatiable thirsts, and you might as well let them go instead of sitting on board, all cramped up, with them climbing the mast for want of grog. They snarl and fight, or sulk, or drive you nuts with bickering. So, I'd turfed all three of them off, Badger with them to try to keep them in order, not least his crazy little brother.'

He waved towards Kino, who was slumped beside the mast, head on his chest, sleeping, and then settled his eyes on Badger, who was sitting on a thwart, gazing ahead. 'I don't know what I would have done over the years if it weren't for the loyalty of that man. A real friend, he is. I call him a lazy dog and a poisoner. He won't lift an oar and he can't cook without burning everything or leaving it raw and he farts and he's ugly and cantankerous and he drinks far too much, and I could list a thousand other faults in the man but he's loyal to me. He has sailed in *Bradan* for more years now than I can remember and that counts for something, even if he is the lousiest, filthiest good-for-nothing crew a skipper could have. He's my friend, and I'll call him it to his face if I have to.'

Badger turned his head and grinned.

'Aye, of course he's laughing. He never misses a thing, that one. Isn't that right, Badger, are your ears flapping?'

Badger poked one finger sharply up, then returned to gazing out to sea as if ignoring them.

'Anyway, there I was, alone on *Bradan*, and it was calm enough in the loch, surrounded on all sides by good green land. The channel in there is tight and forked and no amount of gale can hurt you as long as your anchor bites. There was smoke out of one of the houses and I could imagine the ceilidh. There were plenty of happy-looking black cattle and a prosperous air about the place. I knew the crew wouldn't be back until well into the next day, and that was fine. We weren't going anywhere in that wind and I was looking forward to a bit of head space. You can go a bit crazy on a small boat, crowded together, knowing every intimate detail of everything you'd rather not have to know about your crew. So a night alone was a boon, a treat. I'd checked the anchor a dozen times and I was happy we weren't dragging, then I'd tucked myself up in my bedroll. I must have been deeper asleep than I'd intended, because without me noticing, Ussa blew in. She'd lashed her boat to mine before I was properly awake. She must have been circling, checking me out. I had avoided her so well for years. To be honest, I think she had given up the chase and it was just a coincidence that we were in the same part of the Minch at the same time, sheltering from the same wind, and she took the chance. Her skipper knows all the safest anchorages, just as I do.'

'Is Toma still with her?' Rian said. 'I loved Toma. He always knew the way.'

'I don't know. Do you, Fin?'

Fin shook his head. 'The old man's out to grass. A guy younger than you skippers her boat these days, Eachan. Nutter.'

A frown furrowed Rian's forehead. 'Where's Toma?'

Fin shrugged. 'Dunno. Not well. Maybe even gone west by now.'

Rian pursed her lips. She was thinking of the time the old man had helped her to steal the stone back from Ussa. He hadn't wanted the evil thing on his boat.

Manigan waited to see if she was going to say anything, then continued. 'Anyway, they pulled alongside with barely a bump and it wasn't until there was the lurch of footsteps on board *Bradan* that I knew what was happening. Three of them – two big men and Ussa with a knife at my throat before I'd got myself out of my sleeping roll. With the eye patch over her missing eye, I hardly recognised her. And you remember that big thug, Og, who used to be her slave?'

'Of course,' Rian said. 'He's not back with her, is he?'

'Aye, he went back to her even after he'd been granted his freedom, more brawn than sense if you ask me.'

'I sometimes suspected he loved her.'

'More fool him. Anyway, he had me pinned down, his knee in my groin. It was like having a bear on top of me, and with her blade half-choking me I wasn't moving. Some weasly little slave was rummaging and throwing everything he could overboard, and there are times when you have to do the only thing you can to survive. So before he had completely emptied my locker of every piece of useful tackle I possess, I told her where the stone was. It was over in a moment. My throat was nicked, but I'm still talking, aren't I? She's a greedy, ruthless bitch and I hate her, but blood must mean something because she could have left me a corpse with no difficulty at all, but she just took the stone and a few choice tools and weapons. The big man cut a few ropes out of spite as he climbed back over the gunwales to her boat. I was furious, but to be honest, in hindsight, if I'd been in her shoes I'd have made much more of a mess of the rigging just to make sure I couldn't come after her. As it was, my drunken crew turned up the next day with raging hangovers, long after the gale had eased enough to let Ussa get away, and I never even got to see whether she headed south, east or north at the mouth of the loch. I didn't see her again until more than a year later and the stone had done its worst by then.'

'How do you mean?'

'It took away her glamour completely. Fin, will you take the helm for a while?' He got the young man to take the tiller, showed him how to make sure he stayed at the same angle to the wind, then busied himself with tidying ropes. Once satisfied he sat down next to Rian on the other side from Fin, slung an arm around her shoulder and said, 'Do you remember when she was beautiful? When I was a boy I remember thinking she was like a princess. And she was loveable.'

Rian raised an eyebrow. 'Loveable?'

'She was! She had a way of listening to you as if she treasured your words, as if she was savouring your voice, and it made you want to tell her everything. She must still have it somewhere. Nobody's rotten all the way through. But she is rotten, there's no doubt about that.'

'How do you think she got like that?' Fin asked.

'It started early. As soon as she got the trading bug. At first she did it just for a bit of fun, buying trinkets from smiths then setting up a stall at the fair in Ictis and selling them as fine jewels. The thing is, when she put some tawdry beads in her hair and stood with the sun on them, they gleamed and twinkled. Her beauty shone on her wares and people would pay for a share of that sparkle.

'Later, the beauty and grace became seduction, and she moved on from pretty trinkets to weaponry. She knew it was obscene, what she was doing, going around, unsheathing daggers and swords at every harbour, but once she'd started, she didn't seem to know how to stop. As it got more dangerous she needed a bodyguard, and that's when she got into slaves. Og was the first. She bought him for a sword from a member of his family, his stepfather. I've never understood why he was loyal to her. But there's a lot about Ussa I do not understand.

'Once she had bought a slave, another followed, and selling them was easy for her. As soon as she fell out with someone, off they'd go and she'd buy herself a new one. She knows no one properly. She has no friends. We are not people to her any more. We are all just objects to be traded. If you can no longer see the sacred spark in a bronze-smith's casting, why should you see it in the eyes of a human being?

'When she stole the stone from me, she was already one-eyed, yet she was still trying to look glamorous, but when I saw her one year later she was rotten through and through. Perhaps the stone spoke back to her and made her see what she had become. All her poise and surface charm was based on self-deceit. She didn't believe what she was doing was wrong. It was just trade. But the stone must have made her incapable of hiding from her wickedness and let it eat her up from the inside to her very skin.'

'I wonder whether she has been play acting for so long she no longer knows who she really is,' said Fin. He sounded genuinely sorry for her.

Rian stared at him. What was she doing on a boat with a sympathiser of Ussa's?

Manigan wasn't thrown by the remark. 'She always used to have a spark of that vulnerable girl in her eyes, no matter how much of a queen she was trying to be. There was someone in there who looked out and attended to what she saw with fascination, with curiosity. Even you, Rian. Even though she was cruel to you,

I can imagine her enjoying your beauty, admiring your courage, appreciating you for your fierceness, your independent self. But when I saw her last, the only time I've seen her since she robbed me, her eyes were dead and soulless, with only hunger in them, and she had become blubbery. Don't get me wrong, I've got nothing against looking well fed but she looked as if her body could no longer be satisfied by anything.'

'That wind is strengthening,' Badger said.

Sure enough, the sky was grey to the west and a swell was building.

'Do you know what you're doing, Fin?'

He nodded, and Manigan went forward to help Badger put a reef in the sail. They were kept busy for a while until the shortened sail was back up.

Manigan took the helm and they settled again. Kino whittling a piece of ivory, Badger making some porridge and Fin, with his eyes shut, back against the mast.

'Is he all right?' Rian gestured towards the youth.

'He's napping again. I never knew anyone to sleep so much.'

Badger looked up, 'Every lad's the same, you know that.'

'I suppose that's right, at that age it's normal. But I'm not convinced it's good for you, too much sleep.'

Rian chuckled. 'You're becoming an old grouch.'

'Ach, stop me from becoming that, my love, if you can. I've no reason to be grumpy with you here on the ocean, finally doing what we should have done all those years ago.'

Badger slopped porridge out into mugs and handed them round. He left Fin's by the mast.

Manigan blew on his mug and put it down. 'It's easy to lose yourself out here, to drift away for hours, but I find there is a core of me that floats free when I let go of my thoughts. That's the part of me that loves you best, Rian. It's the part that missed you when I was traveling and would tell me to head home to you. Now you're here, so I don't need any other kind of home.'

Rian reached out and stroked the back of his neck. 'I remember Danuta telling me there's great wisdom inside every one of us if we know how to listen. Whenever Ussa or Pytheas or anyone was being cruel to me, I used to go inside myself. It used to feel like I could climb up a crag within me that had a safe place at the top. It's hard to explain. But up there I knew nobody could really touch me or do me harm.'

He turned and rubbed his cheek against the top of her head and for a while they said nothing, looking out at the water.

'I thought the wind was getting up here, but now I'm wondering if we should shake that reef out again. Don't you love the way the sea surface glitters? This ruffle on the swell. It soothes, like the touch of fingers on skin. I can watch the light on water for hours on hours, those patterns of sheen, as if the light is curdling. See those blobs of colour, the way they distend and stretch and merge with each other, then disintegrate again? It's an endless dance. All my woes slough off and dissolve among the ripples, while all the things I've never done bubble up and dazzle me.'

He took a slurp of porridge, and after he'd swallowed, said, 'I meant to tell you about Fin and how I found him. You know he's Fraoch's little brother? Half-brother, anyway.'

Rian hadn't thought about Fraoch for a long time. At one point she had thought they might be friends, but Rian had never found it easy to forgive people who betrayed her. She dredged in her memory for what Manigan had told her about their kinship. 'So he's Gruach the bronze smith's son?'

'That's right.'

'And Gruach was your cousin.' She remembered Fraoch's bronze smith father with much more warmth, but the connections with Ussa and Fraoch still left her distrustful of the youth.

'Old Gruach was a wily old wizard, and he made special magic happen for more than one woman. I'd heard him claim he had a son, but I'd never set eyes on the boy until he was sixteen, when he ran away from home to live with Ussa, of all people.'

'What about his mother?'

'I've never met her. She's somewhere in the Summer Isles or near there.'

Manigan supped his porridge, and Rian finished hers and handed the mug back to Badger. 'So he's one of Badger's kin as well?'

'No, not Badger's folk, some other lot.'

Badger nodded. 'Scoraig.'

'Why did he go to Ussa?'

'I asked him that. He said she passed through where they lived and invited him along. He just wanted to travel, he said. What other way was there? He wasn't allowed to go with her, naturally. At least it sounds as if his mother was a sensible woman. But the tyke stole a coracle and set off across the sea to wherever it was Ussa had said she was going. Idiot boy. I gather it's not so very far but even so, anyone who tries island hopping in a coracle deserves what they get. I gather it was a bit scary. "I hadn't realised how long it would take to paddle over and the boat seemed awful small and the sea awful big half way across," he told me.

'He's determined, I'll give him that. He didn't turn back, and he reached the island. I don't know which one, you'll have to ask him. He found Ussa's boat and stowed himself away as best he could, which wasn't very well, he said, and Toma found him when the crew came back next morning before they set sail. Anyway, young Fin threw himself at the mercy of his aunt. Can you imagine? And yes, dear old motherly Ussa let him stay. I can bet what she was planning. No, I'll let you imagine. You know her as well as I do. Queen Bitch got herself another lapdog, even prettier than Pytheas.'

'Don't say that kind of thing, you horrible man.' Rian elbowed him as if in disgust, but her eyes were laughing.

'Look, he's awake now. Ears burning, no doubt. He doesn't mind if I talk about him like that, do you Fin?'

'I'm just happy to know I'm so interesting. It was Tanera Mòr, the island.' He was smiling, and clearly not taking offence. Badger pointed out the porridge and Fin grabbed it and started eating. The monkey, which had been asleep in his coat, tried to join the feast.

'See! So tell Rian what Ussa did next.'

'No.' Fin seemed to be absorbed in feeding porridge to his pet.

'You're an arrogant young pup, so you are.'

'I'm eating and you'd tell it better.'

'Would I?' Manigan turned back to Rian. 'Do you know this young fellow wants for nothing? His father's the best bronze-smith the north has ever known and greedy old Ussa has made him her heir. He has gifts lavished on him from all sides, and yet he says they don't mean a damn to him.'

'It's this, the sea, that's the only treasure I'm after,' said Fin.

'He says he only went off with Ussa because she journeyed on the ocean, not for her gold and jewels. Well I reckon you'd have to be mad to throw away an offer like Ussa's for riches beyond counting, just to spend a season chasing walruses. I know what I'd choose if I had the option.'

'You wouldn't taint yourself,' said Rian.

'Perhaps you're right. The riches coming from Ussa would make me pause for thought. For a moment or two, anyway.'

'More.'

'Aye. Maybe three. But not much longer! If I had a chest of golden jewellery to my name I'd give up this chase before you could say Old Gentleman!'

'No you would not.' Rian was laughing.

'Would I not? You really don't think so? Oh try me, why don't you?'

'I don't have a chest of jewels.'

'Aye, well that, my love, makes two of us. So here we are. And here's this rapscallion good-for-nothing sleepyhead nephew or cousin or whatever he is of mine, daft as a sea urchin, that's what I think, and about as useful on a boat. If I have to show him how to tie a bowline properly one more time I'm going to tie it around his neck and show him how it tightens.'

Fin grinned. 'And no doubt you'd tie it one-handed, behind your back.' He got up and went to dip his mug in the water barrel.

'Too right. Hey, don't dip that in there like that, wash it first. I want to drink that water later and I don't want your porridge scum in it.'

Fin slopped some water in the cup, swirled it round and chucked the contents overboard.

Manigan nodded. 'That's better.' Then to Rian, 'See what I mean? He has the boat sense of a farmyard pig, that boy. His damned pet monkey has a better idea of what to do on here, I tell you not a word of a lie. And that says a lot about him, doesn't it? A pet monkey. Not a dog, oh no, no sensible beast like a ferret for this young man. A monkey. I ask you.'

'She's the smartest animal on this boat,' Fin said. The monkey was absorbed in grooming.

'Aye, aye, as monkeys go, it's an intelligent and amusing monkey and yes it's clean, I'll give it that. But it's still a monkey!'

'It seems to have stopped being sick, at least,' Rian said.

'True. Who ever heard of a monkey with sea legs?'

'You'll no doubt make a story of it, Uncle Manigan.' Fin stroked the little animal's head.

'I blasted well hope so. I'll dine on the time I sailed to Iceland with a monkey in the crew.'

'Are we going all the way to Iceland?' Rian was wide-eyed.

'Aye. If we can, that is, but we'll need something other than a westerly. We'll need some wind to go anywhere, of course. We could sit here a long time drifting not very far on this feeble current.'

The wind had now almost died away again and the sea was becoming glassy.

'Come on, let's shake this reef out.' Fin, Badger and Kino untied reefing knots and hoisted the sail to its full extent. Rian saw that despite Manigan's complaints, Fin handled his tasks on board with skill. He'd probably been sailing all his life. They rolled on in the lazy swell, making slow progress.

Manigan gestured west. 'If there's only westerly, we'll go east. Maybe we'll make it to Bear Island, north of the Norse lands. There are islands even to the north of there again, they say, although even my grandfather never went there. I'd love to go.'

'I don't care where we go.'

'Well that's all right then.'

'I can die happy now.'

'Oh don't do that. I'll not be happy if you die, Rian, my love, I'm only just getting to know you properly.'

'Hardly.'

'Aye, you are the love of my life, but that doesn't mean I know you very well. You don't really get into someone's skin until you've sailed with them, I don't reckon.'

'We sailed all the way to Whale island right at the start of it and then to Ictis.'

'Right enough, we had that mad chase down from the Black Chieftain's place, but you can't count that. We were too busy running away to be able to find out much about each other.'

'I found out everything I needed to know about you.' She tilted her head at him, cheekily.

'Oh you did, did you? You might think you did. I never told you half of what there is to tell.'

'No, you leave all your stories unfinished. Like that one about King Ban and the stone. You started that on that journey and never did finish it.'

'How do you remember that? What kind of a strange creature are you that remembers I told you half a story about King Ban nearly twenty years ago? You're a wonder and a marvel, so you are Rian. I shall have to tell you it some day. It's a good one, that one!'

'And you've still not finished explaining about Fin.'

'Fin, what about him?'

'How you have him in your crew.'

'For my sins. Well, Ussa lavished all her riches on him, showed him a good time around the houses of the rich and mighty of Belerion. She did everything she could to bring him close in about her. The monkey came from her, of course, one of many toys. There was a horse too. Still is, presumably, somewhere. A good one, by all accounts.

'Anyway, end of last year I was there selling ivory at the big Belerion fair and he came and introduced himself. Yes, Fin. I wasn't impressed. He waltzed up in his fancy embroidered hose and a jerkin with tassels, mincing about in leather slippers as if the ground's not good enough for his pretty little feet.

'"Hello, Uncle," he says. "Uncle Manigan, isn't it?" He put on a ridiculous high-pitched voice and Fin rolled his eyes.

'"Impudent cub, who are you to call me Uncle?" I reply.

'"I'm Gruach's son," he says, "and I'd like to come to sea with you."

'"You're jesting with me," I say.

'"No, Uncle," he says. "I've wanted it all my life. You're the Walrus Mutterer, aren't you?"

'I could hardly deny it, could I?

'"I'll do the worst job on the boat," he says.

'"You'll do no job on my boat at all," I reply. I wasn't even thinking about it.

'"I don't know much about boats," he persists.

'I could tell that just by looking at him.'

Fin interrupted. 'I told him I'm good at fishing and that animals trust me.'

'Aye, and it turns out it's true, they do. But back then I thought he was just saying stuff to ingratiate himself with me and I was having none of it. And then he says, "My aunt Ussa'll vouch for me." Ha, ha, ha. You can imagine what I said to that!'

'You probably swore', Rian said.

'I no doubt did. And I told him what I think of his aunt Ussa, too right I did, and I filled him in on a bit of history and he didn't look so happy when I sent him packing.' Manigan shook his head. 'But then after I left you and Soyea in Assynt, I headed west to the Long Island and he turned up again. Like a bad smell, I told him. It was Badger who persuaded me to take him on. I needed anyone I could persuade to come with me hunting. It's not easy to get good guys to come north and Badger said he'd take care of him, make sure he didn't get into trouble. The Summer Isles boys are all as bad as each other, you know.'

Badger looked up and lifted a hand. 'That's us.'

Manigan coursed on. 'Anyway, Badger had watched the boy growing up there, reckoned he was all right really, despite all the regalia he had on. He had a bag the size of a big pig, full of his riches and fancy gear.'

'What fancy gear?' Rian pointed at the young man, who was wearing an old, sea-soiled gansy and coat.

'I know, he's a scruff now, isn't he? But see what he had then, how he managed to avoid getting himself robbed travelling up to the Long Island all the way from Belerion is a mystery to me. He'd worked on one of the trading boats from the Amber Coast and the skipper said he wasn't a bad crewman, not very strong but sharp enough and biddable. Young Fin had blagged his way on board in Ictis, the autumn before. He'd been determined to quit life with Ussa, and when I wouldn't have him, he'd gone off with the first boat that would. Him and the monkey.'

'It was Og who set it up. He was leaving too.' Fin said.

'So, he finally saw sense, did he? Anyway, they'd gradually made their way up the west coast, sheltering a lot. Late winter's not a good time to make passage, as you know, but these boats from the Amber Coast are built for all weathers and some of the skippers are fearless. I don't know what he'd have done if I'd not shown up in the Hoil.'

'But you did,' said Fin.

'Aye. I did.'

'I'd have gone to the Amber Coast, probably. Like Og, looking for my fortune.'

'And there'd you'd still be, boy, in a bog probably. Anyway, he came aboard, stowed his big bag of booty and set about trying to persuade me he's a useful seaman, which I'm yet to be convinced of. He's made some damn fool mistakes, I can tell you that for nothing. There was the time we hit a storm off the Cat Isles...'

'Oh leave off, Manigan, we don't need to hear that again.' Fin was blushing now.

'What? They get better with retelling. They do!'

'And it wasn't Badger that persuaded you. It was the stone.' The young man's voice was strident now.

Manigan seemed to acquiesce at the mention of it. He gave a rueful shake of his head. 'True enough, the stone, aye. If I'm honest, that's what swayed me. What power it has, eh?'

THE DEATH STONE

'So where is it now?' Rian said.

Manigan patted the locker lid he was sitting on. 'Here. Fin has it now. Did you not know? That's what's blocking up my stern locker. Aye. The Death Stone, my three-faced friend. Why do you think I'm heading north with a smile on my face, telling stories? Young Fin here has it now and he's with me. He has a healthy respect for it as well, I'll give him that. Fortunately.'

'How come?'

'He bought it.'

'Ussa sold it? You're kidding.'

'I know, it's incredible to me too. But I've asked him a dozen times and that's what he says he did.'

'I never said I bought it from Ussa,' Fin had his back to them and was looking out to sea.

'You what? You did so,' Manigan said.

'I never. I bought it, and she organised it, but it was from her father, not her.'

'Donnal Sevenheads?' Rian was shocked. 'Is he still alive?'

'Aye.'

'He must be ancient. What did you buy it with?' Rian asked, wondering what other dealings with Ussa's family the boy had been involved in.

'A sword,' Fin said.

Rian raised her eyebrows at this, the standard price for a slave. Indeed she had first been traded for a sword.

Manigan nodded. 'I heard it was one of Gruach's best bronze ones. Beautiful, by the sounds of it. But how the hell did Sevenheads get it off her?'

Fin shrugged and didn't reply.

'I'll bet it was a bet,' said Badger.

Fin nodded. 'She told me she staked it and lost, gambling with him, ages before she got it from you, and that was why she wanted it so badly all those years. She owed it to him.'

Manigan snorted. 'I'd guess the stone probably realised pretty soon old Sevenheads didn't need any help with killing. What do you think? I'd believe anything of it. Anyway, it obviously spotted a gullible innocent and got itself into new hands.'

Rian thought Manigan sounded as if he was still in thrall to it himself. 'How'd you feel about Fin having it?' she said.

'Fine. I'm glad it's not mine anymore. I had it for years, and now it has moved on. I wish him better luck with it than I had. It's a relief to know it's out of Ussa's hands and not mine to search for anymore.'

Fin shifted around on the thwart so he was facing Manigan. 'So you'll not be stealing it off me in the night?'

'Nah. You're stuck with it, son.'

'If you really want it you can have it, you know.'

Manigan elbowed Rian. 'See what he's like? He'll give anything away. It's unbelievable. He values nothing.'

Fin thrust his hands down on his thighs and pushed his chin

forward. 'I value a great deal: fine food, a comfortable bed, good company, music well-played, lots of things like that. But I don't value objects for their own sake and I've no interest in having lots of possessions unless they're meaningful.'

'All right. You're rich as a king and not interested in any of it. Amazing isn't it, Rian? Well, give it all away if you like but watch who you're giving that stone to, that's all I'm saying. And watch what you do with it.'

'Because of its powers?'

'Because of what it is, aye.'

'You said there are stories to tell me about it.'

'Don't hold your breath,' said Rian. 'I've been waiting for years.' Fin grinned at her but she returned his gaze with cool scepticism.

'All right, the stone stories. It's as good a time as any.' Manigan did one of his customary sweeps of his head, looking out to the horizon in an arc from west around to east, then called, 'Badger, look to starboard. Do you see what I see?'

Badger roused himself and peered eastwards, then gave a little toss of his head, as if shaking himself awake. 'Are we there already? Aye, land ho!'

'We nearly sailed straight past her!' Manigan was on his feet, turning the tiller, and calling for the sail to be loosened and brought round so it was nearly square on and they could run with the breeze towards what was soon, even to Rian, discernibly an island. It was pyramidal in shape, with a tuft of cloud over the peak, as if it was smoking.

'No story, then,' Rian said.

'Later, my love. There'll be plenty of time later.'

She gave a little smile. She had heard that line so many times before, but later was always full of something other than the end of the story.

SOYEA

FUNERAL

Everyone seems affected by the visit of the Sisters. Buia has a new dress on that one of the sisters gifted her, and because she washed for the solstice ceremony she is sweet-smelling. She is focusing on living things for a change, flowers in particular. She brings back armfuls of blossom, and the broch is soon a bower of hanging bundles of scents. There are baskets of rose petals that she turns and stirs, releasing their fragrance into the air so the whole building is a tower of perfume.

We clean the broch from top to bottom, set a lamp to burn in the cellar and give offerings to the spirits of the underworld. We get a cow from Duileag, and Buia calls her Beithe and loves her like a bosom friend. Donnag is making more pots, and soon Bael's destruction of her earlier batch is just a memory. We conjure a plan to produce jars of poultices and ointments and then trade with them. There are always boats passing and we are short of produce to barter for their fish, let alone the other goods they are often carrying. If a smith visits, it would be good to have something to swap for some repairs to the kitchen ware. There are people in the houses down by the beach who have given us grain since our own supplies ran out, and we need to thank them with something too. They come to us when they need help, but we could offer them more if we had a better supply of herbs. So we are becoming a factory. The broch is a busy hive of activity. I am learning every hour and still each day a new flower opens its bloom.

But every day Danuta fades. It is as if all her essence is being transferred into the flowers. First she asks to return to her chamber and her cough rattles in there like a dry pea in a pod. Then it becomes difficult for her to eat. Some days she finds it impossible to keep food down and starts shaking her head whenever I offer her porridge. She takes a spoonful of soup, then pushes it away. She sups a little at her herbal mead and I add in the herbs that The Wren gave me, but after a while she wants only water.

Then comes the day when she barely wakes when I go to check in on her. Buia and I take turns to sit by her bed, listening to her rasping breath. And one morning, while I am making breakfast, Buia calls out, a wordless wail. I rush into the chamber. Danuta is no longer with us.

I don't know what to do. Buia is sitting beside Danuta and won't let go of her hand. Donnag hovers, then crouches in a corner of Danuta's chamber. The quietness becomes oppressive and I wish Mother was here. Whatever it was that she was hoping to discover from the old woman is gone. All of that wisdom and knowledge. I feel panicky at the thought, and clueless about what needs to happen.

Buia starts singing something strange. I ask her what it is and listen while she sings it again. It's a calling to kind spirits to help Danuta in her passing. The melody is beautiful.

Friends for the westward journey
Guide this traveller on her voyage
Keep the breeze gentle
Keep the breeze gentle
Friends for the westward journey…

She is singing it over and over, interspersed with a chanted jumble of things to do with Danuta that I don't really understand, but in the next chorus I join in and allow my voice to learn the words and tune. Buia nods and smiles at me. After I've sung three choruses I stop and realise Donnag's voice is weaving softly alongside Buia's.

The singing has calmed me. Between choruses I say, 'I could go and get Eilidh.'

Buia nods, so I go, somehow certain that she and Donnag are doing the right thing to keep Danuta's spirit safe.

It is a relief to walk through the woods and along the shore to Achmelvich, and when I get to the beach I see Tormid. I tell him Danuta has died and he sends a boy running for Eilidh and gets me to help him prepare to launch his curragh. Before long there is a boatload of people and in what feels like no time I am walking back into the broch with a crowd.

When Eilidh and half a dozen other voices join with Buia's, she bursts into tears. She sits sobbing by the bedside, but she has kept the vigil and Danuta's spirit must be safe. Eilidh strokes her hair and gently detaches her hand from Danuta's, whispering to her. Buia allows herself to be led to the hearth for some food and then heads off to her hut. After a while she reappears with a basket full of cormorant feathers. She sits by Danuta's bedside arranging them onto threads, weeping quietly as she works the needle. Eilidh helps her to dress Danuta's body with gleaming black plumage.

Tormid has taken Bael to dig a grave, up beside the dragon tooth wall of big upright stones that overlooks the beach.

I make food. I begin with bannocks and carry on. People bring contributions: a goose, a big basket of silverweed roots and lily tubers, mussels, fish and cheese. Ramsons and other herbs are hung from the rafters already. I make dish after dish and women I didn't know before come and help me. Duileag and her mother, who is also called Duileag, sit one each side of me. As we peel and chop and stir and season, the elder Duileag tells me about when she and my Mother were children, and I think Danuta would have been pleased to see this befriending at her hearth. We cry for her, and sing.

Bael paces with a flask of mead until he is unable to stand, then sits, continuing to drink until he collapses and is carried away to his room. Hours later he reappears and sits in Danuta's room, sipping at a cup of ale. There doesn't seem to be anything behind his eyes except anger and if anyone speaks to him, he snarls.

At some point I sleep, and then carry on.

Some of the women from the summer solstice ceremony have reappeared and they feel like sisters. Other people, mostly strangers, keep arriving, and although I am shy of them they are all kind to me. When I am at a loss I look to the hearth and always find something else to do, even if it is just feeding the fire or boiling water.

On the third day we carry Danuta to her grave and lay her in the earth. Eilidh says blessings and there is a storm of wailing, weeping, and more songs.

Then people start to disperse, including Bael, who goes wherever it is he goes. It's a relief.

We try to carry on with life, but without Danuta, nothing can really be the same. Buia begins to spend more time in the broch, and I'm surprised by how much lore she knows, despite her wandering mind. She never seems resentful if I ask her to teach me.

One day I tell her the rhyme I made up for the cough medicine recipe Danuta taught me: 'reed roots and nettle shoots, let them bubble for breathing trouble.' She giggles, then opens her eyes wide. 'That girl. That's it.'

'What?'

'Reed. That was her name. Cuilc.'

'Who?' I have a feeling that name should mean something to me, but I can't place it.

Buia's hair may be a tangle, but her eyes are clear, although they are focused on somewhere far away. 'Her mother.' She looks at me. 'Your mother's mother.'

RIAN

WALRUS

The approach to the island revealed a colony of walrus lying on a beach, just where Manigan hoped they might be. They brought the boat in so Manigan could get ashore, then anchored in shallow water, far enough away not to alarm the animals but close enough to see what was happening. Rian remembered the terrible time she had waited and watched while Manigan performed his ritual killing of the guard walrus in the Seal Isles, only for Jan Bonxie and his fellow fishermen to ruin everything with their slaughter of the other animals.

This time there was no one to interrupt Manigan in his ceremony, as he transfixed the huge tusked 'old gentleman'. Rian so wished she could hear him talking and know what he said and sang and whispered. He had told her and Shadow something of the ritual, with great reluctance, and she could still remember some of what he would be chanting.

'The story goes: This is a story about a walrus
'The story goes: Once upon a time there was a walrus.
'The story goes: The greatest walrus there ever was...'

They were so far away, however, that it was hard to make out where he was relative to the huge animals, let alone whether his lips were moving. Badger kept a close eye on him, and Kino readied himself with tools for dealing with the carcass after Manigan's hunt was concluded. Rian sat at the bow, watching Manigan.

It didn't seem to take many minutes before all but one of the great animals were stampeding into the sea and Manigan was waving to them to approach. Fin lifted the anchor then they rowed ashore. Some of the walrus approached, their curious whiskery faces bobbing up just yards from the boat, on heads the size of barrels.

'Now then, just leave us alone,' Badger said to them. 'We're not wishing you any harm. It's just the old gentleman that Manigan wanted a word with.'

Rian knew that one flick of those muscly back flippers could tip them up, and she didn't breathe easily until they felt sand under the keel.

For hours they were all kept busy dealing with the ritual butchering of the enormous animal. Unlike the first time Rian had witnessed the act, when it had all been done in a rush amid the debacle of Jan Bonxie's slaughter, this time it was quiet and dignified. Manigan had her light a fire just above the high water mark. There were mounds of driftwood, and they built up a blaze as the evening went on, to keep away any curious polar bears and to generate smoke to deter flies. Badger produced a drum from the boat and accompanied Manigan and Kino in a long, chanting invocation of the sea spirits. A few dozen strides down the beach, Manigan set various parts of the walrus on a rock and did not allow the others to watch as he bent over them, muttering again.

They ate some of the flesh of the animal and drank ale and were in high spirits. It never got dark, the sun merely sinking towards the northern horizon. When its journey took it beyond the landmass of the island, they fell into shadow and wrapped themselves up against the chill.

Eventually they were all seated beside the fire. Manigan had the hide slung across his lap and with a sharp blade was cleaning off the blubber. 'Now's the time for that story about the stone. Go and get it, Fin. Let it be here to help the telling. That's one of its names, you know, the Stone of Telling. Aye, stories, secrets, the future, you name it.'

'Even lies?' Fin called as he jogged away from them.

Manigan chuckled. 'No, I don't think so.'

They waited in silence. Rian fed the fire until it blazed brightly again. When Fin returned, he unpacked the stone and set it on its bag on the sand. Its faces sparkled in the firelight. Manigan fetched a piece of walrus meat from where they had packaged it up. He squeezed it over the head until some blood dripped into the dimple on top of the stone head, then gave the meat to Badger, who added it to the pile he was chopping up and skewering. Every so often he swatted at flies or tossed a pebble at a gull whose curiosity brought it too close.

'Where shall I begin?' Manigan said.

Not for the first time, Rian realised that so much of her life had been governed by the Stone of Telling. The man she loved most in the world, and the woman she loathed, had both been in thrall to it, and yet there were still huge gaps in what she knew about it. 'You promised you'd tell us how you got it,' she prompted.

'All right. It was my Aunty Fraoch gave it to me, because she said a hunter needed to look after it. Only a hunter would be able to keep it quiet, to appease it. You know one of its names is the Death Stone. It has a lust for death, an appetite, shall we say. It relaxes when a hunt is successful, after blood is spilled, and it gets grumpy and dangerous if there has been no quarry for a while. Aunty Fraoch said she had urges she could hardly bear to live with when she had the stone, and she'd find herself trapping mice, setting snares for birds, dreaming of ways to kill people. It scared her.'

As he spoke his voice lowered so they all stilled to hear him better. Only the fire whispered.

'She had a favourite cat and when it had kittens, she strangled one of them.'

Rian gasped. Manigan nodded. 'Yes, she told me the next time I saw her that I had to take the stone away from her. She couldn't control herself. She was weeping about that kitten, she said it was a lovely, fluffy little thing and she would never dream of harming it and yet there it was, limp in her hands, its body heat cooling. She didn't know what had come over her and she feared that she would meet the same fate as her mother, my grandmother, who had the stone before her.

'Anyway, I agreed to take it and it drove me on with the hunting. For a while I thought it brought good luck, that its bloodlust gave me a better chance of making a kill, but after a few years with it I decided it simply drove me on, kept me at it. And woe betide the crew if the hunting was poor. Though any old seabird seemed to satisfy it. Fish less so. The bloodier the better.

'And so now I see it in your eyes, Fin, the bloodlust. Watch what you do with it. It has a bad record. I found the only way to deal with it was to make each killing, each hunt, a ritual. I've always been strict about keeping the sea spirits happy, paying due respect, and that seemed to balance out the influence of the stone.' He fell silent, staring into the fire.

'Your grandmother,' Rian prompted.

'My grandmother, aye, that's the next bit of the story. She got it from her father, the Merlin, who got it from his father before him. It's been in our bloodline since the iron forges began, but that comes later in the story.

'My grandmother had it for years and it turned her mad. She had been a gentle woman, my Aunty Fraoch said, one of the Spirit Keepers on Ictis. She used to do magic of course, mostly healing spells, the occasional love charm, rites to ensure good harvests, nothing wicked. It was only after it was too late that anyone realised she had started killing things for bad magic, black spells to meddle with the weather and the tides. She wanted to make the moon eclipse at her will. Why anyone would even want to do that I can't imagine.

'Anyway, she did some terrible things. I don't want to tell you what I know of them. You will have to use your imagination.'

'Oh, go on, tell,' said Fin. He got up to clear fat away from where Manigan was working and packed it into a bowl. Then he sat back down, tucking his knees up under his gansy.

'You ghouls! I shall not tell.'

'You're a tease, so you are,' said Badger.

'No. Not with the boy here, not with the stone around. It would be serving its evil purposes and it has been my mission, all life-long, to keep it in control, to limit its potential for misdoing by feeding it with only what it needs. Are you listening, boy? If you don't take care, my grandmother's fate awaits you, or Ussa's. You've seen her evil eye.'

Fin nodded. 'She told me the stone was hers by right.'

'Aye, she believed the stone was hers to inherit from our grandmother. But Aunty Fraoch was determined only a hunter should have it. And Ussa was one of the stone's victims, she was corrupted by it.'

'What do you mean, corrupted?' Rian asked.

'I see I am going to have to tell you something about my grandmother after all. She was mad by the end, and wicked. She did things that should never be allowed to happen, things with children, things with animals, and more often than not the deeds were preambles to death. She got to like watching death by other hands than hers, to observe one innocent taking the life of another. At first it was a cat and a mouse, a dog and a rat, but then that wasn't enough and she needed to co-opt people. Children, mostly, who she could intimidate into keeping secrets.

'Ussa was one of them, aye. Ussa did a lot of killing for her. She was greedy anyway, her father taught her everything she could possibly learn about greed, and after she went to live with Grandmother Amoa, she got a taste for slaughter. Everything, anything: rabbits, cats, dogs, birds, snakes. And worse. Yes. Another child, in the end. That's what turned my grandmother mad enough to take her own life. The stone must have turned on her. I don't know.'

'Were you involved in that?' Rian said. This was all making her feel sick.

'Yes, I was.'

'What happened?'

'I don't want to talk about it. Really, it was horrible.'

'You can tell us.' She partly didn't want to know, but now they had come this far, she would rather find out the dark secret than not.

Manigan shook his head. 'No.'

'Did you do something bad?'

He said nothing, just gazing into the fire.

'You can tell us.' She put her hand on this.

'I can't.'

'But isn't it part of the story?' She could feel how much he was hurting at the memory.

He turned to her, his eyes bleak. 'I killed my dog. He was my friend.'

'Oh that's so sad.' Rian stroked his head like a child.

Manigan's voice was broken. 'Yes. She made me do it. This was how I learned about death and why I ran away to sea. My grandfather had to heal me of the hurt it had caused me. It was my most difficult and important lesson. Maybe I never really healed. Can you heal from evil? I do not know. I do not want to talk about it anymore, my love. Don't make me cry. I just want to tell my story so you'll understand what I've been carrying all these years and so he can be prepared. Don't make me say anymore.'

'You don't have to say anymore. It wasn't your fault.'

'Thank you.'

Kino handed Manigan his flask. He took a drink and sniffed.

'My poor love.' Rian stroked him again.

'I'll be all right. It's difficult, that's all. We're all bound up in it. It's so tightly meshed. It's a mess. That stone. I can't seem to get it out of my life.'

'You can stop telling us, if you like.'

'No, I'll carry on. This place is big enough for me to lose myself in.' He took another slug from the flask and passed it to Rian who passed it straight to Fin, who likewise passed it on to Badger, who was staring, grim-faced, into the fire. He took a sip and kept hold of the bottle.

Manigan sniffed and breathed out deeply. 'So, where had I got to? Amoa, yes. She got the stone from the Merlin when he had a dream. Are you ready for this?'

Rian reached for another chunk of driftwood and tilted it onto the fire. 'If you are.'

'The Merlin's dream was of a king. You're not ready.'

Rian was poking sticks into the heart of the blaze. She turned her full attention back to him.

Fin said, 'Who's the Merlin?'

'The highest druid.'

'It's Riabach now, isn't it?' Rian said.

'Aye. But back then it was Amoa's father.'

'How did he get the stone?' Fin asked.

Manigan twined the fingers of his hands together. 'I just think the Merlin had always had it, since it was made.'

'You mean it was passed down the line of leaders?'

'From one to the next, aye.'

'So when was it made?' Fin's monkey was lying on his feet, and he stroked it as he listened, without taking his eyes off Manigan's face.

'Ach, I can tell you all about where it came from and how it was made, but that's a different story again. I thought you wanted to know how I came by it.'

'Yes. We do,' Rian said.

Fin nodded.

'All right then, so you'll let me finish the Merlin's dream?'

They all nodded, then Fin said, 'Can we hear how it was made later?'

'Yes, of course.'

'You'll forget,' Rian said.

Manigan rummaged in a pocket and produced a bit of twine. 'There, look. I've tied a knot in this bit of string, that'll remind me.'

'How's that going to help?'

'Tie it around my finger, that's the making story. I won't forget.'

Rian tied the string around his right middle finger.

'Very good. So, the dream first.' Manigan's voice changed to his storytelling sing-song. 'The Merlin dreamed of a king. He had killed a rival; a great warrior called the Raven who had been challenging for years for lands in the east of the kingdom. The dream began with the king returning to his broch with the Raven's head on a spike. He stuck it up in a prominent place so everyone could see he had conquered.

'Well, the head of the Raven watched him for three moons, while birds plucked the skull clean. Then one night it lifted itself from the stake and went to the bedroom where the king was sleeping. He woke to find the skull hovering over his face, taking his breath. Each time he breathed out, the skull sucked it in. The king tried to bat the skull away, but it always hung just beyond reach, gobbling up the air he breathed out. As you know, our knowledge, our creativity, our very soul is in our breath and the skull was gradually emptying him of it all. His last gasp of breath was a scream, and the king was dead.

'Then the skull went to the King's son's bedroom and found him wakening. Just as he yawned, the Raven's skull poured the last breath of the dead king into him, so he woke to all his father's knowledge, including how he had died. The skull grimacing over the King's son sent him raving mad.

'Then the skull went to the nursery where the king's baby grandson picked it up and played with it. Then the wee boy rubbed his eyes, itched his ears, stuck his pudgy little finger up his nose and licked it, as a child would. The young prince was found next morning, blind, deaf and dumb, unable even to feel his nurse's touch or smell her milk.

'The old Queen woke up to find her husband dead, her son insane, her grandson trapped alive inside his senseless body. And then she found the cause, the skull, and lifting it out of the baby's crib she said, "only a woman can avenge this wrong."

'Well then the Merlin woke from his dream, and he was shaken. He meditated long and hard about what it might mean, and he concluded that this was a message from the Death Stone. He already knew the stone was dangerous and he thought the final image of the queen holding the skull meant that only a woman could keep it safe. So that was why he gave it to my grandmother Amoa, his daughter. However, as I've explained, as it turned out neither she nor my Aunty Fraoch could cope with the death lust that came with it. Maybe there's some other way of understanding the dream that we haven't figured out yet, or maybe it is just another of life's many mysteries.'

In the quietness that followed, the fire cracked and sputtered.

'Worth waiting for,' said Rian as Manigan turned to her.

He patted her thigh. 'It's not bad, is it?'

She blinked hard, thinking about it. 'No, it's horrible.'

Fin got to his feet and stretched each leg in turn. 'Good story.'

'Had you not heard that one, Fin? No, I suppose not. Is there a hot drink going anywhere for the skipper of the old tub, do you think? You know I used to be able to last all night and day with only cold water. I must be getting old. The circulation's not what it was.'

Badger stopped slicing meat and poured some ale into a beaker from a bronze flask he had sitting on a stone beside the fire, and stirred in some honey.

Manigan reached across Rian to take it, and she tapped the finger with the string on it.

'What was that for again? Oh aye. The making of the stone. Red the Smith.'

'I've heard that one,' she said.

'Have you? The way she chipped the three faces out: the Master, then the Boy and then the Sage?'

'Yes, you told me years back.'

'Did you hear about the prophecies, though?'

'I don't think so.'

He set his beaker down. 'Ah well, then, you need to hear the three prophecies.'

THE PROPHECIES

Manigan looked around to see if he had everyone's attention. Fin was gazing back at him, and Kino had his head tilted to one side. He was not drinking, Rian noticed. Was the ceremonial killing somehow sufficient for him? Badger was busy with the meat, but looking around, as if watching for something. Rian saw Manigan note this, and a little smile flitted into his face. Then he turned to her and his smile broadened.

'Go on,' she said.

He closed his eyes briefly, then opened them and spoke, as if only to her. 'The first prophecy comes from the Sage. Because he had been waiting so long inside the stone, he was impatient to make it as soon as possible after Red had chipped him a mouth to speak with.'

'What's red?' Fin asked.

'That's the name of the smith who was one of the Bear clan; I don't know her real name, so I call her Red. Yes, she was a smith like your father. She'd discovered how to make iron. This was way back, and the king of the Bear clan, King Ban, asked the Merlin what was to be done with it. The Merlin gave Red this round stone, the size of a head and told her to take it to her forge and listen to it until it spoke to her and whatever it said would be the right thing.'

'She wasn't much of a sculptor, young Red. She mostly made blades. The odd bit of jewellery, delicate things, you know. And here was this muckle stone. What was she supposed to do with it? I've told this story so many times before. Rian, you tell it.'

She chuckled. 'No.'

'Aye, go on. The one about Red carving the three faces on the stone.'

So, Rian began to tell the tale of Red the Smith, who had discovered iron, and was following the Merlin's instruction to carve the stone to find out what to do with the new metal. Rian spoke of how Red found herself carving the three faces, the first of which was the Master. It was easier than she expected to tell this story. She was surprised at how well she remembered it.

Manigan pointed the Master's face out to Fin. 'There, see this face. You tell it well, my love. Aye, the Master.'

'He looks like you,' said Fin.

'I've heard him described as many things: fierce, evil-looking, knowing, but never that, you cheeky little runt. Carry on, Rian.'

She described how the second face to appear was the Boy.

Fin pointed to the Sage and Manigan turned the stone. 'No, it's this one.'

'Not dissimilar to Fin,' said Kino.

'Aye. True enough, same little pudgy nose and piggy eyes.'

Fin kicked him.

'Ow! Listen.'

Rian told how the third face to emerge was the Sage, mouth first, which moaned and howled with every cut until the rest of its face was carved. 'And that's as much of the story as I know', she said.

Manigan turned the stone again. 'Here he is, the Sage.'

'You mentioned prophecies,' said Rian.

Fin reached for the stone. 'Shall I pack it back up?'

'No, leave it here, if you will. The prophecies deserve to be told in the stone's presence. Each face holds one of them.'

Fin sat down.

Manigan looked around. 'This was the first prophecy given to Red by the Sage. As soon as Red had cut the three faces into the stone, she said to it, "I was told to make you so I would understand what to do with this new metal. It is hard and strong and easy to shape, and I call it iron."

Manigan stroked the cheek of the old face carved on the stone. 'But the Sage said, "Bury it back in the ground where you found, it, for it will bring only trouble."

'"I made it in the fire," said Red.

'"But the ore came from the earth. Bury it there and the knowledge with it."

'"Why?" asked Red. "It will take such a brilliant sharp edge and the King has asked me to make him a sword from it. I could make all kinds of tools with it. It could be useful."

'"No. The wielding of weapons made from it will bring more knowledge than a head can contain, more love than a heart can hold, more sadness than a body can bear. Tell that to your King."

'You can imagine Red wasn't very impressed by this advice, but she was more than a bit scared of the stone full of faces, so she did as the Sage ordered and took the stone to the King to tell him what it had said.

'Now, on the journey back to King Ban's broch the stone made two other prophecies. Do you want to hear them now, or shall I go on with the story of the first one?'

Rian chuckled. 'Finish this, then go on with the others. You need that bit of string again.'

He stuck his finger out so she could retie it.

Then he went on. 'So, Red the Smith urged the King to bury the iron and forget all about it. But King Ban had seen the cutting edge of an iron axe head and he'd not hear of any such thing.

133

'He put the stone above his fireplace with the Boy's face outwards and the Master and the Sage facing the wooden beams at the side, and he ordered Red to make him a fine iron sword with the sharpest blade edge she could, or else he'd take a hammer to her kneecaps and she'd never walk again. And so Red went back off home and worked at the new metal until she had perfected the sword. King Ban was most pleased. It was the sharpest sword he had ever had.

'Now, the King had a son called Geevor and he was a spoilt boy. He was their only son and both Ban and the Queen gave him anything he asked for. Ban, as you can tell, had a greedy streak in him, and Geevor acquired it and grew up even greedier still.

'One day, when Geevor was a young man, Ban caught him doing a secret deal with a traveling trader, selling a string of pearls that he had stolen from his mother. The pearls had been a special gift from the King.

'Well, Ban completely lost his temper and in his fury, he cut off his son's head with the new iron sword.

'So then he knew the self knowledge a mind cannot contain, the love for his dead son he couldn't hold in his heart, and more grief than his body could stand. The prophecy of the Stone had come true.

'Ever since then, in the land of the Bear tribe, no weapons are made of iron, and it is only used for practical and peaceful functions like farming and cooking. And Red the Smith gave the Stone to the druids for safekeeping, to guard it from generation to generation and to listen to its whisperings.'

They all sat back and gazed into the fire, thinking.

'That's a powerful tale,' said Rian.

'You liked it?'

'Oh yes, even more than the first one.'

'That was a good telling,' Badger said.

'Thank you. I just told it how I learned it, how my grandfather told it to me.'

'Do you ever tell stories to the old gentlemen?' Fin asked.

'Yes, I told one of them once. There was one who was reluctant to die, way up north, a long time ago. He was a long-toothed old gentleman, he taught me why I am the Mutterer. I had to mutter away to him for hours before I could cut him away from his life. I think he took all my stories to a good place. He was a lovely old creature, smelly and farty and warty, and he lay there on the beach flapping his flippers and twitching his whiskers at everything I said. I'll bet your old man Gruach never had a more appreciative audience at his forge, and I can tell you he drew more than his fair share of eager crowds. Isn't that right?'

Fin grinned broadly.

'Of course, you saw him in action, plenty, I am sure. And you saw him at his tricks as well, didn't you Rian?'

She nodded.

'My wonderful woman has seen everything that matters in this world, I'll have you know. She's a marvel.'

'Ach shut up!'

'I will not shut up. Not a bit of it. I'm going to tell you the story that made me handfast with you all those years ago and has kept me fascinated with you ever since. If I've never told you, and I might not have done, it was because I've never wanted to call a jinx on what we have.'

'What's that then?'

'What we have is love, my love. That's a rare and precious thing to keep for so many years. So, which is it to be, my love, another prophecy or the story that made you mine?'

'Another prophecy. Don't get sidetracked.'

'All right, I'll leave the string on for the other one. Red the Smith was on her way to Ban to deliver the first of the prophecies. She had come down from her home in the high woods to the shore, where she hoped to find someone in a boat sailing south to Ban's broch, to save her the long walk across the land, which she believed to be infested with dragons and serpents and marshes and what have you. She was a sensible woman, she wanted to go by boat. Let the wind do the work. Why walk when you can sail? Aye, she wasn't stupid.

'While she was waiting at the shore, she found a cave to live in. She walked south and north, letting people know that if a boat should be passing, heading south, she would like to go with them. She spent a lot of time in this cave burning driftwood to keep warm. One night Red sat feeding sticks into the fire, watching the rain spattering down at the entrance of the cave, when there was a dreadful coughing from the bag with the stone. She got it out and saw that it was the Master making the noise.' He turned the stone so the Master faced the fire.

'"Now that I've got your attention," the Master said, "I've something to say. Our core power is to kill. See the dimple in the top of our head. It's for blood. You will find as long as you keep us, that you must hunt for us. If you do not kill at all, we will be hungry, and you will suffer terrible pangs. If you can stay within necessity, kill moderately, for good, in rhythm with the seasons and with honour and due ceremony, we will be docile. If you step beyond and take more than you need, then we will corrode your soul. So beware. You must find the balance. To say 'enough' is everything. This is my prophecy."

'Needless to say, poor Red was very frightened by this, but right afterwards, there came a little voice saying, "Let me speak, please." It was the Boy. So Red turns the stone around, and gives the Boy her attention, and he makes the third of the prophecies.' Manigan reached to swivel the stone.

Badger was suddenly on his feet. 'Bear!'

Sure enough, a polar bear was heading their way. There was a mad scramble of building up the fire, lugging the meat, skin, tusks, and other body parts to the boat, and in the melee, the story hung, unfinished. Rian would have watched the bear, fascinated – after all this was the source of Ussa's coat, and she was amazed by its size, its great loping stride, its impossibly hairy feet. She wanted to linger, but the others pushed and chivvied her into the boat.

The bear found Manigan's offerings on the rock, and in the delay this provided them, they set off again, southward, close-hauled into a stiff breeze. The sea state was lumpy and both Rian and Fin were soon seasick. The story remained unfinished and forgotten.

NORTH

The trip was nearing its end. They were in the Seal Isles and the weather was calm, with no wind worth attempting to sail in. Manigan had taken on board a girl called Brue with dark hair and dark eyes who knew all of the tidal streams, and by means of these alone, and a bit of rowing, they were making a passage from the east to the west side of the archipelago.

Bradan was drifting sedately along, the current more help than the breeze, a green land gliding past on each side of the channel and everything quiet on board. Rian was sitting next to Manigan at the helm. He had his free arm around her shoulders. She was gazing around with an expression of rapt contentment on her face. This is what she had dreamed about for years: to be sailing these islands as a free woman with Manigan.

Badger and Kino were snoozing, backs to the mast. Fin was supposed to be whipping sinew around the end of the main halyard, but he'd been struggling to get it tight and eventually Manigan's jibes had subsided. It lay half-finished on his lap while he looked around.

The channel narrowed and the tidal stream was remarkably strong.

'Keep to the left of this skerry,' Brue said.

'It's awful narrow,' Manigan said.

'Yes, the other side looks better, but don't be fooled. Believe me this is the only safe way through.'

On the island to the north, an impressive broch came into view on a rocky outcrop. 'Mid Howe,' Brue said, after noticing that they were all looking at it.

'How far north did your father build the brochs?' Fin asked Rian.

She jerked her head away from the view to look at him. 'My father?' Her voice was sharp. His link to Ussa still made it hard for her to trust him. 'How do you know about him?'

'He built brochs, didn't he?'

'Did you tell him?' She elbowed Manigan.

He shook his head. 'What do you mean?'

Fin picked up the rope from his lap and said, uncertainly, 'Did I say something I shouldn't have?'

Brue, as if sensing that the peaceful mood had broken, or perhaps just to monitor the tide, moved to the bow.

Rian shook Manigan's arm off her shoulder and crossed her ankles, glaring at Fin. 'I asked you a simple question. Who told you?'

'Buia. Is that her name? The grey-haired woman who lives in the hut beside your broch.'

Rian leaned forward. 'Buia told you?'

'Yes.'

'Why?'

'I don't know.'

'What else did she tell you?' Her eyes drilled into him.

'Um. That your grandmother was a great healer. The best. She said she thinks Soyea will be too.'

'What else?'

'That you took after your grandmother. Your hair, your eyes. That you never looked anything like your mother.' He paused.

Rian's mouth was open.

'And she said...' He looked at Manigan who was staring at him as well. He let his eyes fall to the rope. 'She said she was glad your mother didn't drown you. Which I thought was pretty weird.'

'What else?'

'I don't remember.'

'She knew my mother?'

'I guess so. Did you not know?' He met her eyes.

She gave a little shake of her head. 'No.'

There was an awkward silence. Then Rian said, 'Why did she tell you that?'

'I don't know. I asked about Soyea. Whether she reminded her of you when you lived there.'

Rian took Manigan's hand. 'I have to go back to Assynt. I never thought to ask Buia. I didn't know she knew.' She gazed into his face with dazed incredulity.

'We'd better go then.' He lifted their joined hands, and kissed her fingers. 'All we need is a little bit of wind. Brue!' The woman at the bow turned her head. 'We're going to need to head southwest. Any chance you can whistle up a breeze?'

KILN

It was a long, slow sail in agonisingly light winds. But eventually the Assynt mountains were lined up again, Rubha Stoer behind them and the split rock ahead.

There was smoke belching from behind the broch as *Bradan* approached. No one came to welcome them except a small boy who ran for a rope that Manigan threw him and then danced away to where a group of people were gathered beside the blaze.

Rian left the men to make the boat secure and marched up to the broch. A kiln was lit and people had gathered from the village to watch the fire being fed. Bottles were circulating and there was almost a festive air about the place. But Rian could sense there was something missing, something wrong.

Soyea saw her coming and ran towards her, arms wide. 'Mother!'

It was enough to make her want to cry, but she needed to be

focused. She had been trying to be patient ever since Fin had spoken about Buia.

Soyea was tugging her arm. 'You're back! Come and see Donnag's kiln.'

Rian held her daughter close. 'It's lovely to see you. You smell like a bouquet of flowers.'

Soyea laughed. 'Everything has happened since you left. I've been initiated!'

'You clever thing! How wonderful.' Rian looked her new, confident daughter up and down with a smile. Then she took in the crowd. Donnag was at the centre of the activity, stoking her fire from a big stack of birchwood. Rian barely recognised her, she was so transformed from the dour wretch of spring. And there was Buia, sitting close to the blaze, mouth slack, watching the flames with a bovine, glaikit expression. 'Where's Danuta?'

Soyea slumped. 'Oh Mother, we wished you were here. She went peacefully. This is a kind of farewell for her.'

'She's dead?'

Soyea nodded. 'A week and a day ago. On the new moon.'

Tears welled up in Rian's eyes. It was unbearable. The mother she had only just regained, taken away so soon. What had she been thinking, to go off with Manigan like that when Danuta needed her, sailing away from Buia without even asking what she knew? She had missed everything. Her daughter was transformed by her summer. She had never seen her so glowing. 'You're initiated, you said? Into the Sisterhood?'

A smile lit up on Soyea's face. 'Yes, The Wren was here. It was wonderful.'

Rian tried to put a brave smile on. 'That's…well I'm proud of you. So much to tell me about. Have we missed Danuta's funeral?'

'We buried her three days back. Up by the dragon tooth wall. Eilidh led the ceremony. Buia helped. We all helped. Buia's very sad.'

'I'd better see her.'

The loss of Danuta billowed up in her. Crying, she let Soyea guide her in towards the kiln. There were nods and greetings and condolences from people as she passed, but she hardly registered them. She sat down next to Buia, who turned a red-eyed gaze on her and leaned her head sideways until it rested on Rian's shoulder, looking into the fire.

'Mother Danu's gone west.'

Rian blew her nose, mopped up her tears. 'I'm glad I saw her before she died.'

Donnag was standing before her. 'I'm sorry for your loss, Rian,' she said, with a gravity that Rian found strangely soothing.

'Thank you.' She held Donnag's gaze for a moment.

'I must tend the fire,' the thin woman said. 'It is in Danuta's honour.'

'Thank you.' She was crying again.

Donnag returned to the blaze.

Rian turned and saw Manigan and Fin standing talking with Soyea, who was gesturing at the crowd and the kiln. There was so much more assurance about this young woman than the Soyea she was familiar with. Her little girl was grown. She felt something inside herself falling open.

Then Manigan was coming towards her and she let herself sink into his presence as he shuffled her along the bench, squeezing her up to Buia, holding her together while she did what she needed to do. Out of the corner of her eye she could see her daughter and Fin leaning into each other, talking, his hand on her forearm, and then standing, shoulder to shoulder, both tall, both strangers, yet somehow together, watching everything.

Rian took a deep breath. 'Buia. Do you know who my mother is?'

She wasn't sure if Buia had heard her. She gave no reaction, and just continued to stare into the blaze, her eyes not shifting even when Donnag said 'excuse me' and passed between them and the kiln with another bundle of wood to feed the hungry fire. The wall of heat pushed them back on their seats and Rian wondered if they could move the bench away.

With a jerk, Buia clenched her hand into Rian's thigh and turned to her. 'She is a wicked girl. I don't like her. Is she still alive?'

Rian looked into her eyes. They were gleaming with tears and fire. 'I don't know, Buia. I don't know who she is. I never knew.'

'She's a wicked girl, Cuilc. Thin and spoilt. I don't like her.' She had the voice of a child.

'Did you say Cuilc? Is that her name?' Rian didn't so much as blink.

'Cuilc. I don't like her. She said I should feel sorry for her because she has to marry ugly Luachair instead of lovely Farspag, but that's no reason to drown a baby, is it?' She looked past Rian to Manigan, appealing to him. 'Who are you?'

'Manigan.' He spoke gently, but he too had stiffened at the name.

'You're the Mutterer.'

'Yes.'

She gazed intently into his face. 'I like you.'

Between them, Rian had started to tremble.

'Are you sure about this?' Manigan said. 'That her mother is Cuilc? Rian didn't drown.'

'Mother Danu saved her. Pulled her from the sea. She's our little foster girl, Rian. I'm good, but her mother is wicked. It was a secret. I didn't tell anyone as long as Mother Danu was here, but now she's gone.'

'You told Fin,' Rian said.

She frowned. 'I never. I told him I knew her. I told him she tried to drown you. But I didn't tell him who she was. I never told anyone until I told Soyea. And now you. Danuta has gone west and I can't hold it in anymore.'

Rian felt Manigan's grip harden around her shoulders. She looked up into his face and saw reflected there a horror equal to her own. 'This means Eadha is my brother, so Rona...'

'Half-brother, anyway,' said Manigan. 'But it's still…'

Rian finished the sentence he seemed unable to. '…sacrilege. Didn't I say there was something not right about that marriage?' She lifted her hand from Manigan's thigh. 'We have to leave tomorrow.'

Buia twisted on the bench and waved at Soyea, who waved back. 'Mother Danu's gone. Soyea can look after us now.'

SOYEA

STONE

Later, much later, when the kiln has been fired and everyone else has gone to bed, and the sky is starting to lighten again, I find myself sitting with Fin against the wall of the broch facing the sea. We seem to gravitate together. I don't feel tired and he is full of stories. His monkey is sitting on one of his feet, grooming itself.

We have been talking about Cuilc, Rona and Eadha, the realisation that my sister is married to my uncle, and what we think about it. Mother is hysterical, Manigan is furious, and I don't know enough to be sure how to respond but it sounds serious. I'm trying to remember if beautiful Eadha looks anything like mother and I've just hit upon the possible complication that, as Manigan is also from the Winged Isle, maybe he and Mother are related as well.

Suddenly Fin says, 'Can I give you something to look after? To keep safe. Somewhere not obvious.'

'What is it?'

He pushes the monkey aside and pulls a tough hemp bag out from among some boulders below the broch. It looks heavy. He opens it enough for me to see it contains Manigan's stone head, the one Ussa stole, the one Mother calls The Death Stone.

I shudder. It's years since I've seen it.

'I don't want it.' It is out of my mouth before I think.

'I know.' He closes the bag and sits back down. 'I don't know what to do with it.'

'How on earth did you get hold of it?'

'I bought it. It seemed like a suitably crazy thing to do at the time.'

'Who from?'

'Ussa's father.'

I'm flabbergasted.

'I don't want to have to keep lugging it around. I thought about chucking it in the sea, but I'm not sure that's a good idea.'

I don't know what to say.

He's looking down at his monkey, scratching it between the ears. 'To be honest, I'd heard that having the head was what made Manigan a great hunter. So I wanted it.'

'So you want to be a hunter too?'

'I don't know. I want to sail. He's a bit of a hero.'

I snort. Someone else in thrall to Manigan. That's all I need.

'So you should carry the stone.'

He shakes his head. 'It gives me dreams.'

'Bad dreams?'

He nods slowly.

I shiver. I don't like this. I don't want the stone. And I'm thinking of how scared he must be of it.

'You think I'm a coward, don't you?' He doesn't wait for me to answer. 'I know it's dangerous. It's called the Death Stone. You can ask it questions and it will answer, so they also call it the Stone of Telling, but each answer costs a life. It's a ghastly thing. I just have a hunch you might be able to look after it. There's a prophecy...'

'What prophecy?'

'There's stuff I've been told by Manigan that I can't repeat. I lose track of what's secret and what's not. But there's something about the way you avoided that bear. You just seemed to sidestep the danger. Faced it, without being scared, and did the right thing.'

I look at him and he meets my gaze. He has pleading in his eyes.

Buia is here. I never heard her approaching.

She points to the bag. 'That's the Death Stone.'

He nods at her.

'It smells.' She wrinkles up her nose. 'Hide it. That place is no good.' She is pointing to where it was. 'This is better.' She shuffles over to the corner of the pig pen and sticks her hand under the wall. 'Here.' She beckons to me.

'I don't want it.'

'Better hide it,' Buia says. 'This is a good hiding place.'

I stand up. As I pass him, he has a look on his face of pure desperation that I can't bear. He hands me the bag. I take it and stuff it in the hole.

Buia rubs one finger across her lips and closes her eyes, then opens them again and makes a funny pursed expression with her mouth. She twirls her fingers in a gesture of goodbye and wanders away.

The next day, before the kiln has cooled, *Bradan* sails off with them all in their furies and tempers and everything here goes quiet again. There is nobody here but Buia and I to admire the beautiful pots Donnag has made to honour Danuta. We drink a little mead in her memory.

RONA

RUINS

My life is in ruins. It is a cataclysm. It is all Mother's doing.

Cuilc is not here and now I wish we had not let her go. She wouldn't allow this to happen. She'll deny the claim Mother is making, I'm sure of it. It cannot be true.

She says she has come to save me, but in fact she's murdering me. I shall die without him.

I do not believe what she tells me. It is impossible.

I refuse to believe it.

She and Eadha are so unlike they cannot be related at all, let alone sister and brother. He is dark and strong and warm and beautiful, while she is pale and thin and cold. He is like a beautiful stag and she is like a stone.

She has convinced Father as well. She says we have committed sacrilege, that to sleep with my mother's brother is as bad as sleeping with my own brother, which must be punished by death or banishment.

We were in bed when they arrived. I must relish the memory of it. We were perfectly at peace, alone in the building together for the first time in months, taking advantage of an unheard-of indulgence, privacy in the daytime, before our evening dance practice. We had made love and were lying together, murmuring, purring like kittens, when we heard shouting and Mother screeching. Today she was like a hawk on a leash, her voice, shrill and jagged, full of outrage and disgust. And father was like a thundercloud. He pulled me away from Eadha and hugged me, but it was a wrestler's hold. He said they have come to rescue me, but I don't want to be rescued from Eadha. He made it sound like we are doomed. He made it sound like a heavy door slamming shut.

And then I was locked away in here, in the dark and I don't know what they have done to Eadha. Oh my heart, what will they do to him?

They say it doesn't matter that we didn't know. It makes no difference, they say, the spirits know everything. They say our sex is an abomination. They call our desire for each other unnatural, a perversion. How can this be? How can something so beautiful be anything other than the wish of the gods?

I don't believe it.

I cannot believe it.

It is damp in here and cold. It smells disgusting. If I go to sleep the rats will chew my face.

I am alone here.

The darkness terrifies me.

I am losing my mind.

When he touches me, it is like the sun. I become honey. He, the bee, stings me and it is heaven.

I do not care if he is blood kin. He was never family to us before. He was a stranger when we met. We were both adults. There was nothing wrong in what we did. We fell in love as two people meeting randomly and finding ourselves drawn together. It is completely pure. There's no corruption, no perversion. It is not like that. It has never been like that. It is pure.

But what if the force of our love is due to kinship? I have felt it as unique, as a fire that burns more brightly than any that has burned before. Can that be because he is my uncle? Is it a fire of damnation?

I do not care. Let me be damned. I need him.

I must escape.

I hunt around in the dark. It's the grain cellar and there is no way out except through the door, but at some point they must feed me. I shall find a way to make them set me free. I find a sack to nestle in on and think. I curl myself up into a ball and cry until my desperation gives way to fury. I don't believe it. Mother is imagining it. She is mad.

I must get out of here or I too will go mad. I must not sleep. Rats will chew. Listen to them scuttling.

I pace about in the dark. I can take four steps in each direction. Almost every step I feel a slug under my foot. The walls are slimy and foul and there are cobwebs everywhere. They stick to me. There are probably spiders in my hair, weaving their webs, trying to choke me.

I listen. Scratching. Rats again. I can't bear it, but I have to.

I am thirsty. I will not die in this hole.

Eadha. Where are you? Why was it wrong? It was so beautiful.

Surely the spirits cannot limit us with these petty rules. Mother's half-brother, a stranger, my lover, my god, my soul. I pray. The bull, the stag, the drake, the pack leader, they all take whichever female they desire. Why not Eadha the Chieftain, the most beautiful?

My skin remembers you, my lover.

My fingers remember you.

My lips remember you.

ESCAPE

Father brings me food in the end. I am ready and seize my chance. I have to be clever and get it right first time. I weep audibly to make him pause, listen to me, come in a bit closer to hear. He takes a step in and I can see the light beyond him. As he bends to put the food down, I make my voice soft and full of sorrow. 'Papa, is that you? I'm thirsty.' He's my father. He loves me. I've always been his favourite.

He is peering into the darkness and I rush past him, pushing him against the door. It works. As I pass him I smell bread. I am nearly faint with hunger but only one thing matters, and that is to get out. I run up the steps, through the next door, on and out. And luck is with me. No one stops me. As I charge through the main room to the outside door they reach out but I am too fast. I'm slippery as a salmon and the silver river of fortune is flowing with me.

Eadha and I know lots of good hiding places. Once I'm out of the broch it's easy. I didn't know what time it was in the souterrain, but it couldn't be better: dusk, the easiest time to find a shadow to be secret in.

I slip away, running like a weasel and vanish through a crack in a dyke.

The night will be short. I press on along the coast, away, away. Eventually I pause and try to decide where to aim for. Where will Eadha go? Where will he be waiting for me? I wonder whether he has already managed to get away. I hope so. Once we're together we can hide forever, after all, he has known this place since childhood.

At least I have water now. There is always water. And at first light in the woods, I will find leaves and roots and I will live. It is not possible to starve at this time of year. I hide in among boulders where nobody will find me.

At first light I creep out in the dimness and carry on along the shore. I find pignuts, plenty of leaves, enough to fill my stomach. I must keep moving. I have made up my mind what I need to do.

Before sunrise I am along at the nousts where I take the smallest coracle with the lightest paddle and heave it down to the shore. The tide is rising but I cannot wait for it to help me. Fortune smiles on me again: an offshore breeze. I set my back to it and skull. I think about just going across the loch to Brigid's Cave, but that's exactly where they will expect me to go, so I'm being cleverer than that.

My body was not made for this amount of skulling, but I must keep going. I must get over the horizon before they wake, before they find out where I am going. If Father sees me, he will sail me down in minutes and I will stand no chance. I put my back into the paddle.

By the time it is fully light, the shore is far off but I am tiring. Waves buffet me. My hands bleed where the blisters from paddling have burst. The salt stings and I am thirsty again. I do not know if I can make it. But I don't think they are following me. I see no sails when the waves lift me.

Eventually I can skull no more.

Perhaps it would have been better to rot in that hole. No! Anything but that. Eadha, where are you? What am I doing out here?

As the chop gets up, I begin to fear I will die here at sea but then I pull myself together and think. The wind is blowing where want to go. It wants to help me. I stand the paddle up as a kind of mast and let my shawl act as a sail. If only I could find a way to fix the mast in place without having to hold it. I rip strips of cloth from my dress to use as a lashing for the mast and bandages for my hands.

I never knew Father had taught me so much about sailing until today. The boat is gaining on the island. I will be sunburned and if I do not get a drink soon, I will be driven to drinking seawater.

My head is pounding, the breeze is chilly and the glittering sea is blinding but I am on a bearing for Rum and it is getting closer. I cannot miss it now, even if I end up on a rocky shore. At least I am not going to die out here.

The cloth is weak and even with the lashings I have to cling to the paddle to keep it upright. It is hard work trying to keep the shawl functioning as a sail, but I am getting there. I may even reach the inlet where they land their boats. I remember it now and I can see the opening, trees growing in the shelter of the bay.

My shawl-sail begins to flop. I scream at the wind, 'Don't die on me now, wind, please. Please don't fade out on me here. Just a little further!'

The breeze lapses completely and I sit drifting, begging the wind spirits. A skuar plumps down on the glassy water beside the coracle and watches me, its beak like a sickle.

'You can't eat me,' I tell it. 'I'm not going to die just yet.'

I am about to jump out and swim for it when a ruffle comes across the water towards me.

My sail bags as the breeze lifts. It fills! The boat moves. The trickle under the hull is like sacred music.

Life was ebbing and now it is flowing again. I will survive!

I almost don't believe it when I reach the shore. With the last of my strength I drag the coracle up above the seaweed. Crawling, I follow the sound of water and there's a little stream, trickling down towards the sea. It's all I need. I hurl myself down and slurp at it like a dog, weeping with relief. And then I hear something, a cough. I turn around and see a man and realise I am naked. But exhaustion overcomes my shame. It's Aonghas. He says kind words. I can't get to my feet, but he picks me up and carries me back to his home.

RUM

I am weak as a newborn calf, unable to get up, my legs wobbly, my hands like lobster claws. I am alive, though, and Cuilc is here. As soon as I see her I try to tell her what has happened but she hushes me and will not listen. She must think I am raving, crazy. But I have not lost my mind.

I sleep. I don't know how long for. When I wake a scrawny woman introduces herself as Onni and feeds me porridge. She tries to make me eat meat, but I hate it. Deer flesh. They say it will make me strong so I have a little, but porridge is better. I will get strong enough on porridge. I keep asking to see Cuilc and when she comes I tell her we have to rescue Eadha but she acts as if she doesn't trust me. Am I a prisoner here as well? She says I must rest, but Eadha's life is in danger. I must get back to the Winged Isle, try to rescue him. She says if I am so keen to get back why did I run away?

Their barley is wormy and disgusting. This rotten food must have rotted their minds. Why can't they see what is so obvious? Aonghas says a boat won't make it, but I came in that little coracle and he has a big strong curragh. It's an emergency. If I were stronger I'd get up and sail it myself.

When I wake again there is a howling wind, but when I remember the situation I get up and dress. I'm still a bit wobbly but not so weak I can't get down to the shore. Even in the relative shelter of the inlet the surface of the water is lifting in sheets and driving onto the land, waves smashing with great, white explosions and a wild roaring from the stones on the beach. I am soon wet through. It is the kind of wind that will move boulders.

I see that the coracle is well strapped down with all the other boats. Aonghas has taken care of it.

There is nothing I can do. The storm rages, imprisoning us all on the island.

I get back shivering and it takes me a long time to warm through again. Aonghas and Cuilc treat me like a child, complaining if I get up out of bed. I explain over and over that Eadha is in danger and they say that they hear me but then do nothing. Aonghas says I have to be patient but I can't stop worrying. Anything could have happened to Eadha. I talk to him inside my head, trying to reassure him that I am coming as soon as I can, telling him that I am well and safe, as far as I know.

When we were together, so often we seemed to be able to read each other's minds. With no need to speak we would agree where we wanted to go, what to do, our one shared soul guiding us without words. We would say the same thing, together, simultaneously.

I ache for him. I talk to him, but I don't hear him respond.

What if he is dead? I dread it. But if he were dead, surely I would know; my soul, our soul, would be broken and screaming, surely? But I don't hear his voice. I do not know what he is thinking or where he is.

Cuilc is drunk all the time, and she laughs with Aonghas, cackling with him, flirting. It is repulsive to watch in someone so ancient. He laughs along with her, humouring her, as if she is something special. Why is he so deferential towards her? She is just a crone.

Eventually the wind eases and Aonghas announces that we can go. He will take Cuilc in grand state across the water, he says. There is something going on here that I'm not sure I understand. Finishing his bowl of porridge, he winks at me and it makes me feel sick. He strides off saying he is going to check his boat, and if all is well, we can go, but he returns a while later shaking his head. The wind has turned westerly and dropped in ferocity, but there was some damage to the curragh. He has someone fixing it.

'Patience,' he says. 'Tomorrow we will go, at first light if the weather is reasonable.'

I am praying for the weather. I can't wait much longer to see Eadha.

While we wait I confront Cuilc again with what Mother said. We are sitting beside the door of the house, in the sunshine. It is a beautiful day and it seems outrageous for everything to be so wrong, with the sky so blue and clear. If Eadha and I were together of course we would be revelling in it, but as it is, the sun is too bright, too hot, too intense. Horseflies bite our arms and legs and our conversation is punctuated by slaps.

Down at the shore, along from the house, out towards the narrowest part of the loch, the boatsmiths are at work with Aonghas. Hammering is interspersed with the scrape of a saw. It is taking them an age to do whatever it is they must do.

'Do you believe my mother is your daughter?' I say to Cuilc.

She laughs as if I am a stupid child. 'Whatever do you mean?'

'That's what Mother said, that some boy slave, when you were both young, got you pregnant and she was the result. That's why they locked me up. And Eadha.' Has she not been listening to me?

'Don't be ridiculous,' she says.

'I'm not being ridiculous. That's what she claims. That she's your daughter and therefore Eadha's her brother. If it's not true, how are we going to prove it?'

'It's just a silly nonsense someone's thought up.' She emits a high-pitched sort of giggle.

'How can you be so unconcerned? Eadha's imprisoned. I don't know what she'll do to him. His life is in danger.'

'Nonsense. Eadha's a very capable boy.'

'But they've locked him up. Why don't you care?'

'I do care, dear. That's why we're going over as soon as Aonghas has sorted his boat out. It's nothing to worry about.'

I am so exasperated, I could throttle her.

'But what if Mother insists she's your daughter? Everyone believes her. There must be someone who can tell her it's not true!'

She looks at me then, just a fleeting glance, then she stares out at the loch. 'Of course. I can tell her.'

'But what if she doesn't believe you?'

'Oh, it was all such a long time ago.'

'What was?' Nausea grips me. There's an awkward pause and my stomach clenches. 'Is it true?'

'Don't be ridiculous.' She giggles again, that laugh I've never heard her use before. It sounds completely insincere

Suddenly she groans and puckers her face up in pain.

'Are you all right?' I say

'Just a little spasm.' Her voice is taut and she holds her hand tight around her belly. The colour has drained out of her face. She pushes herself up to her feet.

'Excuse me.' She stumbles to the corner of the building but before she can get there, she doubles up and vomits. I catch her as she crumples. There is blood coming up and vile green stuff and the smell is enough to make me want to reel back in disgust. I panic. She is dying in my arms. I start shouting and Onni comes running. Cuilc's not a big woman, but I'm not exactly huge myself. I am glad I've been doing all that dance training. I find the strength to hold her up. She is convulsing as I half-carry her inside, with Onni helping me to get her to her bed. The breath heaves in and out of her, sounding like branches scraping together. She is weeping feebly. She looks like a snotty little child, with all that sick down her front.

We pull the clothes off her and make her comfortable. She swoons away into unconsciousness. I can't bear to leave her side but all that evil vomit needs clearing up.

Onni makes soothing sounds and fusses over everything, making it seem a bit less scary. I don't know what to do so she gives me instructions. She says, 'You keep a hold of her hand there.'

I do as she says and she chunters on. 'The cailleach will be better in the morning, it's just a bit of sick, nothing to worry about, it'll be something she ate, the old ones have a sensitive constitution. Now you just rest there, Cuilc my dear, you take it easy, we're all here looking after you.' On and on she goes like that, then she hands me a cloth and I wipe the old woman's face and front, gently, as if she's a baby.

Slowly her rasping breath calms down a bit and perhaps the pain has subsided enough so she can come back to herself. When Onni has left us alone, she looks me right in the eye and says, clear as anything, 'I do want to see Eadha, before I die.'

It is like a knife going through me. I feel her pain the next time a spasm hits her. I am sitting here, wasting time, when I should be going to find him, but I simply don't know what to do.

When the pain has eased enough for her to speak again, with her eyes closed, she says clearly, 'There is no incest between you, I swear it.'

A bit later, Aonghas comes in and she says to him, 'Fetch Eadha. I want to see him before I die.'

He shakes his head. 'With this wind there'd be no difficulty getting across, but it could be a week before I could get back with him. And from what the girl says, he's a prisoner. You'd be better off letting me take you home, if you must see him.'

It's the brutal truth. I can see that. But how can a woman in her state travel?

She closes her eyes, I assume in defeat, but after a while she says quietly, 'Very well. When we can go?'

'In the morning,' Aonghas says.

'If I live that long.'

'Ach, Onni says it's just something you ate. You'll be right as rain tomorrow. I know you Cuilc. You're tough as walrus hide.'

A wan smile appears on her face and she opens her eyes, but there is nothing in them but pain.

'Tomorrow.' She grips my hand with sudden ferocity and stares at Aonghas. He nods, turns, and ducks out of her view. I watch his back as he strides out of the building.

When I look back at Cuilc she has her eyes closed again. Gradually her grasp on my hand subsides and she seems to be sleeping. I creep away outside.

Aonghas is putting a stretcher together from a couple of poles and some skins. He glances up at me. 'She'll not walk far, I doubt. We may as well make her as comfortable as we can. You'll find some goat skins up in the rafters. We'll wrap her up warm.'

'You're very kind,' I say

'I've known her all my life. There was a time I'd have done anything for her. And if this is the last thing I can do…' He leaves the thought hanging, but it is clear he doesn't really think she will be fine by morning.

As much as we can, we keep up the pretence. I don't want to eat, but to maintain the fiction of everything being fine, I accept the food I am offered at dinner time. We converse in civil tones about nothing and take ourselves to our beds, mine at the foot of Cuilc's so that I am there to help her if she needs anything. I leave a small lamp burning. I don't think anyone gets much sleep.

RETURN

By morning I am exhausted.

Fortunately, Aonghas seems to understand the urgency, or maybe it is just his nature; brusque, direct, letting nothing get in the way. A young man appears who Aonghas addresses as 'Mac', boy, and I don't know any other name for him.

'Hello, I'm Rona,' I say.

'I know,' he grunts, as if I've said my name is Stupid. And that is the measure of our interaction.

Aonghas and Mac lift Cuilc onto the stretcher, carry her to the boat, and somehow manage to get her aboard without jolting her unduly. Mac has the strength of an ox and Aonghas is a giant masquerading as a man. They make Cuilc look leaf-light as they swing her about. It is like watching a dance. I am amazed, respectful. Mac gives the merest nod of acknowledgement when I say, 'Thank you for being so gentle with her. You're strong.' But I can tell from his bearing that he is proud, and I am glad I've said it. I might be stupid, but I am grateful, and there's never any harm in that. Just before we set off I remember the coracle, but Aonghas is way ahead of me and has tied it behind us.

I follow Aonghas' instructions, although there isn't much that the two of them can't manage between them after the initial flurry of casting off his boat, *Sgiannach*, and hauling in ropes. The sea is bouncier than when I sailed over in the coracle, but it is hardly rough, and the wind is behind us, so we glide along at a steady pace. The sea swishes against the bow and a line of froth shows where we've been.

But even this gentle rocking seems to cause unbearable suffering for Cuilc. I stay with her. She is brave, I give her that, and she tries to sound positive about how the sea air will do her good. But she is sick often, and when we meet a big wave and the boat lurches, I can see the motion pains her. She grimaces and closes her eyes. I stroke her hand, murmuring words I hope have comfort in them. I don't know what else to do.

She looks at me and smiles. 'You're a good girl. Eadha made a good choice and I've been a crabbit old bitch.'

I say she's been nothing of the sort, although of course she has, but it's impossible to feel anything other than sorry for her in this pitiful state. I've no doubt I could make a similar confession.

After a particularly horrible bout of sickness she moans. 'Don't let me die out here. Let me see him, I have to see him. I've something to tell him before I go.'

'Can you tell me?' I ask.

She stares at me, thinking hard, by the look of her frown, then shakes her head. 'I want him to know first.' She closes her eyes again.

She looks as if she is dead already with each breath reviving her from the state of a corpse, or perhaps this is just an impression caused by my desperation. It is dreadful, the discovery that life is a thread that may break at any moment.

We reach the coast of the Winged Isle, the Cuillin mountains like the jaws of a great beast. We have to turn up the loch. Aonghas asks me to help pull the sail round. It is hard work, but it doesn't take long. I've sailed enough with Father not to be completely ignorant of what's needed. I take care to coil a rope I see lying, and I get a grunt of thanks from Mac for doing it neatly. Perhaps Mac really is his name. Odd. We've reached a point where I don't feel I can ask his real name.

Up the loch, we partly lower the sail. The wind is perfect for this journey and it pushes us right up to Cuilc's house on the shore. As soon as it is shallow enough, Mac jumps out and pulls us in next to Father's boat. I clamber out after him. Father is in sight and comes running to help Aonghas and Mac to haul the curragh up out of the water.

'Thanks Manigan,' Aonghas says. 'We'll need an extra hand to get the invalid ashore.'

Father frowns. 'Who?'

'Cuilc. She'll die in her own bed at least.'

The two men exchange a look I can't interpret, and I feel a fresh twinge of fear. What if Cuilc's assurance is not enough? What if what she is claiming simply isn't true?

Father ignores me while the three of them try to get the stretcher off the boat without jolting Cuilc too badly. She swears at one point and Aonghas apologises.

Another lad I haven't seen before arrives. He is thin and wispy, like a plant that's grown in the dark, and he has a furry little creature clinging around his neck that I later learn is called a monkey – a revolting thing, no doubt flea-ridden. It gives me the shudders. He looks far too feeble to help carry the stretcher up the steep track to the house, but he puts his shoulder to it and seems to be helping them.

I trot along behind. Father calls him Fin and I can see something difficult between them, but familiarity too. He must have been with them when they arrived here, but I didn't notice.

Back in the broch, we get Cuilc to her bed, and then the men stand around in that way men do inside a house.

'Where's Mother?' I ask. 'We need her knowledge of herbs to help Cuilc. Where is she when you need her?'

'Don't speak of her in that tone.' Father speaks to me like a child.

Then the ghostly boy says, 'She and Badger went off to talk to a priestess.'

'Who? Ishbel?'

He shrugs. 'Wherever your man is. '

Father gave him a filthy look.

Of course, Eadha will have gone to Ishbel. I feel huge relief and say, 'Cuilc says what Mother's saying isn't true and she needs to tell Eadha something that will prove it. I have to go and fetch him.'

'You're not going anywhere, my girl.' Father grips me around my upper arm.

'Let go, you're hurting.'

If anything, he tightens his grip.

'Can't you see she's dying? Tell him, Aonghas. We need Ishbel. We need someone who knows how to help her. And she needs Eadha. She has to tell him something.'

'She needs help, that's for sure,' Aonghas says, as if feeding out rope with a tension on it.

Cuilc's breath rasps. 'Get Ishbel.'

Everyone turns to look at her. Her eyes are fluttering.

My father says to Aonghas, 'Do you know the way to this priestess' cave?'

Aonghas shifts his weight and says nothing, considering the question.

'I do,' Mac volunteers.

'Aye, but there's the crossing to be made, when the wind...'
Aonghas looks at me, but I can't read his expression.

Cuilc moans from her bed and the men just stand there. I suddenly realise that I need to act as if this is my own house.

'I think we all need to eat something. We've been hours at sea. And I must at least make her a hot drink. I'm sorry for the lack of hospitality, Aonghas, it looks as if my father's let the fire go out.'

I turn to the hearth, full of bitterness, and try to get the fire to wake up. It has never been one of my strengths. Fires are fickle, dirty and bothersome. The ghost boy Fin lifts off the sticks that I am trying to warm in the embers and from somewhere he produces a bit of bark and something fluffy. He murmurs over it and suddenly there are flames.

'I've been watching your mother,' he says.

I don't know what he means.

'She handles fire better than anyone I've ever seen. I'm surprised she didn't teach you.'

I fetch a cup and pull some mint leaves from a hanging bunch. Eadha and I gathered them to dry just a week or so back on Cuilc's orders. It is all I can think of that she might like. I find some oatcakes and hand them to the men, who eat the lot between them without speaking.

I make one more try to go to Brigid's Cave. 'I need to fetch someone who can do more for Cuilc than give her a cup of water. Her death'll be on our hands if we don't do something.'

At least this stirs Aonghas from just standing watching Cuilc die. 'You know the way to the cave, Mac?'

The lad seems keen to go, nodding.

As he leaves, I make to go with him, but Father says, 'You're staying here.'

'This is my home. I can go where I like,' I retort.

It is Aonghas who stops me this time. 'It's at your home where you're needed,' he says, glancing towards Cuilc.

The two of them, Aonghas and Father, follow the boy outside.

He sets off at a run as soon as he is out the door. I watch him until he is hidden by trees, while Father goes with Aonghas to the shore to make the boat secure.

A shout from inside takes me back to the fireside, where Fin has boiled water. 'Did you mention food?' he says. 'I can help you make something. You'll be hungry, and they'll have a harder sail back over there, and if Rian comes back with the priestess...' He tails off.

'We should cook a meal.' My heart sinks. 'I can make bannocks. Can you cook?'

He points up at the rafters where some herring are hanging. 'Fish soup?'

I dip into the almost empty barley barrel and sit down beside the quern to start my bannock ritual. Perhaps the grinding will comfort me, although I'm not in the mood to sing as I usually do.

Instead, I answer Fin's questions. Between asking practical things, like where we keep our implements, he makes a long series of enquiries into my childhood, my mother, my father, even Soyea. He is particularly interested in my sister, although I do my best to put him off.

I am halfway through telling him about the way her father went off to wherever he was from with her twin brother, never to be seen again, when Cuilc makes a strange gasping sound. We both turn to her and I know immediately she is dead. Her face has gone slack. My steps to her bed feel like wading through ever-deeper water in which I am sure to drown. Her body is lifeless, frozen. I hold her hand and my head sinks down onto her chest.

Then there's the sound of someone approaching. I hope it's Ishbel but it is Badger who bursts in, panting, in a total lather of sweat, bleeding down one side of his face. 'Where's Manigan?'

He is here, at the door. 'What's the matter man?'

Badger catches his breath. 'A gang of Ussa's slaves has got Rian.'

Cuilc is dead. Mother is gone. Now we will never, ever know the truth.

Father is strangely calm, sitting Badger down, tending the cut on his face and asking him to explain in detail what happened. I can't understand why he isn't chasing straight after Mother, after all he is supposed to love her above everything. But he doesn't go anywhere. He just sits there, his chin on his clenched fist, elbow on his knee.

'What are you doing? You have to rescue her,' I demand.

But he just says, 'She'll be back.'

'What do you mean?' I am shouting. 'She might be killed!'

'No, she won't.'

'How can you be so sure?'

'I just am. This…' He gestures at Cuilc. 'This….'

Everyone around me is going mad.

RIAN

CAPTURE

Rian and Badger followed the instructions they were given by Cuilc's neighbour to find Ishbel the priestess. As they came down to a stony bay the path divided, one leading away up to Brigid's Cave, the other continuing along the shore. It was here that two men jumped out from behind boulders and muscled them to the ground.

Rian heard Badger giving as good as he got but she was unable to put up much resistance to her assailant. He was young, dark-haired, bearded and strong. He carried her at a run along the shore. She fought back, kicking and biting, then he threw her to the ground. Kneeling on her back in such a way she felt sure she would never walk again, he immobilised her completely with rope around her ankles, thighs, wrists and chest. She tried to talk to him but he slapped her face.

She was trussed like a pig. He heaved her across his back and set off at a jog down the coastal track. At a substantial stream, with a noisy waterfall, he tossed her across and she lay winded in the heather on the other side. The ropes were agony; the only way to tolerate them was not to move. He picked her up again, slung her over his shoulder, and continued to jolt her along. Once she stopped struggling, she noticed that he had brands the same as hers.

Eventually, around a headland, they came to some huts. Smoke was coming from two of them. At the shore there was a familiar clang of metal: a smith at work.

It was no surprise when she was unceremoniously dumped at the feet of Ussa. What she had long feared had finally happened. She looked up at the jowls of the trader, seeing her for the first time in more than eighteen years.

Ussa's body bulged out of a belted robe and flabby chins hung below her pasty face. Gold was slung from everywhere possible; earrings tugged her lobes down, a fat necklace with a red gem filled her cleavage. Even her black leather eye patch was embossed with silver. She stood over Rian's contorted frame, hands on hips.

'Well if it isn't the green-eyed witch of Clachtoll.' The big woman kicked Rian idly with a heavy boot. Her movement was ungainly and Rian could tell that her ankles were swollen and uncomfortable. 'I have you at last.'

Rian, having taken in all she wanted of Ussa, closed her eyes. There was nothing the woman could do to her to make things any worse than they were already. The shame of a daughter's incest was an all-encompassing pain beside which a rope was mere discomfort. She became aware that Ussa smelt of stale sweat and rotten teeth. She felt disgust for the woman, yet also, she was surprised to discover, curiosity. She opened her eyes again.

'I've waited for this moment for years.' Ussa's voice was unchanged but her body seemed ravaged. This was no longer the glamorous tyrant Rian remembered. The person she looked up at had twice the weight and a fraction of the power. She was a spent force, or worse, a travesty, a physical wreck. Yet in her one remaining eye there persisted that cruel fixity. The bonxie stared back down at Rian, the gaze of a raptor considering its prey. Ussa may be old and unfit, but she was still dangerous. Potentially lethal.

'I wonder what I'll do with you? That was a good guess on my part, wasn't it? Once I'd heard you were here, that you'd want to go to Brigid's Cave. What do you think? Cunning, aren't I?' Her voice poured like blood from a wound, smooth and deep, though with a tinge of rust to it now. Or had it always had that edge?

Ussa had found a seat and dragged it over so she could sit, watching her prize, nudging Rian's body with her foot from time to time. The exertion made her breath rasp.

With each movement, the ropes cut, but Rian didn't care.

'You never did say anything, you little clam. I remember now. Silent as a stone and about as interesting. What the hell Manigan ever saw in you I never understood, yet you still managed to weasel your way into my family. Imposter.' Ussa poked Rian's belly with her boot, but Rian made no response; she just watched.

'Have you still got my brand on you?' Ussa leaned down, dragged up Rian's skirt. 'Yes. Not much meat on you is there? You'd not give the dogs much nourishment.'

Rian was unmoved. Ussa could put her on a spit, roast her alive and eat her, it would be no worse than knowing her daughter was in the mire of incest and she'd been unable to prevent it. She wondered if Manigan had managed to track Rona down, or whether she had found Eadha and they had escaped together. She closed her eyes as the full horror of that prospect bit into her. She had been feeling sick ever since Buia had told her about Cuilc, but still these sudden realisations would fill her with fresh shame, nausea rising at the image of her daughter being intimate with the handsome man who was her brother.

Ussa mistook her wince for fear and returned to her gloating tirade. Rian opened her eyes again and faced her tormentor with an expression of pure scorn. Nothing the woman could do would touch her. She felt herself rising to the high, safe place she had taken herself to all those times when Ussa tried to conquer her in the past.

Poking her again with her toe, Ussa said, 'I'll have to think how best to handle you. I'll not make the mistake of damaging my goods this time. You think I can't break you, don't you? Well just wait until you're lying there in your own shit begging me for something to drink. Then we'll see how brave you are.'

A girl came out of one of the huts. 'Hey you,' Ussa shouted. 'What food and drink do you have?'

A woman from the nearest hut took it upon herself to wait on her, supplying a plate of fish and bread and fetching her a cup of ale, but it seemed to Rian that the rest of the people of the hamlet were keen to give Ussa a wide berth. Ussa drank the ale, then shouted until the big slave who had captured Rian produced a flask of something stronger. As far as Rian could see given her limited vantage, most of the other people had made their way to the shore to watch the smith's performance.

The day was dimming and a strong smell of sulphur wafted across from the forge. Rian could imagine that pyrotechnics would be under way and thought about asking Ussa which smith was traveling with her.

Ussa shouted for a lamp and the woman brought a little tallow lantern from the hut. Ussa positioned it so she could watch her prize.

Rian continued to listen to the trader's chuntering, a mix of threats and boasts, which became increasingly incoherent and repetitive as the flask emptied. Rian's feet were completely numb and with her arms tied behind her back, her shoulders were a torment, but it wasn't difficult to deflect her attention away to the worse torment of her spirit. The pain kept her alert. She tried to think of ways she might be able to escape once Ussa bored of her and left her alone.

But Ussa's fascination with her seemed unquenchable. She kept returning to her statement, 'I've been waiting for this for years.' The delight would rekindle in her face for a while, but then she would talk herself round into misery and self-pity. By the time the flask was drained she managed to reduce herself to weeping, muttering about the threat of death that loomed over her from her father, Sevenheads, and complaining about the agony she still felt from her missing eye. She seemed to think Rian's capture could somehow pay the price for this injury.

Rian tried to make sense of what she was saying. After years of avoiding this woman, it was, much to her surprise, fascinating to see her seeming to be so poisoned by her past.

In her drunken state, Ussa was entwined by grievance. Over and over, she returned to ranting her anguish about the Stone of Telling and the years she had wasted chasing it only to find it was a torture to her. Now she was lonely and afraid of dying. And all of this, every bit of it, was Rian's fault. Each time she remembered this point, she kicked Rian again, until she hurt her feet doing it. Her kicks were nothing to Rian, but when one was particularly sharp, she groaned and Ussa pulled herself back.

'I mustn't damage the goods now. I'll make a pretty fortune selling you.' With this the cycle completed, and she was back to the smug satisfaction of having captured Rian at last.

Her slave appeared unbidden with a second flask and didn't even cast a glance at Rian before slouching away to the shore again. Rian guessed that the smith must be putting on a good show.

By now Ussa was pathetic. If Rian hadn't known how capable she was of random and irrational violence, she could have pitied her.

Ussa's words became slurred, her statements incoherent, and then her head slumped, eyes closing. With a jerk, she was awake again, eyes groggy. She looked at Rian and giggled. 'I've got my slave back.' But then the struggle failed and she sat back, asleep.

Rian tried to wriggle and cursed the slave who had tied her so effectively. She was on a soft grass sward, and there wasn't even a stone to generate some friction against to wear away her ties. In some ways it was worse to listen to Ussa's snoring than all her evil talk.

Perhaps this was her punishment for having wasted so much time, delaying going to Assynt for all those years, waiting for Cleat to return rather than doing what she had always known she should do to establish her own identity. And now that she knew, it was too late. Her bloodline was knotted. She must accept this curse. Yet she was not made for acceptance. As soon as she settled on it her mind rebelled. Surely the wrong could be redeemed. There must be a way to rescue Rona from the situation. She was young, and pure in heart. There must be ways to appease the spirits. She thought of her own life. She could have given up when she was defiled by Pytheas but she had not. She would never give up. She had paid a heavy price, the loss of Cleat, but she couldn't ever give up hope entirely. It felt the same with Rona, poor girl. She must do everything she could to save her.

Her mind made up, she wrestled and strove and tensed and relaxed but could make no impact on the ropes. All she managed was to roll a few feet away across the sward.

Ussa's lamp sputtered and went out. The night was dark. People were returning to their huts. The smith's show must be over. A chill started to seep up from the ground and it brought despair with it.

Then, through the turf beneath her, Rian felt footsteps approaching. A hand was placed briefly over her mouth, then a finger across her lips. Rian nodded, then lay still as someone worked away at the ropes that bound her wrists behind her back. The hands seemed small, and smelled strongly of woodsmoke and faintly of sulphur. Rian's heart raced. Who was this friend? They had presumably been close to the forge.

Once her arms were freed Rian felt the rope around her ankles being untied. She sat up and rubbed herself. The pins and needles were agony, her fingers were like wood but her rescuer grabbed her hand and tugged her away from Ussa, helping her to shuffle on her dagger-numb feet. She staggered, reaching out for balance, and realised the person helping her was dressed in leather clothes.

'Don't you recognise me?' The voice was hushed, even though they were well out of earshot.

It was cloudy, but Rian could just make out the profile of a woman. It was familiar. With an intake of breath she recognised her betrayer from all those years ago: the daughter of Gruach.

'Fraoch?'

Her face was older but it still had those dimples, the wide smiling mouth, the arched eyebrows. Rian didn't trust her. She had betrayed her once, she could do it again.

'I managed to get something sleepy into her drink and persuaded her thugs to turn a blind eye.'

'Thank you. Why?'

It was years ago, but she was curious about what had changed.

Fraoch whispered, 'Maybe for Manigan, or Fin.' Of course. Fin was her half-brother. 'Or just for yourself. Or for me. We could have been friends.'

'I don't think so.' Rian thought about responding with something about Fin, but didn't.

'I let you down.'

'You're with Ussa.'

'Not necessarily. I sometimes make myself scarce. And so should you. You'd better get going. Her slaves don't feel the same way about you as I do. Do you know where you are?'

Rian nodded, then realised Fraoch might not see her gesture. 'Exactly.'

'Manigan explained why you hate me,' Fraoch said. 'I was foolish back then. I didn't know anything about friendship.'

Rian thought for a moment about pursuing the topic, but it seemed irrelevant. 'You've made up for it now.'

'You have to get away from here.' Fraoch squeezed her hand for a moment then let it go. 'Good luck.'

Rian was filled with a strange sense of lightness. She was free again. At least for now. She set off, her feet finding their way down the track in the darkness, back along the coast. It was slow and painful at first but the circulation soon returned. It seemed to take an age to reach the waterfall. Eventually she was back at the stony beach. Although she never had any doubt where she was going, as the seashore made her direction obvious, her ears were focused behind her all the way. At any time she expected hands on her, a body to leap out and overpower her. But it didn't come.

She continued to pick her way down the track, wondering about seeking Ishbel, but she no longer knew who she could trust, so she pressed on to the top of the loch and across the salt marsh, then started down the west shore. The shelter of the woods was welcome.

Dawn was breaking when she neared Cuilc's cliff-top tower house. Down at the beach Manigan was in the process of launching *Bradan*. He rushed up, and her legs crumpled under her as he held her.

'Well thank the Goddess. I thought I was going to have to break a life-time's habit and start chasing Ussa instead of her chasing me. Badger, look! Fin, Kino. Someone tell Rona her mother's safe and let's get cracking. Time to put some miles between us and this forsaken place.'

BACK TO ASSYNT

The wind was south-westerly and they had to beat down Loch Slapin away from all the wrong. It barely seemed possible, the headway they made so slow that Rian was balled up with frustration, her hand bunched in front of her mouth. It was bad enough to be leaving the body of Cuilc unburied, abandoned, without then being unable to make actual progress away from danger.

The red mountains stood, impassive, their ochre scree pale in the morning light. Beyond them the black mountain ridge, like a huge mouthful of teeth, stretched into a mocking grimace.

First they sailed east towards the spot where Ussa's boat was hauled up on the shore. Rian raked the shore with her eyes but she could make out no movement. Manigan murmured for the crew to tack. Kino, Badger and Fin swung the boom around the mast and hauled the sail back up. It filled and they set off westwards and away. They seemed to be hardly any further down the loch than when they'd started, still in clear sight of Cuilc's broch, when they tacked again. The easterly tack took them once more over to *Ròn*.

'We're never going to get away,' Rian wailed, 'we're just going back and forth in front of her.'

Manigan pointed to a rope at the port side quarter. 'The breeze has plenty of south in it this time. Give me a good hard pull on that sheet and we'll get even closer to the wind.'

Rian tugged the rope as instructed, then sat watching for signs of pursuit. She didn't have long to wait. There were people around Ussa's boat now and it was being pushed towards the water.

Still, *Bradan* was on a more promising course and even Rian could believe they were progressing down the loch. They trickled south east towards green slopes, then crabbed back west, close in to the cliffy shore. It was interminable, but they were gradually putting distance between themselves and Ussa.

Rona sulked on a bench aft of the mast. Rian caught her eye, and said, 'Are you all right?'

'Of course I'm not. How could just leave her there? All your talk of propriety, worrying about me and Eadha, and you leave her body there, unburied. You'd treat an animal better. What do you expect me to think of you when you treat your own mother like that?'

'Oh don't be ridiculous. She is in Aonghas' good hands,' Rian retorted, but the gibe had truth in it.

After that Rona refused or talk to any of them, or to eat. She lowered her head when the boom was swung but took no part in the sailing work. Rian felt herself tearing in two as she watched her daughter's misery. Manigan and she had agreed that unless someone who knew better told them otherwise, they would consider Rona's marriage annulled. Four months would need to pass to rid her of the defilement of the four-month long period of incest. Until that time, she would have to be considered unclean.

She looked back and even her daughter's distraught state couldn't quite quench the excitement at their growing lead over Ussa's boat.

'I can beat that old tub in this situation with no bother at all,' Manigan said, and it seemed to be true. The bigger vessel could not point anything like as close to the wind as *Bradan*, and it was still labouring down the loch when they turned east around the Point of Sleat, then north up the Sound, the wind firmly behind them.

Rian found herself humming the old song that Toma had taught her, and a minke whale surfaced ahead of them, its fin curving up above the water and rotating back down. Everyone, except Rona, whooped with the thrill of it.

Manigan tousled Rian's hair. 'There you are, my love, you're free again. And the whale has come to prove it.'

She smiled. 'Ussa can't have me.'

He chuckled. 'No, she can't. Sometimes it feels like I've spent my whole life trying to keep you out of her grasp. We're getting good at it, eh?' They powered along now, Manigan gleeful. 'We'll beat the tide, I know we will, and if she misses it she'll never catch us.'

By midday the Sound was a narrow channel and the water became complex, whirling and furrowing as they approached the kyle between the Winged Isle and the mainland to the east. Manigan, Badger and Kino were laughing with delight at the speed they made as the boat was swept through Kyle Rhea with the full force of the spring tide. Manigan had to hang onto the tiller at times to keep the boat on course among the eddies and swirls. They had left Ussa's boat far behind and Manigan was jubilant. 'By the time she arrives at the narrows, the tide'll be turning and it'll be against the wind too. She'll have to anchor and wait till midnight, if she dares attempt it at night, which I doubt. And we're away!'

By nightfall they were in open water and it was a clear night for sailing north, the breeze still helping them along their way past the northernmost end of the Winged Isle. By morning, the Assynt mountains were showing on the distant horizon.

SOYEA

PIG

I am preparing the evening meal when the shadow of a man falls across the hearth. Bael drags a carcase in after him, letting it drop to the floor beside the fireplace. It is the sow. She is bloody from the wound at her throat and leaves a smear across the floor. Her swollen teats show she was still feeding her young. From a pocket Bael pulls out a piglet and tosses it down beside her. He stands, legs astride, between the body and the door, then looks up, taking in the flowers festooning the place.

Buia says. 'You're back.'

I can't believe she doesn't express any outrage about the sow.

'What the hell's been going on here?' he says.

'Summer.'

He rolls his eyes at the reply. 'It stinks in here.' Then he looks at me, although I am trying to be invisible. 'I hoped that ugly bitch would go off with the witches. Where's Donnag?'

He addresses the question to me, but I'm not going to speak to him. I point out of the door. She is setting up the kiln again out the back to fire more of our pots, but he can find that out for himself.

Bael's return changes everything. Buia shuffles off to her hovel and flowers are replaced by bones again. Donnag retreats into herself, and although she continues working on the kiln to bake her pots, the fire goes out from her eyes. Instead of eating with me by the hearth, she reverts to her old habit of taking her bowl to her solitary perch on the stair. I feel much more exposed now tending the hearth on my own.

Bael prowls in and out of the broch, peering suspiciously at everything new, sniffing into corners. He stares at me while I cook. It unnerves me, and I drop a favourite bowl, which breaks in two. I cut myself while I'm chopping silverweed roots. He laughs with a wide open mouth, a mocking ha-ha-ha that makes me feel completely foolish. I staunch my bleeding finger and wish the pain on him. When the stew is ready, I take my food up to my cubby hole, leaving Bael to rage alone.

He hung up the sow right beside the door so it's impossible not to see her every time we go in or out. I think he wants us to hate him.

I am sitting by the hearth stripping wood sage leaves off their stalks just outside Danuta's old room. I can feel her presence, as if the aroma is reaching her wherever she is. I need this comfort.

Then Bael comes in. 'Roast the pig. There are people coming tonight.'

I take a breath and try to stay calm. I can't imagine who would want to be his friend and if there's a purpose to his feast he doesn't share it. 'Have you a way of purifying her?'

He looks at me as if I am his next prey and he is deciding where to poke his spear. 'Just roast it.'

There is no way I am going to touch the sow. The curse of the mother-killer is not something I am willing to risk. In theory I know what would have to be done to lift it, but that's for him to instigate, not me, and I'm not confident I could do the whole sequence of appeasements correctly, even if I was willing to try. I want to ask Danuta, of course, and what was once her presence becomes a huge and painful absence. I pick up the next stalk and pluck its leaves, one by one, deliberately not looking him in the eye.

'Well? What are you doing?'

'I'm making sage sauce. You'll be pleased later. Donnag loves it.'

He takes the sow's carcass off the hook and drops it down on the floor at my feet. It is stiff now and the trotters clatter onto the stones. One of them bashes against my foot. I try not to flinch, and slowly pull my leg back, but now I have to say a charm to stop its evil entering me. I mumble it under my breath.

'What witchery are you up to now? If you don't get that pig over a fire, I'll skewer you and give you the roasting you deserve.' He looks as if he is pleased with himself for saying this. He's swinging the meat hook on one finger.

I make an effort not to let my hands tremble as I take up another stalk and start at the bottom, tearing the leaves off one by one.

'Bael. Come here.' It's Buia, speaking from the doorway.

I move my bundle of sage and bowl of leaves aside and shift so he doesn't come near me as he obeys her. I'm amazed that he does, but since Danuta died, Buia seems to be the only one he has any respect for, though until now I have never seen her use her authority.

I can't see what he does now but I'm sure she knows fine well I can hear every word she says to him. The fear slumps out of me. He is like a dog, obedient to just one voice, this voice.

'The Mother is hurting. I feel her pain. You ripped a suckling baby off her.'

'How should I know it was feeding?' He sounds sulky as a child. 'It drove me mad, rubbing its filth on me whenever I went near it, mud everywhere.'

'She's waiting for you to ask forgiveness. Can't you feel her curse?'

'But we need meat. We can't live on flowers.'

'Danu says we need forgiveness.'

'Why can't you just do whatever we need for that? Or the girl? She loves all that witch stuff.'

'Danu says you killed the sow.' Then suddenly she has Danuta's voice, as if she is speaking from beyond the grave. 'It's your breath that must speak remorse,' she says. 'Beg of the mother.'

I get rapidly to my feet and with the bundle of sage in one hand and the bowl in the other, I tiptoe to the guard room behind the door to hide.

'Be good and do what's right…' I can't believe what I am hearing. It's the old woman's voice, back from the dead. Her last few words bring a smile to my face. '…And you should clean yourself. You stink.'

I cheer silently at the cheek of the woman and duck into the dark little room. Then once I've heard him stomp back inside I slip out.

It is drizzling outside but I don't care one bit. I go to see Buia, but she is not in her hut, so I drift on down to the shore.

There's no end to the time I can spend watching waves unfurl onto rock, their endless patterns. I told The Wren this and she said, 'Watch it, if it fascinates you. There is never the same pattern twice, yet just as in life, there is the force of motion and the force of stasis. Some things flow and some things appear to stand against the flow, but the rock that resists is shaped by the water and the water must accommodate the rock. Everything gives and everything must be negotiated.'

I watch the water and think about what she said. It is completely unsatisfactory, this view of the world. I know it makes sense at some level, but the world, life, needs to be less acquiescent than that. Where are the deeds we do? Are they no more than waves lapping rocks on a shore; one act, one wave among all the other waves? If that's all our actions mean, what is the point of doing anything? The next thing, done by the next person, will over wash it all, no matter how strong it seemed.

The persistence of the waves has no limit, and in the end I turn my back on them. There is no soothing to be found on this windy, wet afternoon. Only a long, bright strife seems to be offered by the breeze, lifting the sea into biffing scraps. The sky lowers, threatening a wetting.

I go back in. There is no alternative.

Bael is still there, of course. With the pig. I know I am bound to be roped into it.

He is in a mess: sweaty, bloody, guilty, out of his depth having gutted it and making a poor show of the butchery.

'When are people coming?' I ask.

I make a ceremony for forgiveness of the sacrilege. I don't know what Bael has said or done, but the animal is dead now and it would be worse to let it go to waste. I cook the sow on a spit, and later people arrive, mostly men, and they eat it. I do not touch the meat. That would be one step too close to condoning his action.

Drink flows. I don't know who most of the people are. There are three from Inver Pollaidh, who I have met before, and Alasdair is here again with his three brothers. They all look similar, big and round-faced with scars from fighting. Everyone else is new to me. There is a group of men, women and boys from Coigach, and one of them asks me about Badger so I am briefly inclined to stay and talk, but once they open the second flask of Donnag's father's foul brew I have had enough of them. They repeat themselves, talking endlessly of cattle, and they are all so angry, raging about raids by islanders and blaming the weather for everything.

There are too many weapons in the building and I alternate between boredom and fear. I notice Donnag has made herself invisible in her usual spot on the stair and I feel I must pick up the duty to keep a fire burning in the hearth.

One of the men from the north bursts out with an angry invective about islanders and turns to me with a snarl. 'Where are you from, anyway?' He pinches the skin on my arm.

I want to escape. I tell him the truth, that I was born on one of the Seal Isles and brought up far, far south, so I am new here. There is the start of a discussion about my mother: everyone knows the story of her being sold as a slave. Bael soon puts a stop to it. As soon as he has distracted them with the likelihood of an impending visit by a smith I slide away. I nod to Donnag on the stair as I pass her and take refuge in my cubby hole.

Early next morning I sneak out of the broch and watch my back all the way to the woods. I am soon tripping over golden birch slipper mushrooms. I gather the few that I can bundle up in my scarf but I'm cursing that I haven't brought a basket with me. I love the way they hide in moss, and how, like treasure, they give themselves away with a glimpse of bronze; as you pull back the stems and leaves of grass, primroses and ferns, the big fleshy mushrooms are revealed.

While I am teasing apart some particularly tangly moss I hear a squeak. It's not a bird I recognise. I look up, and high in the birch above me, paws around the trunk, is a bear cub. It makes the same noise again. It's almost a whimper. I back away to another tree and look around. The cub is pretty, with big furry ears and its tongue lolling out. I feel quite sorry for it, but I know I need to be wary. Its mother will be somewhere nearby and is likely to be protective of her young. She may be looking for birch slippers too.

I scour the undergrowth, but it is dense bracken, brambles, willow and hazel. A bear could be just a few metres away and I'd not know it. The cub squeaks again and starts descending the tree towards me. If it is curious about me I'm in real danger from its mother, and I don't know where she is. My heart is racing. I move slowly towards the next big tree, a rowan, and press my back to it. There's still no sign of the mother.

I step around the other side of the tree to try to get a view all around me, scouring the bank above. I'm sweating. If only the mother would give herself away! Is she watching me? I'm prob-ably looking suspicious, skulking here. Should I make a big noise, announce myself? Or will that just frighten the cub? I decide that alarming it is too big a risk and take a breath, then walk as calmly as I can to the next sizeable tree, an aspen. I look back at the cub. It is still up in the birch tree. I hope it is forgetting about me. I tiptoe my way, tree by tree, back to the path, my breath slowing, heart calming gradually as I get further and further away without encountering the mother.

I return to the broch. Bael is still drinking with five other men.

I tell no one about the bear.

PRESERVATION

When our alcohol supplies run out, everyone leaves, including Bael. It has been two days of hell but I recover, gradually, and return to the work of gathering and preserving herbs, experimenting and learning all I can from Buia. She teaches me to make a dye from a lichen that comes out a beautiful red, and it is so lovely I vow to spin more wool so I can dye more next year.

Bael returns three days later and sleeps like a stone for two days solid, getting up only to eat and drink. Finally, he washes himself and seems to come to his senses and purgatory begins again. He wants something from me. He follows me like a mosquito, trying to land on me, touch me if I get within arm's reach, poking and pawing, his sunken eyes leering at me. If I hated him before, I loathe him now. My skin creeps when his hands make contact, as if he conveys disease. I want to spit on him.

Today is blue and breezy so the daily chores are a pleasure. I take mash to the remaining piglets. Buia is milking the cow and singing to her.

I notice that there's lots of yarrow in bloom and I remember Danuta told me it's an excellent thing to preserve in mead, as it's helpful for so many ailments. Buia might know the recipe. I'll ask her. And if not, I'll just experiment.

I wonder how the mead I made earlier in the summer is maturing, but I know it won't be ready for months. I am not sure if there will be any of the old stuff left after Bael's last blow out. Normally he leaves it alone, preferring the dark ale he brews, but there were people with him who might drink anything.

On my way back into the broch, Donnag is coming out, wearing boots and an old shawl, carrying a spade.

I back out of the entrance to let her past. 'What are you doing today?'

'I'm going for clay. There is some in a stream bed down towards the beach.' She points south. 'The old man there told me I could go and dig some and he'd show me where it's good. His father made pots.'

It's a long speech for her. She is taking our project far more seriously than I expected. I wish her good luck.

'It'll be good to have fresh clay,' she says.

'And it's a beautiful day,' I say.

She looks around, seeming to notice for the first time that the sky is blue. 'So it is.' She smiles.

I take her gentle mood with me into the broch and feel my own smile on my face as I sprint up the stairs and go rummaging for mead. The case where I found it last time I looked is now empty, but I know there are others stashed under the drying loft. Between here and there, though, is a clutter of empty flasks and upended boxes, all mixed in with a tangle of fishing gear. My eyes see the empties as opportunities, now that I have a barrel of mead underway, so I grab a box and start gathering them, trying to match bungs and stoppers to the ceramic flasks that still seem to have life in them. I fetch another box, into which I chuck the cracked and broken pots. They may as well be ditched. Given her burst of fervour for pottery, maybe Donnag will make some more for me to use.

'Poking about where you're not supposed to again, I see.'

His voice is a whip.

I swivel round to face him. There is too much clutter in the way to give me much room to keep my distance from him. He steps closer. Buia is right. He stinks. I don't know what it is. Dried vomit, maybe. That would also explain the stains on his jerkin.

He is grimacing at me, his scarred face distorted by a grin, one eye half-closed as always. His face doesn't know how to smile properly. It makes him look as if he is in pain. The falseness of it is uglier than a scowl would be.

'If you want to see something secret, I can show you something.'

The smile becomes a leer.

'I'm just getting some mead. I'm going to get Buia to show me how to preserve yarrow.' I don't want to be cowed by him, but it's impossible not to be frightened. I've seen him when he's violent, lashing out. I've heard Donnag's stories. His boast of having chopped someone's fingers off for touching her.

'Where is the mad bat? She's not in her hut.'

'Around the back, with the cow.'

'So, nobody here but me and you. My slut wife has gone for a mud bath. It's the perfect opportunity to show you what you really want to see.'

'What do you mean?'

'What do you mean?' He imitates me in a whiny voice. 'You know damn well.' He grabs me by the wrist.

'I don't want to see anything of yours.'

He tries to slap me but I flinch away.

'Playing coy, eh? I know you're gagging for it.'

His hand on my wrist hurts.

'Let go of me.'

'Why should I?'

He pushes me back and I lose my balance and stumble, knocking over one of the boxes of flasks with a clatter of breaking pottery. I look down, relieved to see it was just the damaged ones, but just that momentary loss of attention is all he needs.

He is standing over me, and with his other hand he grabs the arm I try to steady myself with. Clasping both of my wrists in one of his hands, he pushes my arms up over my head and thrusts me back onto something hard, one of the chests probably, pinioning me there with his knee. With his other hand he starts pulling aside his clothes.

'No. Don't hurt me.' I don't know exactly what I'm saying but it is all refusal.

I wriggle and tug my arms but all that achieves is his knee rammed between my legs and his hand pulling my wrists to an excruciating angle.

'I like hurting people.' He brings his face close to mine.

I try to look him in the eye but there's nothing there except an animal. I look instead at the scar on his face. I see how it healed and imagine it as a gaping wound.

'Who caused that scar on your cheek?' I say. Is there a person in there, with memories?

'Shut your ugly mouth.'

There is an angry boy inside this monster. 'Did Danuta stitch it up for you? Or someone else?'

'I told you, shut it.' He jerks my arms almost out of their sockets. I daren't speak now.

He has pinned me at an agonising angle over the box and my lower back feels as if it will snap. His leg has my thigh and hip slammed against a sharp corner and his foot is crushing mine. He is trying with his other hand to get his clothes off without loosening his grip. Then he starts on my skirt, but I do all I can to hinder him.

'Look at me,' he says.

I will not. Not if that's what he wants.

He starts calling me filthy names. I try an old trick my mother taught me, going completely limp so he will loosen his grip and I can make a spring for it.

'You think I'm stupid, don't you?'

He pulls my arms into an even more painful position.

'You might as well faint. I'm going to skewer you anyway, just like that pig. You'll probably enjoy it, though, you slutty little bitch, gagging for it.'

His breath is foul against my face. He is tearing my skirt. I can hear it ripping. My legs are bare. I am crying now. He's going to force himself into me.

'Weepy, weepy.' He is laughing. I shut my eyes. I can't bear to look at the scar anymore and I'm breathing through my mouth trying not to smell him.

Then he's ripping away my moss pad. It's my bleeding time of the month.

He makes some filthy statement about my blood and I call him a bastard. He pauses.

'Perking up, are we? Go on, call me more bad names. I love it.'

'Bastard,' I say again.

'Is that the only one you know?'

'You bastard.' I'm screaming at him and he has paused. Perhaps, even though I can't fight him physically, my voice is a kind of weapon. I yell it again and again.

And suddenly he's off me and somebody is pulling at him. He draws a knife and there's Mother, yelling at him.

'Get your filthy hands off her.'

Then he has her down on the floor, but she has hold of his wrist, so he can't use the knife. They're struggling and he's kicking her.

I try to pull him off her, tugging at his jerkin. Something I do – or maybe it's Mother's hand on his wrist – makes him drop the blade. It skitters towards me. All I have to do is bend down and pick it up, and when he turns towards me and lunges, I stick it in his neck.

I see his anger turn to astonishment. His hand goes towards his throat and touches the knife handle, a gesture that seems almost delicate, as if he is stroking it. There's blood streaming from the wound. Then his eyes glaze and he crumples, toppling sideways among the bottles. When the clattering stops, all that's left is a wailing sound, and when I close my mouth it stops.

I slump down on the casket and look at Mother, who is sitting on the floor, staring first at Bael, face down, blood pooling among broken pottery, and then at me.

RIAN

AFTERMATH

Rian sat on the chest looking at the body. Soyea was crying beside her.

There were footsteps on the stairs. Fin took one step towards them, then stopped. He bowed his head and retreated.

Rian heard shouts and then Manigan was beside her. She did not know what he was saying.

Fin took Soyea to her cubby hole. She seemed pliant with him, sobbing, clinging onto his arm, babbling about the knife, the blood. 'Shh, shh,' he was saying as he led her away.

Rian allowed Manigan to persuade her to go down to the hearth. She turned her back on Bael and took the stairs slowly.

Once downstairs, Manigan said, 'Get that fire going. Heat some water.'

She reached for some kindling and began to do the one thing she could always do.

Manigan went back up and he and Fin carried the corpse down the stairs and laid it out under a sack. Then he went out. A while later he returned. He and Badger dragged Rona between them. Once inside the broch Manigan shut the door behind them.

Rona was tousled and furious. 'It's not fair. Mother, tell him.'

Rian got up and hugged her little daughter. 'I know it doesn't feel fair, little bird, but you're going to have to bear it. Just for a while. You'll get over him.'

Rona pushed Rian away. 'Get over him? I won't ever. Why can't you see that?'

Rian tried to hug her again but Rona kicked out, inconsolable. She seemed oblivious to the corpse. Rian returned to the hearth, and patted the stool next to her. 'Come and sit here, we'll talk about it.'

But Rona made a burst for the door and when Manigan caught her she tried to bite him. He picked her up like a child and carried her away upstairs. There was banging and shrieking for a while, then he reappeared and pulled up a stool beside the fire.

'I've shut her in one of the chambers. There's a bed in it. I don't know what else to do for now.'

'We can't just keep her locked up,' Rian said.

'She's still going on about running away to find Eadha. That's all we need. I'll let her out when she calms down.'

'Let me go and talk to her,' Rian said.

'Given the names she was calling you, I don't think there's any point.' Manigan shook his head.

Rian couldn't bear the idea of her daughter caged in a cell, but what could she do? The punishment for incest was unambiguous. She was just going to have to endure it.

Badger and Kino were standing just inside the door. 'Shall I go and find someone?' Badger asked. 'Who's the big man around here these days? Is it Alasdair?'

Rian registered that the question was directed at her, and nodded.

Manigan got to his feet. 'He's in another broch up the coast, we'll need to sail there. Do you know where it is, Badger?'

Badger scratched his head. 'It's up around the Rubha, I think. Culkein, isn't it? Or is it Drumbeg?'

'Rhu an Dunain.' Rian said. 'You'll be quicker walking. It's just up the hill and over across the other side of the peninsula.'

Badger nodded. 'I can go on my own. You'd better stay here, Manigan, with Rian and your daughters.'

They clarified the directions, and then Badger set off. Kino said he would go and see if he could find Eilidh and Tormaid in Achmelvich.

Fin remained, perched on a stool, his back to the wall. Manigan paced, then, hearing bangs from upstairs, went up to see what Rona was doing in her fury. Downstairs, the hush was intense. Rian could not look at Fin and sat poking the fire.

After a while Donnag came in, muddy with clay. She took one look at the body and put down her bag, then lifted a corner of the sack, saw who it was, and let it fall. Rian waited to see what she would do. She gazed at her and at Fin, then poured some hot water from the pot by the hearth into a bowl. Rian held her breath. It looked as if she would head up the stairs to wash without saying a word, but instead she turned to Rian. 'What happened?'

Rian couldn't hold the fierce gaze of the thin woman. Looking down at the fire, she wondered what to say.

Eventually Fin spoke. 'He tried to rape Soyea.' His voice reverberated into the pause.

Donnag's forehead crumpled with concern. 'How is she?'

'Distraught.'

'Did she kill him?'

'It looks that way.'

'Poor Soyea.'

Rian looked up at Donnag and saw that she was more saddened for Soyea than for the dead man on the floor, who she barely glimpsed at before slipping away upstairs with her bowl.

Rian put more water on to heat and fed the fire. Before long Buia came and looked and sat beside her, and Rian, in a soft voice, explained what had happened. Buia made little moaning sounds and shook her head, then went out to her hut, returning a little later with a basket of grey gull feathers. She lay them in a line, end to end, from Bael's throat, down his body, then across the floor of the broch and out of the door. Rian followed her, to see where she was taking the line.

Outside in the breeze, it was harder to make the feathers lie still, and Buia was painstakingly fastening each one down with a stone. Rian helped her by bringing her big pebbles. The strange grey river flowed right around the back of the broch, stopping when it reached the midden. Rian felt an involuntary shudder go through her at this channel of evil made manifest.

Her task completed, Buia took a deep breath and allowed Rian to lead her back inside.

Men's voices signalled the return of Badger with Alasdair, who took a long hard look under the sheet. As he stood up, Rian met his gaze.

'We just sailed in today. He was raping my daughter. I tried to pull him off and he got a knife out. You can blame me.'

'You don't need to take it on yourself,' Alasdair said. 'Nobody needs to hide anything.'

Manigan, who was standing in a shadow by the staircase, said, 'I don't think anyone's trying to hide anything. It was Soyea who stuck the blade in him. He was raping her. Rian caught him, heard the girl shouting up there, and in the tussle Soyea got his knife. I'd call it self-defence.' He took a step forward, his voice rising. 'That man Drost, Bael's father, sold Rian into slavery, and if you ask me he taught his son everything he knew about treating people like dirt.'

Alasdair faced him. 'You didn't like him, I take it?'

'No, I didn't like him. That's one way of putting it. Did you?'

'Sit down, man. Has anyone sent for Eilidh?'

'Yes. My brother went for her,' Badger said.

Manigan sat down. 'Did you like him or not?'

Alasdair didn't respond. 'When Eilidh gets here, we'll talk it through. Is there any ale in this house, do you know? We've had a bit of a walk.'

It wasn't long before Kino arrived with Eilidh who shook her head and sat by the hearth beside Buia. She held her hand and nodded as Rian gave her version of events.

'So there doesn't seem to be any dispute that your daughter is the murderer,' Alasdair said.

This brought Manigan to his feet, indignant. 'This doesn't count as murder.' He appealed to Eilidh. 'You know what healers the women are, they wouldn't hurt anyone. Young Soyea's been learning herbs from her mother all her life, and she had it from Danuta. They save lives, they don't take them. Alasdair. They're not murderers.'

'He's not alive any more though, is he?' Alasdair said. 'Someone killed him. Are you sure it wasn't yourself? You're a professional killer, I gather.'

'I'm the Walrus Mutterer. I hunt the Old Gentlemen of the Sea. I don't kill men, if that's what you're getting at.'

'Well I was only asking. When I first came in Rian was suggesting she had done it. I'm just trying to get clear what went on.'

Manigan sat down again and spoke as if to a boy. 'Rian even made out to me that it was her at first, she was wanting to shield her daughter, it's the mother's instinct. I guess she knows she'd have done it if the knife had been in her hand.'

Rian gave a little nod, feeling her face burn red with embarrassment at Manigan's angry outbursts.

'What exactly did you see?' Eilidh said to Manigan.

'Me? I just saw the man with his arse bare and a blade in his gullet, lying in a pool of blood and enough empty bottles to prove the man was a drunkard as well as a rapist.'

As if Eilidh could sense Rian's discomfort at his behaviour, she said, 'You don't need to be disrespectful, Manigan. Life is short, we all know it. Men die. Children die. It's what happens. But not like this. It's not the kind of thing you can easily accept. I think we should all calm down. It's a horrible thing but it's not going to be helped by insults and foul tempers.'

Eilidh and Alasdair left, saying they would go and tell other people in the village what had happened. For a while Rian tried to stick to doing practical things like cleaning up the blood.

At one point Soyea came out of her room. Fin seemed best able to calm her down, and persuaded her to wash and put on fresh clothes. Buia took her away upstairs and for a while there were sounds of chanting and a drum.

When it fell quiet, Buia appeared at the bottom of the stairs, red-eyed, carrying a small drum and beater. She stood by the body of Bael and banged wordlessly: a short, brittle repeated pattern of two single beats and a triplet, each phrase directed at a different part of the body, a spell against evil spirits. She worked her way slowly from the feet up to the head, then with a drum roll she stomped away out of the broch. Rian heard her bang away furiously outside the door and then grow fainter as she walked around the broch, presumably following the trail of feathers. Eventually the drumming stopped.

They covered the body with another layer of sailcloth, trying to limit the smell, then Rian set about clearing up all the empty bottles and flasks upstairs. Donnag emerged from her room and helped, and it was she who opened the big chest.

She stopped moving. 'What's all this, do you think?'

Rian came to look. Donnag propped the lid open. The chest was full of bronze: cups, plates and cooking implements, but also knives and an embossed shield. Most of it was intact, but there were also broken bits of riding equipment, handles, and scrap pieces no good to anyone. It was all mixed together, with no order.

'I wonder where it all came from?' Rian picked up a chain and ran it through her fingers.

Donnag pulled a knife with a long slim blade out of the tumble of metal, then laid it back on the surface. 'Why would you have things like this hidden away?'

Rian picked out a goblet. It had an elegant shape, curving in at the middle.

'That was my mother's.' Donnag reached for it and Rian handed it to her. 'It went missing. I remember her complaining about it.'

'Is it all stolen, do you think?'

Donnag turned the goblet in her hands like a sacred vessel, her bottom lip trembling. She said nothing.

Rian gently shut the lid of the chest. 'Perhaps we should show it all to Alasdair and Eilidh. See if other people recognise things in here too.'

They showed it to Alasdair when he passed by on his way home that evening, and he also recognised several pieces from his own home: two cups and a necklace. He suggested they bring it all into the light, and helped Fin, Badger and Manigan to carry the chest downstairs. They laid out all its contents. It glittered like guilty secrets beside the corpse.

Rian took herself to bed as soon as Alasdair had left. When Manigan made his way there later, she was lying awake, red-eyed, and fresh tears flowed as he hugged her. 'Murder and incest. My daughters. I can't bear it. What punishment is this?' She wept as if her heart would break.

He held her until the tears subsided. 'I don't know what you'll make of this, but I promised I'd tell you.'

'What?' She got up to find a cloth to blow her nose, then got into bed again.

'Well, I made some comment about Soyea – who would want her now, a woman who stabs a man in the throat and her not exactly a beauty,'

'You didn't. That's not fair.'

'It was just a joke, you know. We've had a few. You can smell the evil from the corpse. You have to drink to stand it. No body of an animal I've ever killed has stunk like that one. But the point is, Fin said, "I want her." I hadn't realised what a shine he's taken to her. When did that happen?'

'I saw them together the last time we were here.'

'Well, I never noticed. He says they love each other. And then he said, "Can I handfast with Soyea? Will you give us your blessing?"'

'Oh for goodness sake. This is hardly the time is it?' She sat up in bed, shaking her head. 'What's he doing here anyway? I don't trust him, he's got too much of Ussa about him.'

'Steady on. There's no need to get cross with Fin. He's trying to be helpful. Is it not Bael who deserves your anger?'

'Don't tell me what to feel.'

Manigan opened his mouth as if to speak, then shut it again.

Rian was kneading the blankets between her hands. 'You didn't agree he could have Soyea did you?'

'No. I told him I'm not her father and it's up to you. He looked disappointed.' Manigan took a breath. 'I offered to ask you for him. Apparently Soyea thinks you don't want her to be free.'

'I don't know what I want. I want none of this to have happened.'

'You know, he's grown on me. There's something about him makes me think he could be the Mutterer. I always thought I'd know the man by the way he hunted. But it's not that at all. I think I've found him by how he loves, not by how he kills. Perhaps that's just another kind of hunting.'

'Huh.'

'He has a grin that lad, it'd melt the heart of a polar bear. Do you know where he's sleeping?'

'No.'

'He's outside Soyea's cubby hole, at the top of the stairs, him and his monkey guarding her like a pair of dogs.'

STENCH

The next morning, no one said much, except for Buia who was chuntering incoherently, swaying on a stool, her eyes barely straying from the corpse. Earlier she had brought black dung beetles and dropped them on the body. Rian was becoming scared of her.

There was banging from above them. Rona was awake and clearly not happy to be locked up. Rian still didn't like the idea of her daughter being imprisoned but Manigan was probably right that it was the only way, for the time being, to stop her doing something stupid. It was an unbearable situation. She poked at the fire and prodded one of the oatcakes baking on the stone beside it.

Eventually, from her spot on the staircase, Donnag spoke up. 'We should fetch The Wren.'

As soon as she spoke, Rian knew it was right. They needed someone powerful to help them deal with this evil turn of events.

Donnag came down and faced Manigan across the hearth. 'Would the wind let a boat cross to the Long Island and back?'

He tilted his head in assent. 'It's a southerly. I reckon we could make it over by dusk. And after a southerly it'll usually go westerly later, so if that's not too soon, it might be possible.'

'And good for getting back,' Kino said.

Donnag stared, as if only registering his presence for the first time, and said to him. 'Who do you think might be willing to go?'

Manigan and Rian exchanged glances, and she knew he was thinking what she was; that if Ussa was intent on following Rian north from the Winged Isle then she might arrive at any time. A southerly wind was perfect for her.

'I'll do it,' Manigan said eventually. 'It'll be easier to cross over with *Bradan* than try to find someone else to make the trip. Alasdair'll look after everyone here.'

Rian knew he'd said that to try to reassure her.

'Are you up for it Badger?'

Not surprisingly Badger and Kino were both keen to get away from the stifling atmosphere of the broch. They set off almost immediately, taking Donnag with them, aiming to head straight back the next day if they could. Only Fin showed any reluctance, but he went too. At the last minute Manigan suggested they take Rona with them and Rian agreed. Rona made no sign of wanting to stay or go and mutely followed her father, perhaps on the basis that escape from the boat could be no harder than from the broch.

Rian watched *Bradan* shrink away over the horizon and dragged her feet back into the broch. The corpse stank.

Only she, Soyea and Buia remained. Buia had retreated to her hut and Soyea was sleeping in there with her. Since Fin had left, she was unwilling to enter the broch because of the corpse. Most of the time she would not, or could not, get out of bed, where she lay with her face to the wall.

So Rian was left alone to tend the fire. It was so quiet that even its crackle seemed to intrude on her thoughts. By evening, she was surprisingly drowsy. She couldn't bear to climb the staircase to the top floor where she and Manigan had put together a makeshift bed. Instead she slept a dark and dreamless sleep in Danuta's room.

It was already fully light by the time she woke and the first thing she was conscious of was the stink from the cadaver in the main room. Danuta's presence seemed to hover beside her as she brought the embers back to life and greeted the morning fire. Feeling sick, she began the process of making bread, setting the yeast stick in warmed water and measuring flour from the sack that had appeared down in the cellar since the last time she had been there, one of several signs that care had been taken and that life was being lived a little better in the broch. Until this cataclysm.

There was a cow now, she remembered. She had seen it the last time she had been here, when they had fired the kiln. Later she would go and find Buia and ask if she could milk it. But for now, she sat sifting the flour, her fingers idly loosening lumps and picking out stray pieces of chaff.

Footsteps alerted her to someone outside. The shadow of a person loomed in the entrance and Rian watched, as if from a great height, observing evil personified.

With a perfunctory knock on the open door, Ussa stepped into the building. The walk up from the shore had clearly been an exertion for her; her breath rasped, heaving in and out of her chest. Her face contorted into a grimace of disgust. 'What the hell is that stench?'

Rian felt only calm. Perhaps this was a new form of fear, or maybe she had no capacity left for negative emotion. Yet she tasted blood in her mouth as if someone had punched her. She had bitten her lip. She unclenched her jaw. 'Bael's corpse,' she murmured, watching as Ussa took in that she was alone.

'I've caught you in the cuckoo's nest, haven't I? Little bird.' She spoke the affectionate phrase with acid, but this reminder of Danuta only gave Rian strength.

She picked up her blow-tube and fed the fire with breath until the embers flamed, then laid three more sticks across them and sat back as they crackled. 'Take the weight off your feet, Ussa.' She pointed to a bench. 'Are you thirsty? Hungry?'

Ussa ignored Rian, her attention riveted on the dead body on the floor, the chain of feathers, the beetles crawling about. Then she switched her interest to the chest of bronze. She bent over it, picked up a necklace, fingered it, then let it drop.

She took a step towards Rian and thumped down onto the wooden seat. She had brought a new smell into the place, the stale sweat of a long journey.

'I met a boy at the shore. I hear your brat is the murderer.' Her breath still came in rasps.

'He was raping her. She defended herself.'

'So you've a lie in place already to cover it up. It won't work.

He had a lot of friends, me included. People much more powerful than slave scum and their bastard spawn. Which is, after all, all that you and she are. I'm not sure I still want her, by the way, now she has done this. I'd been thinking she was the one in the prophecy, but now that looks unlikely. But you're different. Our old score still needs to be settled.'

Rian poured the yeasty water into her bowl of flour and began mixing it with one hand. She was determined to show no fear, letting only a slight frown line her forehead. She wondered what sort of prophecy Ussa might mean but wasn't willing to flatter her with curiosity so merely said, 'I'm not a slave, Ussa.'

'You are mine.'

Ussa leaned forward on her seat, hands on knees like a man, in the wide-legged stance so familiar to Rian from all those years ago. Whatever it was that had frightened her about it was gone. Now it was just the ugly pose of an old woman.

'I'm not a possession.' Rian's hands kneaded rhythmically in the bowl. 'I'm a mother. But even my daughters don't possess me, just as I don't possess them, although I am theirs and they are mine. I am Manigan's also. If I belong to anyone, I belong to them. It's a belonging made of love, but maybe you don't understand that.' It felt like the longest speech she had ever made and part of her was amazed to see that Ussa seemed to be listening.

Words came out of the trader's mouth, but her eyes were uncertain as she said them. 'There's no such thing. Home, love, happiness, these are all lies we tell children. Did you never grow out of believing in them?'

Rian put the bowl down, pulled a board onto her lap, sprinkled flour on it then scooped up the dough and began to knead it with both hands, squeezing and stretching and rolling. 'Saying you can't see the yeast won't stop the bread from rising.'

'Don't try to be clever.'

'I'm just being me.'

There was silence as Rian pummelled the dough.

Ussa's eyes returned to the corpse. 'He was a real man.'

'He was a monster,' Rian said. 'He was a thief and respected no one. Have you seen what he stole?' She pointed at the pile of bronze beside the body.

Ussa scoffed. 'He just liked pretty things and he was clever at getting them.'

'Is that how you see yourself?'

Ussa lifted her chin as if trying to look coquettish. 'Possibly.'

'Why on earth are you still chasing me? Why can't you just give it up? A slave is just a slave, any old slave will do, I heard you say it so many times. So why me?'

Ussa shrieked with laughter. 'You'll never understand.'

Rian stretched out the dough and folded it in on itself. Then an idea struck her. 'Am I one of your debts?'

Ussa had been fixated on the Death Stone, despite claiming that every object was interchangeable for something else and nothing was sacred, not even people. But the stone had been different because she owed it to her father, Donnal Sevenheads, the son of a legendary warlord, the first Donnal Sevenheads, so called because he had murdered seven of his rivals for power and put their heads on stakes outside his house. Her father had a way of holding her to her promises. Theirs was no normal father-daughter relationship. It wasn't beyond the bounds of likelihood that Ussa's obsession with capturing her had something to do with all of this.

Ussa frowned, 'What do you know about my debts, you little witch?'

'Is it your father?' Rian pursued, and seeing an involuntary flinch in Ussa's face, she went on, 'Why are you frightened of him?'

Ussa's knees were together now and she was staring at Rian as if her words were hurting her. 'I'm not frightened of him.' But this was a different voice from before, more like that of a fearful child.

'Ach, be free of him, Ussa.'

'What do you know about it?' The big woman's mouth drooped. 'Are you on his side too?'

Rian stopped kneading the bread for a moment, made a guess and took the plunge. 'If you took me to him, he'd just tangle you up in something else. Better to accept that I'm free. And then you're free too.'

Ussa's mouth was slack with incomprehension.

'He must be ancient. When he dies, you'll be free. Why wait until then? The fear's in here.' Rian tapped her head. 'Just let it go.'

The child in the eyes before her stared as if she was offering something wonderful, but then snapped out of sight as men's voices and footsteps sounded outside.

Alasdair stomped in, followed by two men Rian recognised as Ussa's heavies. Her composure began to dissolve. Physical fear of the big men set her shoulders back. She tried to continue kneading as though she was calmer than she felt.

Buia sidled into the broch after the men. Seeing Ussa, she pointed at her. 'What's she doing in here?'

Alasdair faced Ussa. 'I met these guys at the shore, said you were here.'

'I'll not be long.' Ussa stood and smiled graciously at Alasdair. 'You two know what to do.' She waved towards Rian.

The two big men started for her, one around the left side of the central hearth, the other around the right side. The first took her by the arm. The kneading board started to topple. He grabbed it from her and dropped it on the floor. 'This way, then.' He pulled her to her feet.

The other man found his way blocked by Alasdair. 'What's going on?'

'Get off me.' Rian was trying to shake the man's hold from her upper arm.

'I'm just taking back what's mine,' Ussa said.

'What do you mean?'

'Her. She's my slave.' She pushed the second man towards

Rian, around Alasdair.

'She is one of us.' Alasdair stepped in front of the man.

'No. You only need to look at the brands on her arm.' She reached over and pulled down the top of Rian's dress to reveal her shoulder. 'There's the same on her thigh. You see? She's mine. I bought her from Drost years ago. I did him a favour.'

Rian pulled her dress back up with her free arm.

Ussa turned to Alasdair. 'I've been waiting a long time for her to move away from Ictis, away from the Keepers who have been harbouring her. But there's no asylum here, is there? I respect the rules on Ictis, I may not necessarily agree with them, but I'll abide by them while I'm there, but here? This is a free land, and I can take back what's mine, even if I did buy lamb and now all I'm getting is mutton.'

Rian writhed away from the man holding her. Jabbing him with her elbow and stepping forwards towards Ussa, she threw him off. 'You don't understand, do you?'

'What don't I understand, my cross little slave?' Ussa sounded confident but she took a step back as Rian approached, eyes blazing.

'I am a free woman and you could be too, any time you choose.'

Alasdair stood tall against the doorway and gave a grunt that sounded like solidarity.

Rian gave him a little nod to acknowledge his support.

'Well if someone's wanting to buy you back, that could possibly be arranged.' Ussa grimaced pointedly at Alasdair and gestured to the heap of bronze lying beside the body. 'Some of that will do as payment. After all, I bought her with bronze in this very room.'

Buia had been shuffling around the side of the room and suddenly she leapt at Ussa, tugging at the long gold chain around her neck.

'You're a crow. Mad bird. Bad bird.' Her voice was high, almost a shriek. 'Bad bird. Craw. Craw. Craw.' She was hopping like a great crow, foot to foot. 'Craw. Craw. Mad bird. Bad bird.' She flapped her arms like a bird landing. 'People say I'm mad but it's you that's crazy. They say I'm mad to gather up the good things our Mother makes – feathers, flowers, bones – but you, you gather only dead things – metal and polished stones. You're like a big bird. A big mad crow.'

Rian stepped aside in amazement.

Buia's words poured out, tumbling over each other. 'You come here looking for a slave but what are you? You're a slave. Look at your chains.' She tugged the necklace again. 'Slave to gold, slave to silver, slave to the shiny stones, slave to your own greed.' She poked her in the chest. 'Slave to yourself. Chain around your neck, brand on your face.' She poked again, this time at Ussa's eye patch.

Ussa staggered back, then tried to push Buia away, but she skipped out of reach. 'You've still got one eye, can't you see at all? Look at your hands. Look at your fat feet. Slave feet, bird in a cage feet.' She pretended to be a crow again. 'Craw. Craw. Craw.' She turned, lifted her elbows and hopped away out of the broch, head bent, arms flapping. 'Craw. Craw.'

Everyone, including Ussa, stared after her.

Ussa's two men were smirking at each other. She faced them, clicking her fingers. 'You take those grins off your faces.' She lowered herself down onto the bench with her back to the hearth, facing the corpse and the pile of bronze. 'I can wait,' she said, primly, although it was not at all clear what for.

'It's not looking to me as if you're welcome here, Ussa,' Alasdair said.

'This man was my friend.' She flicked her hand towards Bael.

Rian and Alasdair exchanged bemused glances. He gestured at the two men with a thumb, jabbed it towards the door, and they slouched out after a curt nod from Ussa, who clearly intended to stay exactly where she was.

Breathing out slowly, Rian looked at Ussa's back. Then she returned to her seat by the hearth and tried to dust the muck off the dough.

Alasdair pulled a stool across to the middle of the space between the door and the hearth and sat down. 'Is that bread you were making?'

She squashed the gritty dough. The floor was filthy. 'Yes,' she said, 'but it looks like it's ruined.' She nudged it into the fire and put some sticks over it.

She remembered what she had said before in response to Ussa's denial of love and home and happiness. She needed to believe in love. Perhaps that was what had always enabled her to rise above Ussa. And then there were those five words of Alasdair's: 'She is one of us.'

She looked at the big, kind man. 'I can start again,' she said.

She took the bowl of sourdough down from a shelf, and fetched some more grain, the knocking stick and quern from the cellar. While she thumped the barley in the knocking stone, beating out her fury at Ussa, her grief about her daughters, the smell of baking bread briefly overwhelmed the stench of the corpse, then the dough in the fire was just a charred lump. She emptied the husked grain into a bowl and for a while she hummed as the quern turned. Alasdair's head nodded. Ussa sat with her back to Rian, her head bowed, a hand over her face. Her only movement was the occasional twitch, the odd silent shudder.

When the new dough was kneaded Alasdair roused himself. 'Come on, let's go and get some fresh air.'

SOYEA

PROPHECY

I come into the broch with more trepidation than I've ever felt anywhere. The corpse on the floor, stinking, is enough to keep me outside and knowing Ussa is in there makes it feel like I am entering a viper's den or putting my hand into a hole in a tree trunk with hornets inside. But Buia drags me in, insistent that I must 'deal with the mad bird'. She shook me out of my bed saying it and when she had said, 'Please, please, Soyea,' for the twentieth time I relented. So I am here, feeling as if I'm wading through mud, my whole soul splattered by Bael's blood.

Buia grips me by the hand. 'Rian's away. Alasdair's gone,' she says. 'The mad bird will play. You have to stop her. Come on.' She tugs me over the threshold into the broch.

It takes a while for my eyes to adjust to the gloom. The fire's damped down. The only light is a little tallow lamp beside the corpse. Beside it, glittering, is the metal-dressed woman: bangles on arms and legs, necklaces, earrings, even the eye-patch is jewelled. She is like a trinket stand at a macabre fair, crouched beside the cadaver and his loot, draped in gold and silver. She must rattle where ever she walks.

She turns slowly towards us and I see her eyes are hungry. I thought I had destroyed myself by killing Bael, every vow I've taken for the Sisterhood and every fibre of my body despoiled, but in Ussa I see what being broken really looks like. Even I am not like this. I am whole compared to her. She is utterly riven. She must be starving to be healed.

'Big bird,' Buia whispers.

Ussa turns her gaze on Buia. She looks scared. How can anyone be frightened of poor old Buia? But I remember how, earlier in the year, her strangeness had alarmed me too. Now I just feel sorry for her when she's having a sad day and love her for her crazy wisdom.

I say, 'Shhh,' and Buia makes a growling sound.

'Let's light some lamps,' I say. I have an instinct that there's something I can do here. 'Let's make the shadows dance.'

Ussa is staring at me as I pick two lamps from the shelf and light them from the embers of the fire with a taper. It would be easier to use her lamp but my light won't work if it's contaminated by hers.

'You're a real pair of witches, aren't you?' I guess it's supposed to be sarcastic but there is something in the way she says it that confirms she is fearful that I may have power like Buia's.

'Don't be frightened,' I say. I pick up her fear like it is rope through a ring in a bull's nose and lead her with it. 'I think I can help you.' It's as if I'm tugging gently on the string. 'You can trust me.'

I sit down with my back to the wall so she has to turn away from the corpse to face me. Her face falls into shadow as she puts her back to her lamp. I move mine forward so now her jewels gleam with clean light.

'Tell me,' I say, amazed by how honey-smooth my voice is, 'what's the matter?'

It's obvious what the matter is: her friend is laid out before her with a stab wound in his throat that I made. No wonder she is frightened.

'Why are you still here?' I ask. If I were in her position the last thing I would be doing is lingering with the corpse. Yet she is here in vigil, allowing its stench to penetrate her.

She half turns back to the body and then looks back to me and I am amazed to see tears in her eyes. What's more unlikely, that anyone would love Bael or that this woman cares enough about anyone to cry? So I understand that these tears are for herself. Nonetheless they are a way into her. The rest will be easy.

I reach for a cloth, kneel forwards towards her, touch her gently on her forearm and offer the rag. 'Are you crying for him?'

She looks startled, as if I've pricked her with something sharp, but all she manages to say, through her weeping, is a strangled, 'No.'

She blows her nose noisily and Buia makes a little bird squawk in reply. She is plucking mint leaves off a dried bunch into a bowl. I catch their scent, a waft of freshness.

Ussa snuffles again and this time Buia emits a loud crow's croak in response. It is enough to flick Ussa into anger. She pokes a finger out towards me, her voice tart. 'I know who you are, you know. You're the Greek's child. And this is your handiwork.' Her finger wavers towards Bael's body. 'Killing even without the Stone.'

'What do you mean, even without the Stone?'

'The Stone of Telling. Until this I thought you were the one in the prophecy but you can't be, can you?'

'I don't know. Tell me.'

Ussa blows her nose again and wipes her face. Her voice is broken but it strengthens as she gets into the telling of the tale.

'The stone has three faces and all made prophecies. The first is the Sage, and it prophesied that the first man who owned it would kill his son, and he did. The second is the Master, who said all the owners would kill and go on killing and we all have. The third is the Boy and he said...' Her voice changes to a squeaky sing-song, mocking a child's, '"My Master is wicked and I am only a little child. I can't undo his curse, but I can promise you this. We will

205

cease to do this evil when we are in the hands of the first free child of three generations of slaves."'

She grabs me by the wrist. '"A slave woman and a high-born free man, then a slave man and a high-born free woman, then a slave girl and a stranger."' Her voice reverts to her own. 'Your mother was the girl, your father the stranger. Uill Tabar told me Rian had a slave for a father whose mother was a slave as well and both bred with chieftain families. We should have had you strangled at birth. It's a good job the stone is with someone else who likes pretty things, and who doesn't know its worth.'

'Who's that?' I ask, interested to see where she thinks it is but shuddering inside at the implication of what she has just told me.

'Fin has it now. He's a sweet boy and it'll make a hunter of him. Now he's got a taste for blood, he'll make sure it's safe from the likes of you.'

'Thank you.' I loosen Ussa's hand from my wrist and get to my feet. I'm reeling. Was it the stone that made me kill Bael? Almost as an afterthought I say, 'Why were you crying?'

Ussa just shakes her head. It's as if her angry outburst has exhausted her ability to speak. Then, in a tiny voice, she says, 'Because what Buia said was right. I'm the slave. Rian's the one who's free. Nobody understands how horrible he was to me.'

This is what it is all about. 'Who?' I say, in my softest voice, crouching back down again.

'Sevenheads. Him. My so-called father.' And then she is crying again, a bitter weeping, and in amongst the tears words pour from her and all I have to do is sit and listen.

'Rian asked me if I've ever been happy. How can I answer that? I have always scorned those ideas: happiness, love, home. They are all things for children to dream about, no more real than the gods your fool father Pytheas made libations to. Imagine a god that appreciates you pouring good wine into the sea? It's almost as stupid an idea as his navigation by shadows. Yet he believed in them. I'm coming to envy the people who have the certainty of their convictions. I have nothing.

'Buia is right. My true north has been gold and it has not satisfied me. She's not the first to call me greedy and I've never cared. Greedy is just what poor people call rich people.

'But Rian was the first to call me a slave. How did she work out that my relationship with Sevenheads is no different from how I wanted her to behave with me? And that he succeeded where I failed? I should be able to overpower her with my mind so she feels like my slave, but I can't. I don't understand it. She resists. No, it's more than that. She makes me cease to believe it myself, that's the uncanny thing. She has overpowered *my* mind, made me question fundamental things. Just like he did. I don't know how.

'Is this why I was chasing her all along? So she could show me how not to be a slave? She never saw herself as belonging to anyone else. She never behaved like a slave. Whatever fear she may have felt, that's not real slavery. As long as she felt fear that still meant she had something to lose. Slavery is when you feel safe and know your role and go along with it, no matter how awful it is.

'But even when I had her bound and gagged I could see in her eyes she hadn't lost her freedom, that there was no possibility at all of me breaking her. And I suppose something had to break.'

She clutches her hands together and twists her face into a knot, taking a huge breath and letting it out. She looks into my face, as if searching for something. 'I've played the role of Ussa for a long time. A big, brave, fierce woman. And I want to be free now, not trapped by all my history.' Her voice becomes a whine. 'I've been so lonely. Nobody understands me. That boy Fin, he's come close but even he doesn't know a fraction of it. The nights of horror, remembering.' She peters out but I sit quietly. I don't think she has finished.

When she speaks again her voice is croaky. 'It's not natural for a father to use their child as bait for other children, to lure them in so he can torture them, is it?'

I shake my head, trying to keep any look of judgement from my face and then she rants about her father, a string of abuses that are so foul I don't ever want to think of them again. When she starts on what her grandmother used to do I am speechless with disgust. She has every reason to feel sorry for herself. It is all I can do to keep my expression neutral.

When she pauses, I say, 'And now?'

'Now I give up. I'll send my boat away. I don't care. I'm not doing it anymore.'

I let her words sink into the floor, then say, 'Good.' I hope I say it with conviction. With finality. Something needs to happen now to help Ussa keep this window inside herself open.

There's a sound of trickling and both Ussa and I look round to see Buia pouring water from a height into the bowl of mint leaves. I realise she must have had a pot warming in the embers. The mint-steam rises, scenting, and Buia carries it over ceremoniously and puts it down in front of Ussa. She makes another bird noise but this is gentle, a raven's 'croo', an offering.

I catch Buia's eye and she winks.

'Splash your face, Ussa,' I say in a voice for a child.

She reaches meekly for the bowl. Buia and I make eye contact again. I stand up as if trying not to wake a sleeping baby and we back out of the broch.

Our work in there is done.

Outside the evening is grey and blustery and Mother is walking with Alasdair back from wherever they have been. At the sight of her I feel myself going weak. All that self-control in there with Ussa, I don't know where it came from and now it evaporates. Great shuddering gasps of tears engulf me as the horror of it all sinks in: the corpse, my victim; the slaver-woman's gruesome past; the madness and cruelty we are all steeped in; this endlessly repeating cycle of killing; and at its heart, the stone going round and round, wreaking its damage. So when Mother reaches the broch I just want to hug her and bury my face in her skirt like a little girl and listen to the crooning of her strange songs. I need her to tell me everything will be all right even though I know inside it cannot possibly be true.

RIAN

STONE

Rian hadn't held Soyea like that since she was a little girl. Buia led them into her hut and then retreated. Soyea curled up on the nest of fleeces and Rian sat by her, stroking her hair, murmering, explaining how sorry she was for not understanding how difficult it was for Soyea, apologising for running away with Manigan, saying how unsettled she had felt being back in this place after so much time.

After Soyea's tears eased she told Rian what had happened with Ussa. 'Do you know about the third prophecy of the Stone?' she asked.

Rian shook her head and Soyea repeated what Ussa had said.

'So am I the one who has to stop the stone from doing evil?' Soyea held her head in both hands. 'How am I supposed to do that?'

'Forget the stone,' said Rian. 'I'm so tired of our lives being dominated by that thing.'

'What if I can't just forget about it?' Soyea said.

'I don't know. Just ignore it. Fin has it now. Let him keep it. It's his problem now.'

There was an awkward silence, then Soyea said, 'Perhaps sometimes things can be safer if they are out in the open, not hidden away, not secret.'

—

Rian nodded. Her life seemed to be a long struggle to unlock the secrets about herself.

'It's like you not knowing who you really are. It has eaten you away for years.'

'I know. I'm sorry, Soyea. I try to be calm on the surface.'

'What Danuta said about being stone makes sense, doesn't it?'

'Do I seem like a stone?'

'We're both stones. It's all right.'

'I'm not unfeeling really.'

'I know. Manigan is water. Rona too. But we're stone.'

'And fire, sometimes.' She stroked Soyea's forehead. 'The odd blaze of passion.'

Soyea winced and frowned. 'He was...'

Rian shushed her. 'You don't need to explain, or go back over it, little bird. What happened was coming. I'll defend your right to protect yourself to the end of my life. Now you try to get some sleep, little bird. Who knows what tomorrow will bring.'

'Will you sing me a song?'

Rian smiled. She hadn't known how much she loved her daughters until the clouds of shame had gathered. They could call it murder. They could talk of incest. But no wrong could stop her instinct to protect her children.

She thought for a while, but the only tune that presented itself was the old one she had learned from Toma in the northern ocean, the song of freedom. She sang it softly, her fingers becoming lighter and lighter on Soyea's head, until she saw the girl's eyelids flicker and her breath settle into the rhythm of sleep. She sat for a while, then crept away to her own bed in the broch, tiptoeing past Ussa, who was slumped, sleeping, in the corner, and Alasdair, nodding by the fire.

Next morning, Rian looked up from chopping vegetables and shredding fish into a big pot to see Soyea standing at the door. 'Hello Mother, Alasdair.' Her voice was monotone, her face white.

Alasdair muttered a greeting.

For a while, Soyea stared at Ussa, who was sitting beside Bael's corpse, with her head bowed, twitching. Soyea raised her eyebrows, then made to leave again. Just before slipping out of the doorway, she turned to Rian. 'There's a boat coming.'

Rian jumped to her feet and followed her out.

The broch was soon full of people. Ussa moved to a stool in the corner where she sat silently and after a brief period of embarrassment everyone began to ignore her. Manigan, Rona, Donnag and the *Bradan* crew had returned with The Wren. Soon, they were all handing round the bread and soup, devouring in minutes what had slowly emerged during the previous day.

Rona, calm and composed, accepted a bowl and took it away to her room. Seeing Rian's amazement, Manigan said, 'The Wren has performed a miracle.'

The diminutive priestess smiled. 'I just listened to her and told her that if her love is true, her destiny will out. We talked about dignity and choice. I suggested she save her effort for asking the spirits to help her. She's a sweet girl. She took it on board.'

'Well, I can't thank you enough,' said Rian, realising that what she had taken for a sulk was perhaps how she herself had always tried to act as a slave, holding her feelings in and presenting an outward air of indifference and poise.

After Rian had eaten, she noticed Soyea loitering in the doorway clutching something wrapped in filthy cloth to her belly. She was trembling and pale. Fin was behind her, the monkey on a string. Rian had not noticed them slip away. Something about the way they were standing gradually attracted everyone's eyes to them, even Ussa's.

Manigan was the first to take it in. 'Is that the Stone? What on earth are you doing with it?' He was on his feet, looking scared.

'Fin gave it to me.' She took the stone out of its bag. 'I think it wants to be with the corpse.'

'What makes you think that?' asked Manigan.

'The Master told me in a dream.'

'Explain.'

'He told me he wanted Bael. That he was his responsibility.'

'His responsibility?'

'Exactly those words. And that he wanted to look at what he had done. Now I've heard the prophecy, I have to do something with the stone but I don't know what.' She was holding the stone in both hands, in front of her, as if it was an offering. Her eyes were red-rimmed, beseeching Manigan, all of them, to help her.

Manigan looked at The Wren, and then at Rian, and then back to Soyea. He plonked himself down. 'Do what the Master says. Don't mess with him, that was always my rule. You don't want to be on the wrong side of him.'

The Wren nodded agreement.

Soyea put the stone on the chest of the man and pulled down the sheet. She was trembling. Everyone peered. The corpse was white and gruesome. Soyea turned the stone around so all three faces saw what there was to see in turn, then covered up the cadaver again.

There were sighs and murmurs.

Soyea backed away to the wall, Fin beside her, not touching her. They were both staring at the corpse.

Drinks were refilled and an attempt made at normal conversation, something about that day's crossing from the Long Island.

Then Alasdair said, 'Is it just me or is that disgusting smell fading? It was minging beforehand, really, wasn't it?'

'Aye.' Badger nodded agreement. 'Now it's just like a dead body, before it was pure evil.'

Manigan was gazing at the stone. 'You know, I swear the expression on the faces has changed. Honestly, I spent years with it, and they've changed.' He got up and looked more closely, then started pointing. 'The Boy, see, he used to be innocent-looking and now he's got that shocked expression. The Sage, that's this old fellow, he used to be just peaceful, but now look how sad and sorry-looking he's become. And the Master's the one with the smile now. If that's not a look of satisfaction, what is? I always used to say he had greed in his eye, but it's gone. It's like he has done what he's been wanting to do.'

As he spoke, Soyea began crying. At first a gentle weeping, then she collapsed into a storm of tears. Rian and Fin helped her away up to her room between the walls.

When Rian returned downstairs they were discussing what to do with the corpse. 'You're the headman here,' Manigan said to Alasdair. 'Surely it's up to you or Eilidh.' He gestured to the old woman from Achmelvich, 'One of you elders needs to decide what happens. All I know is I want to put that body in a fire or a hole in the ground, or chuck it in the sea, preferably before the day is out.'

Fin volunteered to do some digging. Badger and Kino too. Even Donnag.

The Wren got slowly to her feet and everyone fell silent. She had a piping, strangely musical voice. 'We need a ceremony to cleanse us of all this grief and evil and confusion.' Then she sat down again.

Everyone was quiet.

Rian became aware of Ussa, still staring at the stone, transfixed. She had nodded at what Manigan said earlier about its faces changing, but had otherwise been motionless, as if she herself had turned to stone. With a shudder, she prised herself up from her stool like an old woman and after one long look at the stone she shuffled out of the broch door, without a word to anyone.

Alasdair said. 'How about a fire on the split rock? There's not been one since I was a boy.'

TELLING

The next morning, breakfast was being taken in dribs and drabs. Rian sat by the fire, doling out porridge as people got up. Fin, who had gone out early with his monkey, burst in and announced that the boat *Sgiannach* was coming into the bay.

Manigan, Badger and Kino headed out to see, and before long, there were more voices, including Eadha's, distinctly saying, 'Where is she? Can I see her?'

Rona must have been able to hear him from upstairs, because she began calling out, 'I'm here. I'm here.'

Rian got up from the hearth and shut the door at the bottom of the staircase with a bang, then returned to her stool. The Wren, who was sitting close by, raised her eyebrows at Donnag, but said nothing. Fin joined Soyea in a shadowy corner, on a deerskin on the floor.

Manigan came in first, leading a big, rumbling-voiced seaman who introduced himself as Aonghas, an old friend of Cuilc. A youth shadowed him in. 'And this is Mac,' Aonghas said. Behind him was Eadha, looking about with darting eyes, and then an elegant, dark haired woman.

Rian got up again. She recognised them all from the handfasting, including Ishbel, who had led the ceremony then with grace and style, but who now seemed shifty and on edge.

Rian showed Aonghas to a bench by the wall, the boy to a mat close by, and nodded to the priestess, indicating a seat near the fire. She studiously ignored Eadha, who remained standing, placing himself between Ishbel and the door, like a guard.

The staircase door opened a crack, and then a bit more, and then Rona was flying into the room, charging across towards the entrance. Badger caught her as she passed but she wrenched her wrist free of his hand. Then Kino got her by one ankle, and as she toppled, Manigan grabbed her around the waist. She kicked and bit and wriggled, but he got his other hand on the scruff of her neck.

'Get yourself back up there.' Manigan pushed her towards the stairs.

'Let her stay.' It was Ishbel's voice, like two stones hitting together. 'She needs to hear what I have to say. It affects her most of all.'

Manigan stopped pushing, but didn't take his arm from around Rona's waist, or off the scruff of her neck, so she continued struggling. She was half choked by him with her wriggling, but it was to no avail. He turned her so she could see some of the room, and looked over at Rian with exasperation on his face. Rian rolled her eyes in response and raised her hands. What could they do?

Rian watched the new arrivals. Eadha's eyes were pinned on Rona, a look of pleading and encouragement in them. He didn't look as worried as Rian expected. Rona had stopped straining so hard against her father's hold. Ishbel's watchful gaze tracked between the two youngsters.

Rian offered drinks all round and soon everyone had a cup in their hand. Rian looked to The Wren to make a blessing, but she deferred to Ishbel, who in turn insisted that The Wren should thank the Goddess. After all this politeness everyone was grateful simply to drink.

Rian sat down next to Ishbel on a low bench. She urged Soyea and Fin to come closer to the fire but they indicated that they were fine where they were, against the wall. Buia was also on the floor in the corner by the cellar, Donnag fiddling with clay beside her.

Ishbel shuffled along and patted the seat beside her. 'There is room for Rona on this bench,' she said. 'Beside her mother.'

As Manigan let her go she almost fell forwards. She squeezed in between Rian and Ishbel, seeming awed by everyone watching her. Soyea gave a concerned lift of her eyebrows, as if to ask if she was all right. In response Rona put on a brave smile and raised her chin.

Once Manigan had sat down beside Badger, Rian said, 'So, Ishbel, what is it that you have to say?'

But before she could begin there was another man's voice, and Alasdair bowed through the doorway. Manigan stood up and offered his seat.

'Alasdair, welcome,' said Rian. 'We've more guests as you see. Aonghas from Rum and Ishbel from the Winged Isle, and they bring news, apparently, so you may as well join us to hear it.'

Alasdair sat down and Manigan joined Eadha in the shadows by the door. All eyes once again returned to Ishbel.

Rian gestured with an open palm. 'So, Ishbel.'

With the crowd's attention on her, her words at first came in no more than a whisper. 'I've little to say,' she began. 'But before I say it, I want to ask forgiveness...'

'Speak up,' said Alasdair. 'What are you asking?'

'Forgiveness,' she said, more clearly.

'Ach, we'll decide if you need that.' He laughed, and Badger and Kino chuckled too. Rian frowned at them.

'Don't be frightened,' The Wren piped up. 'We all want to hear your story.'

Ishbel took a breath. 'I'll get straight to the point. As some of you have discovered, Rona's mother-in-law Cuilc was Rian's mother.'

She paused, as if to allow this fact to hit home to anyone who had not heard the rumour. But of course everyone had.

Rian's heart sank into her belly. She felt utterly sick. Rona's head slumped forward onto her chest. Ishbel put a hand lightly on her thigh.

'We buried her, Eadha and I, before we set out here. She wore this all of her life.' She held up a bracelet, a mixture of leather and silver and an orange-coloured stone, then offered it to Rian. 'I think you should have it.'

Rian held it between thumb and forefinger as if it might be dangerous. The stone in it was unmistakably amber.

Ishbel didn't wait for her to speak. 'Some of you have, quite rightly, been worrying that Rona here and Eadha are too closely related for bearing children. But I can set your minds at rest.'

Rian glanced up from the bracelet to Ishbel. Her heart was pounding.

'Rian was not her only secret. Eadha was the other one. I must now make public what I have already confessed to him. Although Cuilc loved him dearly, she was not Eadha's mother.'

She paused again, but only for a moment, then pointed her finger at her heart. 'I am.'

Rian looked across to Eadha. There was, now she looked, a resemblance between them. Their big-boned faces and sharp chins were similar in shape.

Rian reached for Rona's hand as Ishbel continued talking.

'His father was Callum, Cuilc's husband's little brother. So Eadha is Luachair's nephew, so he still has the bloodline to lead the Clan of the Winged Isle. But he's not your brother, Rian. He's not even remotely related to you.'

Rian let the bracelet fall into her lap and clutched Rona's hand. She turned and saw relief flooding her daughter's face.

Ishbel went on. 'The union of these two youngsters is still perfect, and their child, although not Cuilc's grandchild, would still be her great grandchild through Rian's line. So they still unite the two clans.'

Rona switched her gaze to Eadha. He stepped forward to take her other hand, standing behind her and Ishbel. 'I'm very pleased not to be your uncle.'

'How do we know this is true?' Rian said.

Ishbel nodded. 'I don't know how to persuade you other than by telling the truth. I loved Callum, we were crazy for each other. But he drowned three months before I came to term. I was carrying the baby in secret, because we weren't handfasted. I wasn't what the family expected in the way of a wife – Luachair wanted his little brother to make a good political marriage.

'When Callum drowned, I was mad with grief and Cuilc found out. I agreed to give Eadha to her, for she was desperate for a child and Luachair had been threatening to throw her out for barrenness. She pretended to be in the last stages of pregnancy for those three months and I hid away. Perhaps, after she had you, the guilt of it meant she couldn't bear another baby. Maybe it was Luachair that was the problem. Anyway, I was so young. I didn't want the responsibility of a child, or so I thought, and although I've loved the boy and tried to do what I could to help him growing up, I've kept the secret until now.'

'So there is no incest?' Manigan said.

'No. The man he thought was his father was actually his uncle, so that line of the family still runs through him. But he has no blood link to Cuilc at all.'

'Thank goodness.' Rian buried her face in her hands and gave a huge sigh, then took Rona's hand again.

There were more questions, but Rian no longer cared. It was enough to look at Ishbel and Eadha and know that they were mother and son.

Everyone was talking at once and Rona was beside herself, clambering off the bench into Eadha's embrace, babbling. 'I knew it, I knew all along. I want to shout, I want to dance!'

The Wren stood and somehow the babble of side-chat stopped. She was tiny, and it was not clear what this little old woman did to gather the attention of everyone in the room, but she managed it.

'Alasdair should speak,' she said.

Everyone looked to the big man.

He bowed to The Wren, then stood with his hands on his hips. 'I'm not sure what the significance of all this is, but if you've finished deciding whose mother is whose, I'd like to suggest we go back to the business of Bael.' Heads nodded, and so he continued. 'I've spoken with Eilidh and the village folk, and I've sent word to my brothers and I expect they'll be here soon. It seems to me – and everyone else seems to be in agreement – that we need a ceremony to move on from all the strife in this house and to settle the area generally. We should do it on the split rock.' He seemed to be addressing himself primarily to The Wren.

She nodded. 'Give the body to the air and the ill-gotten gains to the water.'

'You mean burn him?' asked Manigan.

'Aye.'

'And his hoard?'

'Dump it in the sea,' said Alasdair.

'Offer it to the ocean as propitiation,' The Wren corrected him. She pointed to Ishbel. 'You may not be aware, Alasdair, that Ishbel is the Priestess of Brigid's Cave.'

Alasdair gave a bow. 'I was not. You're most welcome.'

The Wren went on. 'There is no one who understands the spirits of the edges as well as she does – the edge of land and sea, the boundary between life and death. Will you help us with the ceremony?'

Ishbel nodded. 'I can guide people along and across the borderlands. But this is your place. You should lead, together with Alasdair, as chief. The spirits will only listen if it is the people of this land who are asking them for help. But I can play the lyre. The spirits of the shore and of the borders to the other worlds will recognise my tunes. I hope we can include Cuilc in the ceremony in some form, as her spirit also needs to be guarded in her passage west. Eadha and I brought some tokens of hers, which I would ask to be built into the pyre. And those two should dance, I suggest.' She pointed to Eadha and Rona.

Everyone looked at them as she explained that they had been preparing for months. 'They have an energy when they dance that will open a channel between the worlds. It will please the spirits.'

Soyea got to her feet. 'Perhaps we can also remember Danuta,' she blurted, then sat down again.

'Yes, please let's,' Rian said.

Alasdair nodded. 'That's decided then.'

Rian turned to Rona and for the first time in what felt like an age, she was able to let a hint of approval come into her stony face.

More drinks were offered and a hubbub of conversation swelled as everyone took in what they had heard.

Rian was reeling from what Ishbel had told them. She swayed on her seat and looked at Manigan across the room, focusing her gaze on the fixed point of his eyes. Nothing else in the room could be trusted. The spectre of incest had evaporated, the threat of Bael's violence was gone, but the horror of it all still hung around her like a fog of midges, threatening to suffocate her, tormenting her. There were hidden dangers, invisible again, and change was everywhere.

All the other people were stirring, talking, shuffling and preparing to go on with whatever was next. But Rian felt unbalanced.

Rona beside her was being absorbed into the body of the man who had been, briefly, and would perhaps always be, tainted by a curse: the brother who wasn't her brother after all. Rian was still awash with confusion at their mothering; the deceit of his, the lack of hers. It was an ambiguity that could take a lifetime to adjust to, and her favourite daughter, until so recently her child, was stained by that confusion.

Meanwhile, Soyea was unrecognisable; a tall priestess who could stab a man to death.

Rian had gained and lost a mother and in some way both daughters had separated from her in the process. She was alone but for Manigan.

All she needed now was for her tormentor, Ussa, to walk into this daze, to swoop once more into her world; for her shadow to fall again across the doorway, and for her to stand with golden talons, preparing to devour her. But she did not. Instead, Manigan made his way through the hubbub, and held her upright, when she no longer had the strength to stand.

RONA

PREPARE TO DANCE

We'll dance tonight. What could be more exciting?

Eadha, Ishbel and I walk up to the rock where the ceremony will be held. Ishbel is in front, with Eadha and I holding hands behind. We have to cross the beach to get there.

I've not been practicing so I'm nervous. 'I dread to think what condition I am in,' I say.

Ishbel stops. 'It'll be fine. Remember no one here knows the detail of the steps. No one will notice if you improvise a little. Only the spirits will see and if your soul is pure and the energy is strong, they will bless you for the personal touch you bring to it.'

'But what if I'm not strong enough?'

'You are strong enough. Anyway, this place will give you all the strength you need.'

We stand, watching the waves roll in across the smooth blond sand, paler than Eadha's hair. They foam, then slide back out again.

'Perhaps our separation was destined to bring us together just for this.' He squeezes my hand. I think of what the Wren said about trusting destiny, and squeeze back.

'The Great Mother has done stranger things,' Ishbel remarks.

Hearing her invoke The Mother makes me remember she and

Eadha are now mother and son. I can't see any change in how they are together. Of course, it is not news to her. I suppose she has always been motherly towards him, if a rather strict parent. She is a magnificent person to have as my mother-in-law.

I am determined to make tonight's dance as good as it can be, but I'm conscious of having only this dress, and nothing to change into. How can we possibly do justice to it in these rags? 'It's a shame we've no costumes,' I say. It can never be the same without the dancing clothes.

'I brought the gear,' Eadha says.

I look at him and he's grinning.

'How did you know we would dance?'

'I didn't know. I just hoped. I thought we might at least get to practise.' He looks a bit sheepish. 'They're all I have of yours.'

I love how proud he is when he realises I am delighted. I feel as though I may actually jump for joy.

A wave foams up the beach and he pulls us back. We stagger about, giggling. He hates the sea and I torture him by making sure we walk as close to the margin of the waves as I can drag him, so we have to run back when the big waves come. We're shouting and screaming with laughter. Ishbel has marched on ahead of us, over the stream, up the bank on the far side of the beach.

'Come on,' Eadha says. 'We don't want to annoy her.'

He's right, of course. We run to catch her up and we're breathless with the steep climb.

'Get used to panting,' she says as we reach her. She doesn't look at all put out by our playfulness.

Soon we're pacing out the space we'll use for the dance, working out where we'll stand, how we'll bring people in and how big a ring we can make. If everyone wants to join at once, it'll be chaos.

This is the most incredible place, a rocky promontory with sheer cliffs down to the sea below. Beyond it there's a gap, then another chunk of rock that looks as if it has been sliced off into the sea. It is all made of huge slabs that lie at an angle, so we'll be dancing on a slope. I'm a bit daunted; the dance is hard enough without adding uphill to some of it. We practice the moves that will be challenging. At least it's grassy, but we'll have to be careful nobody stumbles over the edge.

On the way back to the broch we pass a bunch of men hauling wood, presumably for the fire. Father is among them, and Fin, the ghost, who gives me a shy grin. When he smiles he's not so spooky, but I can't see what Soyea sees in him. He's as gangly as a daddy longlegs.

Eadha only forgot one arm strap of my costume, but now I have the bracelet with the silver-clasped orange-coloured gemstone. It used to be Cuilc's, then Ishbel gave it to Mother, who has given it to me. She says it is amber. Soyea declares it has magic in it that is right for the night. She is one of the Sisterhood now, so she should know. I am just pleased to wear it for its beauty.

Soyea dresses in her priestess robe with a white band around her hair, and for the first time ever I can honestly say she looks beautiful.

There is a debate about how to get The Wren to the ceremony. She is so frail. But she is adamant she doesn't want to slow the procession. Soyea says she will help her, will carry her there on her back if necessary! The other women pay heed to what she says. I'm proud to be her sister. I don't think I've ever felt that before. Eventually the decision is made that all the women will go first and all the men will come in procession with the body later. Eadha is asked to play a drum for the men, so I must leave him behind. It is almost painful to let go of his hand.

'Think how good the dance will be after all this separation,' he whispers. 'And afterwards I will never let you go again.' He touches me so delicately, a feather-light stroke across the back of my neck. His thumb brushes my chin as he lifts my lips up to kiss them so gently I could melt. I swear no woman has ever burned for a man the way I do for him.

So, we women all trudge along, trying to keep the pace slow enough so the old ones don't feel bad, until The Wren tells us to get up there and make sure the fire is ready to light. Mother hurries ahead. That's her role, of course. That and cooking. She and Soyea have left plenty of food for when people return to the broch later.

I scamper up with Mother and pace about at the top, double-checking how much space we will need.

It's so slow to get dark at this time of year. The sun has sunk down into a layer of cloud to the west, which is still glowing rich pink, almost foxglove. The air is mauve and the rocks have taken on a red, blushing glow. You can tell magic will happen tonight. The sky spirits have dressed the world specially for it.

Mother has a small fire burning. There's a gorgeous smell of heather smoke.

Donnag has been making torches. They smell of resin and look impressive; stout sticks with a clay bowl on top. I don't know how she carried them up here, she is so skinny, but they arrived somehow and are in a neat stack. As other women start arriving, I find myself handing out the torches and placing people in a ring, leaving space for the dance and pointing out the sheer edge down to the sea. There are dozens of people, women and children mostly, I don't know where they have come from, and they are all very co-operative. There is a tangible atmosphere of excitement. Everyone knows there is going to be a spectacle.

The three priestesses are last. Soyea and Ishbel have brought stools for the older women. I place them where they'll have a good view.

The Wren refuses to sit and asks for a torch. Of course. She will light the pyre. It may be her last ceremony, by the look of her.

When we can see the men's procession, Mother starts lining up the torches.

I kept one back for Soyea, but she shakes her head. She has that wretched stone head clutched to her chest in its filthy bag.

She and Father had an argument about it earlier. He wanted her to leave it with the body, but she insisted she was going to carry it. He kept saying it had a hold on her, and it was using its power to make her its greedy keeper and enslave her. He was really horrible about it.

But she was adamant that she knows what she's doing. She has a plan, she says, and the Master might not like it, but he will have to put up with it. 'The Sage and Boy are stronger together than he is,' she kept saying. 'His time is over. Trust me.' Father doesn't trust her with anything. Eventually Mother intervened and told him to let her do what she wanted. 'She's the keeper of it now, Manigan. You have to let it go. Please?' It was the way she said that 'Please' that did it, as if she were asking him the biggest favour possible. You could see him struggle, as if he were having to let go of something more precious than life. The stone has a bigger hold on him than on anyone, I think.

When she pulls the stone out of its bag, it has a cloth wrapped around it, like a blindfold.

I hand an unlit torch to Ishbel and she steps forward to the fire to light it. The local wise woman, Eilidh, also has one, and three other local women whose names I don't know. As the torches are lit, the sky seems to become darker, as if it is preparing for the ceremony too.

Then the men arrive. Alasdair, along with an even bigger but younger man who looks just like him, is at the front end of the stretcher, carrying the body. Two others are at the back. These must be the brothers I've heard Soyea talk about. Indeed, you would not want to get on the wrong side of them. They take great care down the stone slope to the grass platform where we're waiting, and then heave the body up onto the rock. Alasdair and one of the brothers climb up first, then the other two lift up the corpse while the upper two pull from above. They eventually get the body up onto the pyre, with a bit of difficulty it has to be said. It's such a precarious place.

While they're struggling, Eadha slips to my side. As he takes my hand it is like the keystone slips into place in some inner wall. I didn't realise until then how nervous I've been feeling. But with him here, I am suddenly strong. We are going to be magnificent.

THE PYRE

And we are magnificent.

But not before the Wren has spoken and some of the men have been given torches. And not until Soyea has done her strange and mystifying performance with the stone.

She makes Father remove one cloth to reveal the Master's face. Then ghostly Fin pulls the second off the Boy's face. Finally, she takes the last bit and walks around the ring, showing us all the old, sad visage of the Sage. Everyone is sitting down. It's so exposed here, you feel safer at ground level, yet Soyea walks across the steeply-sloping outcrop as if it's level, even lifting the stone up above her head. People are gasping at her bravado. She picks her way past the pyre onto the extreme edge of the pinnacle rock. We all hold our breath. I can't believe what she's doing and for a moment I think that the guilt has got to her and she is going to throw herself into the sea or dash herself onto the rocks as some crazy penance.

She raises the stone above her head. She is going to pitch it into the ocean. I can see her mouth moving but I don't know what she is saying. The breeze is snatching her voice away.

There is a shriek. Out of the darkness looms a fat woman with an eyepatch. She's wearing a long wide skirt and far too much jewellery. She is making for the rock and waving at Soyea.

'Do it. Do it!' she shouts.

I don't know if she means for Soyea to jump or throw the stone in the sea or what. I realise this must be Ussa and that she is not a fiction of my mother and father's imaginations after all. She is far stranger than I ever expected. Suddenly Fin is right up against Ussa, his face in her face, talking in a furious whisper, holding both her hands and making her walk backwards, down to the flatter ground, then away round to the edge of the crowd. She moans, but whatever he is saying to her is effective, because she quietens down.

I look back at Soyea and she's lowering her arms. She plonks the stone down right at the edge, the face of the Sage facing us, and shuffles back past the pyre and down the rocks. It's a bit of a let-down, really. I wanted her to chuck the damned stone into the sea. It has caused nothing but trouble. But I can see Father is pleased. He gives her a formal bow as if she's a real priestess, which I suppose she is, even though she's still only Soyea really. Mother is wiping tears away. Relief, I guess, that she didn't do anything stupid.

The fire in the sky has almost completely gone, there's just the purple glow and a small smudge of bronze on the horizon. The rock looms above us.

Once Soyea returns to her place, the three priestesses are in a line, chanting, and they get the whole crowd chanting along with a slow hand clap. Then they set off, The Wren at the front with her torch, then Ishbel and Soyea behind her. They are tiny, medium and huge. It's almost funny, but the chant they have going doesn't make anyone smile. It's weird, almost painful. They step their way in time, slowly, out beyond the edge of the crowd, and then back towards the pyre. We turn as they pass us, and watch The Wren.

She brings us all to silence with a single gesture. Then Soyea and Ishbel help her up the rock. She places her torch on the body and the shroud begins to burn.

Once she is back down in relative safety, the three of them turn as one and retrace their steps, singing loudly, 'The fire and the sky and the earth and the water'. Everyone joins in again, and this time it's a proper song. It is ages since I heard so many voices together. Some of the men are belting it out, it's magnificent. Those four brothers, Alasdair and his lot, have huge deep voices. I can't let myself go, although I try to sing along. I'm too nervous. It must be us soon. I can't even remember the words, although my mouth seems to know how to follow along.

The song goes on, verse after verse, until they get to the point where only the priestesses know the words for the verses. I've never heard these before, but we can all do the chorus, and there are harmonies growing as younger voices learn the shape of alternative lines. It's like musical petals opening. I find myself following an inner line, not as high as I usually sing, and it is lovely to be here, in the middle layer of the music.

Now here come the four brothers. The fire is high, its journey begun. The flames are up and billowing like sails.

The two younger brothers have a sack between them.

It's the bronze.

They tip it out onto the grass with a great clattering that makes the song stumble. I can't think of anything but whether it's cutting up the surface we'll have to dance on. I need that grass under my feet. How else will I endure it?

Alasdair dismisses his brothers after the sack is emptied. The song's chorus repeats, so we all know it has reached its end. Maybe others were following the words. I am just watching where I'll have to put my feet later.

At the end of the song there is a pause.

'I greet the spirits.' Alasdair's voice is huge. 'Accept this small change, this modest token of our sorrow at the disturbance we have caused. We mean no harm. We ask forgiveness.'

He speaks few words, yet they are powerful in their simplicity and directness. They say so much about this man. I can't believe anyone can feel anything but fondness for him. He is straight and true and big in every way. Big boned. Big hearted.

Then he starts picking up the pieces of metal and throwing them off the cliff, southwards into the broiling waves, battering off the rocks on the way down. He is chanting as he throws.

'Here's an end to greed.
Here's an end to badness.
Here's an end to hunger.
Here's an end to drunkenness.
Here's an end to a life.'

A cup, a plate, a bowl, a pan, chain links, a sharp unidentifiable piece of blade, broken strips of metal from who knows where; over the cliff edge they go.

We are mesmerised. I see that to some of the people here – Eilidh among them, Donnag too – these pieces of metal are shards of the man who gathered them. They weep openly as each gleaming item flies out, catching the firelight, carrying Bael's soul out to sea. It hadn't occurred to me until now that anyone might actually mourn his passing, but of course they will. I didn't know him, other than by reputation as a brute and a tyrant-child from Mother's childhood and Father has told me something of how horrid and inhospitable he was to Mother. And of course he tried to rape Soyea, so I can only think of him as a monster. But even tyrants are loved, sometimes even by those they tyrannise. He grew up here, he was part of the fabric, and threads are torn by his unravelling. Even I, who didn't know him at all, am moved by the event and stirred by this coming together to make amends for the violence, to say a final goodbye and open the way to what will follow.

There is no shying from the truth of what has happened, even with all its difficulties. Even big men, like Alasdair's brothers, have wet cheeks and sweep their sleeves across their faces.

And then there's nothing left except a sword, which Alasdair raises into the air above him. It is beautiful, catching the light of the flames, gleaming and glinting.

'Here's an end to the sale of our people as slaves.'

He is looking at Mother, and there is a wind of affirmative murmuring from the congregation. Something momentous is happening. I'm not sure I understand what it is.

And then the sword is spinning in an arc, out, out, up and over and away. It is such a beautiful thing to give to the spirits. Ussa lets out a long howl as it flies. The ocean eats it in one gulp.

As if in answer, my mother sings a strange song, one I have never heard before. It is in a language I do not know. I have never heard a more haunting melody. Father joins in, adding a deep harmony. After they stop, I realise Ussa was singing it also, and she goes on with the melody, alone, her voice cracked and weak and eerie. It is a spirit singing.

When she finally ceases, there is a stunned silence.

It is time.

DANCE

The fire crackles and spits above us and the sea roars below. The body is burning, the evil is roaming, everyone knows this is the hour of danger when the space between the worlds is open, when the spirits will decide what to do with the dead man and with those, living, who are attached to him. And we're all linked to him, in one way or another. That's why we're here.

So we have to hold the space open. That's our job, Eadha's and mine.

And when the lyre begins to play it's actually a relief. The waiting has ended. We can begin.

We lift the headdresses; Eadha has antlers, and I have cow horns. We help each other with the leather strapping. It's heavy, but once it's on my head I stand taller and straighter. I am ready.

Ishbel walks down the slope, plucking a single note on her lyre repeatedly, and takes a seat on a stone at the foot of the split rock. Once she's settled, she begins the tune that sets the pattern for our feet, the sixteen-beat motif that is the basic step-set, which we will vary and return to endlessly, or at least until the world is ready to settle back into stillness.

As we begin to dance I hear the drum. I had not expected it. It is The Wren. She has a little leather instrument across her chest and a stick that she is playing it with. It helps my feet, and I am glad of it.

Eadha and I make the first few sequences as simple as we can, adjusting to the lumpy, uneven ground, getting used to how far left and right and back and forward we can afford to go. This is a terrifying place to dance. One step too far to either side and there are precipitous drops onto waves and rocks. Behind us is the crag and pyre with its smoke belching and billowing, and in front of us that stone incline, which makes a good place for everyone to watch us from. I lift my head and look out at them. They are all ranged up the slope, crouching and sitting, tapping feet or moving hands and heads in time to the rhythm that Ishbel and The Wren are weaving with us. We have our little patch of grass to dance on, our green stage, and as our feet grow more confident we begin the variations we have been taught. Ishbel starts her incantation and her invitation to the people to ready themselves to come forwards and join the dance.

We dance the worlds open.

Our hands are together, his touch as sure as the waves on the shore. My skirt swishes against my legs as he spins me. His smile is as pure as the moon.

Once through all the variations, we return to the basic steps. They feel so easy now. We've warmed up and we're loose and smiling to each other as we do the double clap on the eighth beat and the double stamp on the twelfth. This is the best part. I feel so alive. I could dance all night if I have to.

We dance the next round side by side, beckoning to the crowd. Ishbel raises her voice, exhorting them to come forward, take a turn at the dance, to keep the space between the worlds open, to help the spirits to travel. She tells them that the spirits of people who have died in recent times will be waiting for them, to dance with them. She invokes Cuilc and Danuta, who was Mother's foster mother, who I never met, and I dance some dainty steps in the way an old woman might dance.

I try not to let my smile fade with my dismay. Nobody is willing. They have even reduced their toe-tapping. They look intimidated. I try to make it look easy, fun, and I see that Eadha is doing the same. Nobody comes.

Then, to my amazement, Mother gets to her feet. She never dances! Yet there she is, teetering down the slope, clinging onto hands, until she is down here with us on our patch of grass and joining in. She may never normally dance, but she can! Her feet do the crosses in perfect time, and she looks at me when we clap together and gives a little lift of her eyebrows. When we stamp our feet in synchrony the crowd is alive. There's a whoop and hands are slapping thighs.

I don't need to force a smile anymore. My mother's up here in the Lyre Dance and she's good at it. I offer her my arm and turn her before the next clap, and then Eadha does the same before the stamp. She doesn't miss a beat and she has a sweet grin on her face. She looks younger than I've ever seen her. Some blithe child spirit is here in her.

Then there's a cheer from the men. Father has handed his torch to Fin and is on his feet, making his way to join us. Of course, he dances like a warrior and the energy lifts immediately. He does big high claps and he jumps with each stamp down. He swings Mother round so she shrieks with fear and delight. Now we're in pairs we can do the full weaving pattern as the partners cross, then cross back again. I've never known my parents to dance like this, it's as if I'm seeing them for the first time. And they have channelled such warm spirits that all the watchers are lively now. Surely others will want to dance after this?

Ishbel has responded to the injection of enthusiasm with

laughing, skipping grace notes, and The Wren is augmenting her beat with pattering hops that lift my feet. I can feel the sweat starting on my back and my chest, and my breath is fast and strong. This is what we trained for. All we have to do is keep the rhythm and help others in.

Mother is panting and at the end of the next section she stops and steps back. Father falls in behind her and, still holding her hand, leads her up the slope of nodding, appreciative faces.

Now a young couple scramble forwards and take a turn with us, and although they don't dance as well as my parents, they're full of verve. They're clearly popular in the area because there's lots of clapping and whooping to support them.

Aonghas is up next, and he throws himself into the rhythm with gusto, arms flailing like gybing booms and legs kicking so wide I'm really scared he'll go over the edge or push one of us off. Half way through he invites up a pretty local girl, to whistles of appreciation.

Next up is an older local couple who dance formally and with perfect command of the steps. They know some of the variations too, and the crowd falls quiet as we work hard at it. For the first time, perhaps it is clear that this is a ceremonial act. They take it so seriously, I start to feel tingles up my spine as the spirit world gapes wide open and our reverent bodies entice frail souls into expression. They complete thirteen sets and bow out, and we bow back deeply, then rest our upper bodies for a set, although our feet never miss a beat.

I can feel it in my calves now and I know it will involve varying levels of pain from here on in, unless something extraordinary happens. The headdress is getting heavier with every set.

No one wants to follow that couple, they were so perfect, and I'm left wondering who they were. But then two old ladies come forward and we dance a stately and simple four sets with each of them, and then the four of us together. We reduce our steps and move ourselves more gently to accommodate them. Their frail old legs can barely cope, but they hold themselves with such gravitas that it is plain to all that anyone and everyone can do this.

After them a mother gets up with her little boy, and after them two bigger girls come to take their turn. A vivacious young woman, and then an older man, two giggling teenage boys, trying to lower the tone, and then Alasdair himself, with a young, startlingly beautiful red-headed woman. Together they return the dance to sober ritual.

We dance on and on, keeping pace with each of Alasdair's brothers in turn, then Father's crew. The brothers together, one fit and one shambolic, both adding their sailor's steps and gestures to their sets. In one flourish with them the strap of one of my slippers gives way, and I tear it off my foot without missing more than two steps. Then I carry on, knowing my feet are blistering on the grass as it wears down to the soil under the pounding dance steps. The pain in my thighs is brutal, the headdress digs in above my ears, and my hands are sore with clapping. But we must dance on.

I can see Eadha forcing his smile over a grimace, sweat pouring down his face. For a while after the sailors it is just us, keeping the border open, and I want to stop. Maybe they were the last dancers. But the lyre plays on and as long as the strings are singing our feet must follow their rhythm.

We begin the ghost variations: that's what the Lyre signals us to do, replacing the claps with silent arm movements, the stamps with heel taps that stretch the legs in a different way. It is a huge relief. And in the fourth, strangest variation, which I think of as close to a swimming movement, I see we are being joined by my sister and Fin. I would never have expected anyone to actually want to dance in such a strange section, but when they begin it is oddly exotic, almost other worldly.

My sister hates to dance. I've cringed so often watching her ungainly performances when people have insisted she joins in. But here, with the pale, lanky youth beside her, she makes mere gestures towards the dance's movements. She sways, elegant and minimal, and he jerks and twists beside her and around her. Yet somehow, they look like light playing on ripples, or the flicker of the Northern Lights. There is such grief and passion in their postures, they barely need to move to express the spirits speaking through them. Perhaps our brother is here, Cleat, her twin. Eadha and I soak up their power, wafting around them like breezes. They are wonderful. And after they stop, the pain in my legs has gone.

The dance goes on.

More strangers come. Then at last, Donnag from the broch gets up and dances manically, alone, ignoring both us and the rhythm of the drum and lyre, stamping out some inner fury. Even Buia the mad woman comes and flails about. She is the only one I have to physically stop from going over the edge, as she channels some crazy spirit, but after a while it leaves her, and she calms and finds the musical patterns with her feet. A childlike smile settles onto her face as we lead her through the weaving sets of steps.

When Buia finishes she goes to Ussa and pulls her hand. There is resistance at first and then the big woman gets to her feet, and as she approaches there is a rhythm to her steps. She knows how to dance. Buia lets go of her and returns to sitting while Ussa comes on. By the time she has joined us she is jigging. It is like dancing with a bear. Somewhere within her is a memory of music, an impulse in her feet and hips that her old, overweight physique is no longer capable of fulfilling. Only her arms can still perform properly. At first she lets them lead, hardly moving her feet, but it is as if the beat takes over more and more. She wants to do the turns with us. She is determined to stay for the variations. There is a dancing spirit inside her who is desperate for this, which takes over and demands that she dance and dance, jerking her panting, sweating body like a puppet. She is possessed. Her eyes are staring ahead. We try to bring her to a gentle halt but at each return of the main tune, each skip of the drum, she kicks again, her breath rasping and wheezing.

She dances on and on, twice as long as anyone else. She seems incapable of stopping. Perhaps the spirit that is dancing through her will not allow her to cease. Her breath is going like bellows. Her face contorts and sweat is pouring from her. She is staggering and I'm sure she's going to topple over the edge into the sea.

All of a sudden, she stops. She sways to one side, her eyes closed. Her legs buckle. She slumps to the ground, her neck flopping.

Alasdair and others rush forward and carry her off. The Wren and Ishbel don't miss a beat. Trying not to let horror show on my face, I turn wide-eyed to Eadha and he urges me on. The world is open to all the mad and desperate spirits and we must dance to keep it open.

The gaps get longer between the dancers now, only the most reluctant or incapable people are left. They stumble down and jerk a few token steps, then stagger back. I cease to notice unless they are in the dance, and when they're not it's us alone, Eadha and I, fulfilling the role we found each other for. We are keeping the gateway between worlds open, allowing the spirits to express themselves.

We dance the agony of our separation. We dance the eternity of our love. We dance the power and purity of sex. We dance our life's blood at death's precipice. We dance the world open.

We dance the borderline of sense and madness.

We dance to the edge of frenzy and beyond.

We dance the pyre to embers.

We dance and dance and dance.

Until at last the lyre's song is ended.

AFTER THE DANCE

I stare into flames and see how alive they are. I learn from them how dancing began.

Mother does a lovely thing. As the pyre dies down to a glow, she builds up the little fire she made earlier, nestled in from the edge in a safe place for lighting the torches. Then she sits beside it with her whistle, playing simple melodies from time to time. It becomes a kind of shrine to the life to come, and as people ebb away they pass by it, adding the handles of their burnt-out torches, or some twigs dropped by the pyre builders earlier. Eadha and I gravitate towards her.

Mother has the art of fire. This one is small, gentle and soothing. People speak beside it, weep again, and are invited to go back to the broch for food and drink. I think many have gone. Soyea went there early, immediately after the dance finished, with The Wren and Donnag, and I imagine they're all handing out bowls and beakers right now. I have no desire to go there.

Buia stands with her arm wrapped around Mother for what seems like ages. They seem to find comfort in each other. Something from very long ago is being healed tonight. Then Alasdair stands there with Mother and afterwards she retreats into shadow. I suspect she is crying. It is so like her not to want us to see her expressing her feelings.

Ishbel stops at the fire for a while and congratulates us. We talk about all the dancers, and Mother tries to explain who all those are who Ishbel, Eadha and I don't know.

Ishbel hands Mother a belt. 'I spoke with Ussa.'

Mother strokes the buckle as if it's alive. 'She's impossible.' She shakes her head.

'She said to tell you she was sorry and gave me this for you. She was saying a lot that I couldn't make any sense of. I told her she should take more care when dancing and she said it was her freedom dance.'

'Her freedom dance.' Mother repeats. 'Good.' She passes me the belt. Its buckle is engraved with a beautiful pattern of ivy and a bird.

'She said she wants to learn to play the lyre, and asked if I would teach her.' Ishbel laughs. 'Perhaps I should take her back to Brigid's Cave.'

'Would you?' Mother looks up at her.

Ishbel shifts her lyre and gives a little strum. 'Yes. I might. I quite like the idea.'

'It was more than Bael that crossed a threshhold tonight.'

'Indeed. And I'm hungry as a result.' Ishbel leans in to kiss each of us in turn, then leaves us to the fire.

Now it is only us: Mother, Eadha and I. I don't want to go to the broch, back into the crowd.

Eadha produces a flask of mead as if by magic, and it helps to ease my aching muscles and blistered feet. We sit on rocks within poking distance of the embers of Mother's fire. It is dying away, leaving only a glow and flicker, an echo of the great pyre of death, which is still glowering on the split rock.

Mother flips a half-burned fragment of wood, bringing a flame to life again. Her little blaze feels like renewal. I get up and gather some more sticks so she can keep it going, then tuck in beside Eadha again. He passes me the flask and I sip, then offer it to Mother. She shifts her poker to her other hand and takes the mead.

'What did Alasdair say?' I ask.

She swallows.

'A lot of things I didn't know I needed to hear.'

'Like what?'

She looks as if she won't tell me. She swallows again. Perhaps she might cry. I've never seen my mother cry.

'He said he hoped I had never doubted I was worth more than the sword. He said Drost should never have exchanged me for it.'

'The sword that went in the sea today?' Eadha asks.

She nods. 'Bael's father sold me for it. He put me up as the stake in a gambling game.'

Eadha shakes his head.

She takes a deep breath. 'He said something even more important than that. He said they're glad that I've come home.

That's what means the most. The rest is in the past.'

'Does this place feel like home?' I ask.

She nods. 'Until I was nearly your age it was all I knew.'

'I don't know that feeling,' I say. 'Ictis never felt like home.'

Eadha reaches over and cradles my hand in his.

'You can share mine,' he says. 'Rian, do you think that feeling can grow for a place even if you've not spent your childhood there?'

'I don't know. I just know mine is here. But I don't think I ever really believed it until today. I have spent so long being unable to come here.'

'Will your home still be the same to you now you know Cuilc is not your mother?' I ask him. I am thinking about that stone tower. Ishbel has said it will still be his.

'It's the place I love,' he nods. After a pause, he says, 'I always knew Ishbel was special.'

'For a while there, I thought you were my brother,' Mother says. 'I have to apologise for what I thought. It was not kind.'

'Forget it,' he says. 'It was never true.'

We all stare into the embers. Mother prods a stick in from the edge and we watch it blaze.

'You each have new mothers. I have a new grandmother. It should be a song.'

'I'm happy to have lost a sister and got back my wife's mother. And my wife.' Eadha strokes my hand.

'I'm happy about that too,' Mother says. 'Greatly relieved.'

'What is it like to finally know who your mother is?' I ask her. 'I can't imagine not knowing something so basic. It must be strange.'

'Well I'll never know her now, other than through you.'

We've all been changed by this.

'How is Soyea, do you think?' I can't get her pale, agonized face out of my mind.

'She's strong,' Mother says.

'She and Fin love each other,' I say.

'They danced like flames,' Eadha replies.

'Do you like him, Mother?'

She doesn't answer at first, then she says, 'I don't know yet. He is close to Ussa. But I have feared she would never love a man, ever since Cleat was taken.'

She never mentions his name. I hold my breath. The islands are invisible but she gestures out towards the dark sea.

'Do you know they were named after the two islands out there, Soyea and her twin brother, Cleat?' She is asking Eadha, I suppose, because of course I know. His absence has been an unspoken presence in our family my whole life. He was never spoken about with Mother, but Soyea carried him around throughout our childhood, left him gifts, made space for him in our dens.

'When did he die?' Eadha asks.

'Die? Cleat's father took him to his home when he was almost three. He never came back.'

'Where was that?'

'A place called Massalia. Far, far to the south.'

'Have you been there?'

'No.'

'So do you think he is still there?'

I can't believe Eadha is asking these questions. I would never dare. Yet somehow the night has broken barriers.

'I don't know. No. I fear the worst. I can't explain otherwise why he has never come back. But I hope, obviously, that one day... He'd be a young man now, almost your age. His father, Pytheas, was a writer, and there was a rumour some years ago that he had sent a document to Soyea. Manigan met an Armorican trader who said he'd seen it, said it was supposed to go to the Spirit Keepers.'

'But it didn't appear?'

She gives a little shake of her head. Her face is forlorn. It is an expression I recognise. All my life, when caught unawares she

241

has looked like this. All those years of waiting. Then she looks at me and smiles.

'You danced well tonight, the two of you. I'm very proud of you.' She lays her hand on my shoulder and rests it there while she flicks a stick so its unburned end is on the hottest embers. Then she lifts her hand and steps around to the far side of the fire, knocking in two other twigs. They lie neatly across each other and almost immediately flames ripple up from them, licking along their length.

'Thank you,' Eadha says. And I don't know if it's for the fire, or her words, but she looks up at him and nods, with that little smile she has that I have always thought came from a sad place, but which, tonight, looks more like peace.

SOYEA

DOCUMENT

I am rid of the stone. It can stay where I left it, up on the split rock.

Everyone in the area seems to have been to the broch. I could never have imagined such a feast, such a fire, such extraordinary energy.

After everyone else has gone, Ussa lingers late into the night, slumped on a stool in the corner where Bael's body had been. Her breaths come in shudders.

I offer her something to eat but she shakes her head. I turn away.

She grabs my sleeve and thrusts a package at me. 'This is yours.' Her voice is deep and smooth, incongruously beautiful coming from such a lumpy body, from such a blotchy face.

I take what she's offering. It is wrapped in a leather cloth and inside is a codex of a material far finer than any parchment I've ever seen. It is covered in a script I am not familiar with. As I pull it free of the cloth, a small box drops out with a clatter.

Ussa bends to pick it up but I'm far more flexible than her. I grab it and it falls open in my hand. Inside are three little animals – a white dolphin carved out of walrus ivory, a metal owl, maybe bronze, and something made of amber. I hold the flame-coloured gem stone to the light – it is in the form of a bear.

'Your father travelled the world to find that stuff,' Ussa says.

I look at her in amazement. 'What are these things?'

'An Armorican trader gave me them years ago. I said I'd pass them on to Rian, but I wanted to do something more interesting with them. I was never quite sure what that would be, but I knew I'd know at the time. I don't want them anymore.'

She gestures with her hand that I should leave her alone. I bundle the contents of the parcel back together, carry it gingerly to the hearth and lower it into Mother's outstretched hands.

RIAN

LEAVING

The morning after the fire, Ussa was sitting beside Ishbel, with the lyre on her lap. Manigan rushed in saying Ròn had sailed away and asking Ussa to explain what was happening

'I told them they were free to go.' Ussa blinked slowly at Rian, and then at Buia, then turned back to Manigan. 'We're all free now. She,' she pointed at Rian, 'she plays the whale tune and says it means freedom. I did my freedom dance. Now I am a whale. We're all whales now.'

Manigan looked at Rian, who gave a little shrug.

'Whales,' he said.

'Whales,' Ussa echoed.

Rian picked up three little objects from between her and Soyea and held out her hand to Manigan, who took them.

'What are these?'

'They came from Pytheas.' Rian nodded towards Ussa. 'She has had them for years, she says.'

Manigan examined each one in turn, then dropped first the amber bear, then the bronze owl back into her hand.

She stood them back on the hearth stone. 'The bear must be Soyea's. The owl, perhaps Rona will appreciate it.'

He held the ivory dolphin, fingering its detail, before placing it back on her palm. 'And this is for who?'

She reached up and touched it. 'Fin?'

Their eyes met, and she saw her instinct was right. She saw him glance at Soyea, who simply smiled.

He bent down and tried to get Ussa to look at him, but except for a few tentative notes on the lyre every now and again, she remained silent and withdrawn.

Manigan pulled a stool close in beside Rian and sat down. 'What now, for you? Will you come hunting with me again?'

She took his hand. 'I feel like I belong here.'

He blinked, waiting for her to say more.

'I'm going to stay.'

'Good,' he said.

She turned to check he meant it.

'This'll be a good place to spend winter,' he said.

A smile emptied her face of all its worry. It was decided, then.

The other boats all left together the following day. An easterly breeze blew up out of the sunrise. The preparations for departure were punctuated by discussion of the fickle nature of the winds from the east, the way they always gusted, funnelled down glens into lumps as if to be hurled at passing ships by mountain giants.

Rona was returning to the Winged Isle with Eadha and Ishbel on Aonghas' heavy curragh, which he sailed with only Mac for help. Rian didn't know if Eadha was handy on a boat. She knew very little of him, really. But there would be other summers. Rona and he had promised to make her a grandmother and return.

Ishbel the priestess had the look of someone who would be competent with ropes, somehow. Ussa was going with them to learn the lyre and she would be no help on the boat at all.

Alasdair's curragh would run with the wind directly behind it. He had offered to take Soyea over the Minch to the long island to serve her penance for the killing. She would be out on the moor on her own for a whole moon. The Wren, before she left, held Rian's hands in her tiny clasp and said, 'I will be watching over her. She will be healed by it.'

To everyone's surprise, Donnag had packed a little bundle and demanded to go with them. She wanted to return to her father's and brother's home, she said. Taking the spirtle down from where it hung above the hearth she handed it to Rian. 'This is your home now.'

'It's surely Buia's home now?' Rian said.

Fin stopped packing the food box and looked up. Soyea, seated on a stool in her grey gown, was watching intently. The Wren too.

All eyes seemed to be on Rian. She proffered the spirtle to Buia, who waved her hand in dismissal. There was nothing Rian could do but place it back on its hook herself. It swung from its leather thong, then settled, and its motion was mirrored by the thump inside her chest.

The third boat to cast off, but the first to get its sail up, was *Bradan*, reaching north, Manigan at the tiller. Rian watched them leave, knowing exactly what would be happening now: banter between Badger and Kino as they trimmed the big sail, Fin's monkey asleep on his coat while he tidied up the mooring warps in his quiet way. Once he was ready, he would take the helm. Later, when they found walruses, Manigan was going to teach him the muttering.

Just before climbing aboard, he had said, 'It will be my last walrus and his first,' nodding towards Fin, who was waiting with the rope to cast off. 'And then I will become your wood gatherer and learn to milk the cow.'

She smiled at him through tears and kissed him one last time. Then she pushed his chest. 'Get away with you.'

He ruffled her hair. 'Are you sure you're not coming?'

She nodded.

'Fair winds,' she called as the boat floated and its sails unfurled, the two brothers hauling ropes in rhythm.

Buia waved from the broch entrance, her cat draped over her shoulder. Rian walked from the shore up onto the headland towards the stone tower, then looked back out to sea. A boat for each of her daughters, the third for her man. Of course, everything always came in threes in her life. It no longer surprised her. Quite the reverse: it confirmed the rhythms of the world.

Later they would come home, and Manigan and Rian could grow old together, maybe even live happily ever after, just like in the best stories.

She made the sign for fair winds and good sailing and banished the fear that always came when she thought of all the widows made by the Northern Ocean. She remembered the great sea spirit and murmured a wish to it to keep the men safe.

When the sails shrank and dipped over the horizon, she turned back to the broch to tend the fire. She hummed the melody that Toma taught her, all those years ago, which seemed to have been constantly in her head since the night of the lyre dance. The whale's song. The song of freedom.

THE END

ACKNOWLEDGEMENTS

It all began with Clachtoll Broch, so my first thanks must be to the Iron Age architectural genius who worked out how to build a 15-metre-high, double-walled, dry-stone tower. John Barber of AOC Archaeology calls him Ug, so thank you Ug. You not only left a remarkable legacy on the shore of my home parish, but you sparked in me a fascination with your period and with the people who built, inhabited and visited your implausibly wonderful building, who are fictionalised here. I must also thank, as well as John, Graeme, Andy, Alan, Charlotte and all the other members of the AOC team, who have helped to bring the Iron Age (and indeed other periods) to life through their work in Assynt and indulged my wonderings about what Pytheas may have found here when he came, way back in 320BC.

Huge gratitude also to Gordon Sleight, who has repeatedly hired me to hang out with this brilliant team on their various digs, and to pick their brains while ostensibly writing blogs and media releases for them. Gordon has also read these books with a meticulous care and pointed out the many mistakes, anachronisms and pieces of wishful but implausible thinking that I wove into earlier drafts.

Professor Barry Cunliffe was also very helpful in his insights about Pytheas and in encouraging my ideas about what he might have been getting up to in this neck of the woods. Professor Donna Heddle was similarly key in helping me imagine the cultural world Pytheas found here. Martin Wildgoose showed me into High Pasture Cave and helped me to envision its ceremonial use. Staff of the National Museum of Scotland in Edinburgh, and the museums in Kilmartin, Stromness, Kirkwall, Wick, Inverness, Pendeen, Penzance, Copenhagen, Oslo, Krakow and Longyearbyen, have helped me in my research over the years. Particular thanks to Neil Burridge for showing me his bronze-smithing magic, to the captains and crews of the Ortelius and the Noorderlicht, for amazing adventures in the pack ice and northern ocean, and to Ian Stephen for sailing wisdom and stories about the sea in times gone by. And thanks to everyone else who has talked to me about the Iron Age and helped me to time-travel back to when Pytheas made his amazing journey. All remaining historical inaccuracy is entirely my fault.

The book could not have been written without the chance to take some time out of the day job, and this was made possible by a generous bursary from Creative Scotland, for which I remain hugely grateful. It came about as a result of urging from staff at Moniack Mhor, who also gave me retreat space and moral support by simply believing in the project.

Margaret Elphinstone was my first reader, critical friend and mentor, and the long conversations and convivial times with her and Mike were priceless waypoints on the journey to the finished books. Jane Alexander and John Bolland were crucial readers of early drafts, so thank you both for the encouragement and helpful suggestions about story and characters. Thanks also to all my other writing buddies: Romany, Jorine, Anna, Maggie, Becks, Anita, Graham, Kate, Alastair, Phil and everyone else who has come to join in writing events in Assynt, not forgetting Ed Group, Helen Sedgwick, Peter Urpeth and Janet Paisley. I'm grateful to Lesley McDowell and Madeleine Pollard for editorial advice, and to all at Saraband, especially Sara Hunt, for bringing it to fruition.

My Mum sadly didn't get to read this book, but her pride in me lives on and I'm grateful for it every day. Thankfully I have my Dad and my uniquely wonderful sister, Alison, offering endless support. Thanks to you both and to all the rest of our far-flung tribe.

This book was largely written at sea, thanks to the crew of *Each Mara*, the most precious of whom is Bill, my patient mate and co-skipper, to whom I offer buckets of love and hugs, onshore and off.